DECEPTION

What Reviewers Say About VK Powell's Work

Side Effects

"[A] touching contemporary tale of two wounded souls hoping to find lasting love and redemption together. ...Powell ably plots a plausible and suspenseful story, leading readers to fall in love with the characters she's created."—*Publishers Weekly*

To Protect and Serve

"If you like cop novels, or even television cop shows with women as full partners with male officers...this is the book for you. It's got drama, excitement, conflict, and even some fairly hot lesbian sex. The writer is a retired cop, so she really writes from a place of authenticity. As a result, you have a realistic quality to the writing that puts me in mind of early Joseph Wambaugh."—Teresa DeCrescenzo, *Lesbian News*

"*To Protect and Serve* drew me in from the very first page with characters that captivated in their complexity. Powell writes with authority using the lingo and capturing the thoughts of the law enforcers who make the ultimate sacrifice in the fight against crime. What's more impressive is the command this debut author has of portraying a full gamut of emotion, from angst to elation, through dialogue and narrative. The images are vivid, the action is believable, and the police procedurals are authentic...VK Powell had me invested in the story of these women, heart, mind, body and soul. Along with danger and tension, Powell's well-developed erotic scenes sizzle and sate."—*Story Circle Book Reviews*

Suspect Passions

"From the first chapter of *Suspect Passions* Powell builds erotic scenes which sear the page. She definitely takes her readers for a walk on the wild side! Her characters, however, are also women we care about. They are bright, witty, and strong. The combination of great sex and great characters make *Suspect Passions* a must read."—*Just About Write*

Fever

"VK Powell has given her fans an exciting read. The plot of *Fever* is filled with twists, turns, and 'seat of your pants' danger...*Fever* gives readers both great characters and erotic scenes along with insight into life in the African bush."—*Just About Write*

Justifiable Risk

"This story takes some unusual twists and at one point, I was convinced that I knew 'who did it' only to find out that I was wrong. VK Powell knows crime drama, she kept me guessing until the end, and I was not disappointed at the outcome. And that's not to slight VK Powell's knack for romance. ...Readers who appreciate mysteries with a touch of drama and intense erotic moments will enjoy *Justifiable Risk*."—*Queer Magazine*

Exit Wounds

"Powell's prose is no-nonsense and all business. It gets in and gets the job done, a few well-placed phrases sparkling in your memory and some trenchant observations about life in general and a cop's life in particular sticking to your psyche long after they've gone.

After five books, Powell knows what her audience wants, and she delivers those goods with solid assurance. But be careful you don't get hooked. You only get six hits, then the supply's gone, and you'll be jonesin' for the next installment. It never pays to be at the mercy of a cop."—*Out in Print*

"Fascinating and complicated characters materialize, morph, and sometimes disappear testing the passionate yet nascent love of the book's focal pair. I was so totally glued to and amazed by the intricate layers that continued to materialize like an active volcano…dangerous and deadly until the last mystery is revealed. This book goes into my super special category. Please don't miss it."—*Rainbow Book Reviews*

About Face

"Powell excels at depicting complex, emotionally vulnerable characters who connect in a believable fashion and enjoy some genuinely hot erotic moments."—*Publishers Weekly*

By the Author

DECEPTION

by
VK Powell

2016

DECEPTION

ISBN 13: 978-1-62639-596-1

This Trade Paperback Original Is Published By
Bold Strokes Books, Inc.
P.O. Box 249
Valley Falls, NY 12185

First Edition: August 2016

Credits
Editor: Shelley Thrasher
Production Design: Susan Ramundo
Cover Design By Sheri (graphicartist2020@hotmail.com)

Acknowledgments

I've been blessed to pursue two careers that brought me great satisfaction. The first allowed me to help people and promote advancement for women in a profession that often overlooked them. In the second, I parlay that career into stories of survival, the struggle to balance love and livelihood, and the fight between good and evil. To Len Barot and all the wonderful folks at Bold Strokes Books—thank you for giving me the chance to tell my stories.

My deepest gratitude and admiration to Dr. Shelley Thrasher for your guidance, suggestions, and kindness. You always take time to talk me off the ledges in my mind, even when you're up to your neck in projects. Working with you is a learning experience and a pleasure. I'm so proud of our collaborations and of your success as a Bold Strokes author.

For BSB sister author, D. Jackson Leigh, and friends, Jenny Harmon and Mary Margret Daughtridge—thank you for taking time out of your busy lives to provide priceless feedback. This book is so much better for your efforts. I am truly grateful.

To all the readers who support and encourage my writing, thank you for buying my work, visiting my website (www.vkpowellauthor .com), sending e-mails, and showing up for signings. You make my "job" so much fun!

Special thanks to Christine Mitchell (and your generous friend) for graciously allowing me to use your name for one of my secondary characters. I had fun creating my Chris and hope you enjoy her part in the story.

Dedication

To all those who work to eliminate
homelessness in the world.

CHAPTER ONE

"H ey, you dead or what?" A gruff, unfamiliar voice seeped into Colby's consciousness. Irritated. Unhappy.

Her nose stung with the pungent cocktail of stale booze, urine, and rotting food. She inched away from the stench. Her body ached all over. She licked dry lips and tasted the coppery tang of blood. Her stomach churned.

"I said, you alive, airman?" Someone nudged her in the back.

"Sir, yes sir." Her throat burned as she spoke, her voice a scratchy whisper.

"Good. Now get your ass out of my spot."

Colby tried to open her eyes, but only one worked. The ground under her was damp, and something hard pressed against her tender ribs. Her head felt like an over-saturated sponge and her insides roiled. She stared at a pair of snakeskin boots that had begun to shed and an empty Thunderbird wine bottle with ants crawling around the neck. "Where am I? And how did you know I'd been in the air force?" she asked the owner of the boots.

"Just covered that. You're in my spot. And that tattoo is a dead giveaway." He pointed to the wings creeping up the back of her neck that would've normally been covered by hair.

She grabbed her head with both hands, the shock of a shaved scalp and bruised ribs registering at the same time. "What the hell? I feel like death warmed over."

"Look like it too, but that ain't my problem. Now move your ass."

Colby rolled onto her side and pushed up on one arm. The sick feeling in her stomach surged up her throat, and she dry-heaved. She swallowed hard to suppress the bitter taste of bad liquor and something more chemical. *Was I drugged? I'm a damn DEA agent. That shit shouldn't happen.*

Turning slowly to quell the nausea, she took in her surroundings: dark, an embankment beside a bridge underpass, a group of men huddled around a small fire, cold rain, all eyes on her. No one else spoke, as if deferring to the man giving her orders. *How did I get here?* Her last memories before waking up in a hobo village were bits of conversations about an undercover job, a last meal, and a drink she didn't want.

"I think Agent Vincent would be perfect for this assignment." Leon waved for the waitress to bring another round of drinks.

"What? You've been telling me for months that I'm not ready."

"And you keep insisting you are." Her boss turned to Ted Curtis, the DEA agent who'd asked for their consult on the case in Greensboro, North Carolina. *"Don't you think a woman with military experience would be a good cover for a drug-diversion operation involving homeless veterans?"*

Curtis tilted his chair backward away from her. "You've worked the streets of New York, and if your boss thinks you can fool a grizzled pack of vets, who am I to argue? We'd have to change your clean-cut-agent look into a woman of the street. That life is tough for veterans, especially women, who've been war heroes and then lose everything."

She breathed slowly to control a rush of sadness as she recalled her father hunched over the kitchen table apologizing once again for not being able to work. "Yeah, I know. My dad was one of those vets, and we were nearly...homeless for a while.

"I remember waking up at night to his screams. He couldn't function as a psychologist anymore because his PTSD was too bad. My parents struggled for years until Dad met a guy in the carpentry business. Working with his hands quieted the mental turmoil."

"Did you suffer from PTSD after your service?" Leon asked.

"Not really. I was an air-force computer-systems analyst, perched in the back of a Boeing 707 with a big Frisbee on the top, sending real-time data to troops on the ground, always a bit removed from the action."

Curtis chimed in. "But you've been around vets all your life, so you know the issues they face, and you've worked with the homeless community in New York. I'd say you're the agent for this assignment."

Snake-boot man nudged her with his foot, still towering over her. A graying beard covered part of his face, and the remainder appeared almost as dark in the low light. Scabby knees poked through worn patches in his jeans, but the cowboy hat he sported looked almost new.

"You reek, airman. Somebody worked you over pretty good, but it happens out here. You got to be careful." He'd started to sound almost sympathetic. "Get the hell out of my spot, and I won't tell you again." *So much for compassion.*

"Where am I?"

"Disney World. Don't you recognize the Magic Kingdom?"

The other men laughed as he shoved her with his large hands. She recoiled, lost her balance, and rolled down the embankment. Her ribs and the side of her face ached with each tumble until she landed at the bottom in a puddle. The cowboy dropped his backpack on the spot she'd vacated, while the rest of the group pointed at her and yelled obscenities.

She shivered as a cold breeze penetrated her wet sweatshirt and jeans—clothes that didn't belong to her. She felt helpless and scared, like the first day of basic training when she'd been physically stripped of her trendy outfit and verbally demeaned to the point of tears. Now she was alone again in a city without friends, family, or coworkers and without the resources of her profession.

Glancing at the men clustered together on the cold concrete, she saw people who shouldered more than their share of challenges. She thought of her father's struggles and vowed to make him proud. If they could do it every day, she could handle it temporarily. She was just an interloper. "What am I supposed to do?"

The cowboy shook his head. "It's not my problem as long as you don't do it in somebody else's spot and don't attract the cops. Lessons one and two for sleeping rough, and probably the only advice you'll get free." He tossed her a backpack she'd never seen. "You might need this."

The bag and attached bedroll toppled into the puddle at her feet. "Thanks." She grabbed the bag and hefted it onto her shoulder, hoping Ted Curtis had left something useful inside like a manual for street survival. She turned a three-sixty in the street to get her bearings.

"Hey, if you decide to off yourself, trains come through here thirty-five to forty times a day. Lots of opportunities." As if on cue, the ground beneath her reverberated, and an ear-splitting whistle sounded as a train rumbled overhead.

She covered her ears and headed west toward the area with the most lights. The cowboy had obviously sized her up and found her lacking in street survival skills. She'd just have to prove him wrong. As she passed the train depot, a shrieking female voice sang out from the shadows. "Poor little cherry out in the rain. Nowhere to sleep, what a pain."

Colby pulled the hood of the smelly sweatshirt tighter, realizing how cold her head was without hair. She ducked under overhangs as she walked into what appeared to be a central business district in flux. The sepia tones of streetlights gave the buildings an old-world glow. When she looked south, she vaguely remembered being at Natty Greene's pub earlier with her boss and the Greensboro DEA supervisor, Ted Curtis.

She walked, trying to remember exactly how she'd ended up in a homeless camp in the middle of the night smelling like three weeks of bad hygiene. Her memory of actually arriving had more holes than the shabby jeans barely clinging to her hips. She walked north, thinking the streets seemed longer and the rain wetter with nowhere to go. This was only her first night, but she already felt the burden of loneliness and the uncertainty of disorientation that had plagued her those first months in Iraq.

As she struggled to recall the past several hours, the muffled ring of a phone sounded from her backpack. She stepped into a doorway and dumped the contents on the street, located the mobile, and stared at it for several seconds.

"What the…" She turned the primitive model over in her hand. "You've got to be kidding." This antique only made and received calls. Forget texts. It would take way too long to punch the number keys repeatedly to find the right letters. She flipped the unit open and answered.

"Well, hello, sunshine. How are you enjoying your new assignment?"

"Leon?" Her boss's original confidence in her undercover potential had faltered when Curtis started talking details. She wasn't sure if his reluctance was about protecting her, which she understood from a supervisory perspective, or doubting her skills, which she resented on personal and professional levels. She'd had a distinguished career in DEA so far, but vetting intelligence, running a surveillance operation, or managing an undercover agent didn't carry the same level of accomplishment and clout as being a field agent.

"Of course it's Leon. Who else were you expecting?"

"How did I end up in a homeless camp so quickly?" Somebody had taken liberties with her body that she didn't normally allow.

"You volunteered for the job, remember? They're your people now. But to answer the question, I don't know exactly *how* you got there. I left those details to Agent Curtis. I imagine it was creative and not very nice. Am I close?"

"You could say that." Details of their earlier meeting surfaced, but everything after that was still fuzzy until she woke up under an overpass. "They shaved my freaking head and beat the crap out of me. And I might've been drugged because I can't remember the past few hours very clearly."

Leon was quiet for a few seconds. "We're fucking government agents. We're supposed to follow the law and procedure. I certainly didn't authorize *that*. Are you all right?"

She didn't want Leon stressing about her first UC job, and she certainly didn't want the Greensboro agents thinking she'd cried foul to her boss. "I'll be sore for a few days, but I'll survive. Don't make a federal case out of it. They were just helping me blend in."

"I guess you needed to look the part. Just take care of yourself." He paused. "I insisted on the phone, but your minutes are limited. Use it sparingly until you get some resources of your own."

"And where do you suggest I find resources?" She struggled to keep her voice calm, panic threatening to choke her. She couldn't just walk up to a bank, flip out her card, and withdraw cash. Leon hadn't been beaten by his peers, woken up in a completely foreign environment, or been kicked out of a homeless camp. But she couldn't let him suspect she was already second-guessing her decision to take this case. Had she ever put an agent in such an untenable position with no support?

"How should I know? I've never been homeless. You know your assignment?"

"Someone's using veterans to run a prescription-drug diversion operation."

"Did you establish a credible legend?"

Colby pieced together shards of memory about the undercover persona she and Curtis had agreed upon. "Using my real name and background, minus the DEA bits. The techies added a job in computers to jell with my military specialty. Bouts of PTSD, a gradual spiral from unemployment into homelessness, and alienation from family drove me South." She scrubbed her shaved head, satisfied with her summary. "I was robbed on a bus and dumped near the depot on Washington Street, Greensboro, North Carolina. I'm good to go." In theory, assuming this new identity sounded like a good idea. In reality, it was a little frightening, given all the things that could go wrong.

"You asked for this and you're ready. Just watch and learn. You'll get the hang of it." He sounded more certain than she felt at the moment, but his words boosted her confidence.

"Right." She thought about her reception under the bridge. "That won't be easy."

"Your handler's number is the only one in the phone. She'll contact you when she can. Don't call her unless it's an emergency. I'm always here, but Ted Curtis has the lead." Before she could ask how he knew all these details and if he'd contacted her family, Leon hung up.

Her parents would be worried. They were used to her checking in on a semi-regular basis when she wasn't on assignment. She'd have to call and explain the situation. And what about her girlfriend, Kali? Last time they were together she'd been pressing for a commitment. Colby was only interested in friendship and an occasional sexual romp. Kali seemed happy to settle down and follow her family's footsteps into philanthropy, but Colby wanted it all—chemistry, great sex, compatibility, and real intimacy. She'd promised they'd talk about their relationship soon. Not much chance of that now.

She tucked the mobile phone into her boot and inventoried the items from her backpack strewn on the street: another pair of worn jeans, a Hooters T-shirt, one sweatshirt, a pair of wool socks, one kitchen-sized trash bag, a new toothbrush, travel-sized paste, Axe Dark Temptation body spray, a facecloth, and two pink thongs. Somebody had enjoyed himself.

She pulled at the waistband of the ratty jeans and looked down, releasing a breath when she saw her own briefs. The army-issue boots felt big, but with thick socks she'd manage. Apparently the guys who'd packed her go-bag included things they thought necessary to survive on the streets, but she had no money, no credit card, no safe house, and no gun. At least the air force had given her shelter and a weapon for protection in a hostile environment.

Digging to the bottom of the backpack, she pulled out the final item, an old leather flight jacket. The chest patch said AIR FORCE, but the colors were wrong. Still, it was comforting in an odd sort of way. She checked the street in both directions and dragged her belongings farther into the recessed entrance of the business.

Laying the fresh garments out around her, she stripped off her wet, smelly clothes and pulled on dry things. She inhaled the scent of mothballs as she eased her aching body into the heavy coat and zipped it to her chin. The jacket fit like it had been made for her, and she snuggled into its warmth. Wrapping the wet items in the trash bag, she stuffed them back into her pack.

As she started down the sidewalk, a patrol car slowed in the street. She ducked her head and kept walking, following the cowboy's lesson two. Tucking her hands into the coat pockets, the fingers of her right hand curled around a piece of paper. She pulled it out, expecting trash from the previous owner, but saw a twenty-dollar bill. It wouldn't get her far, but it beat nothing.

Now she needed a safe place to sleep. *A warm, dry hotel room would be great.* Homeless people didn't have that luxury, and she didn't have enough cash. Where would a criminal hide? Her body ached, and mental exhaustion was making it hard to think clearly. Would she be able to pull off this operation? If she could just lie down for a few hours, she'd be ready to face anything. She headed toward the first dry spot she saw, a parking deck, and slid under the exit ramp.

Someone had inhabited the spot before. A used condom hung from a thorn branch, and the stiff ivy covering the ground was matted down in places. At least the space was dry and faced a one-way street, which made it hard to see from a passing police car. Colby stretched her sleeping bag out on the ground, grateful for the additional plastic sheet and water-repellent down. She zipped the closure and, using her backpack as a pillow, tried to relax. The warmth and comfort of the home she shared with her parents felt almost like a dream.

When she'd joined the air force to test her independence and begin her career, her parents had argued that the move was extreme. After she'd returned from Iraq and joined DEA, she'd worked all over the country, trying to find her specific niche. Her parents would probably have trouble seeing the value of this particular assignment among the homeless as well.

Maybe tagging along with her dad to visit soldiers at the VA Hospital and listening while he unofficially counseled them had made an impression on her. On some level, the thought of deceiving people like her father for the sake of making a case seemed wrong. She'd wanted an undercover assignment but wasn't convinced this one was the right fit. Or maybe this was exactly the place to make her mark. Only time would tell. For the moment she was dry and starting to warm up a bit.

She tossed and turned, visions of rats, lice, and other crawling creatures making sleep impossible. Vermin hadn't been on her list of concerns with this assignment, but it was probably only one of a long line of things she hadn't considered. There were so many ways she could screw up. How did the homeless survive worrying about things most people took for granted?

As she waited for morning, she flipped open her mobile phone and checked the stats. Eight minutes of airtime and one contact, Frankie. In the morning she'd call her parents and let them know she was okay, then reach out to this Frankie person. Leon had said to call only in an emergency, but she needed to know she had at least one ally close by.

She stared at the ramp above her, which seemed to be closing in. How would she protect herself if someone accosted her in this confined space? She'd always felt safe with her weapon handy, but she'd been stripped of that for this assignment as well. Her pulse raced and she felt hot and sweaty. Breathing deeply to calm her anxiety, she counted slowly in her head. She'd be fine in the morning when she focused on something besides everything that could go wrong. *What the hell have I gotten myself into?*

CHAPTER TWO

Jeez-us." Adena shook hot coffee from her hand and pulled the fabric of her once-clean blouse away from her chest as the brown stain spread and burned. The coffeepot teetered on the edge of the bathroom sink slash makeshift kitchen, and she grabbed it just before it fell. "I've got to finish this renovation before I kill myself." She poured another cup with one hand while unbuttoning her blouse with the other.

After she'd changed and cleaned up the mess, she settled into the lone chair in her living room and opened the morning paper. Her second cup of coffee almost ended up in her lap as she read the headline: DAYTIME RESOURCE CENTER A YEAR LATER.

Adena skimmed the first paragraph about her father's murder. Writer Martin Linen, who'd originally reported her father's homicide, retold the story. Her breath stuck in her throat as she read his emotionally charged phrases and evocative descriptions of the incident. She shivered and fought back tears as she stared at the photos of the crime scene she'd visited over a year ago.

Linen quoted police officers that spoke vaguely about leads they'd chased down with no results. DRC guests past and present mostly praised the center and the benefits to the community, but one man, John Tabor, criticized the center for refusing him shelter one sub-freezing night.

To his credit, Linen asked co-founder and board member, Oliver Worthington, if the DRC had suffered under poor leadership since her father's death and to comment on Tabor's criticism.

Worthington stated, "We had a few issues with our former director, but those were reported at the time and proper action was taken. We're very fortunate to have our current director, Florence Chamberlin. She is dedicated and makes sure the center runs at peak efficiency. The DRC administrator and I have the utmost confidence in her. As for anyone being turned away, I'm not familiar with that particular incident. All I can say is, perhaps we were at capacity, but alternate accommodations would've been suggested."

Poor leadership? Her father had given every free minute possible to the DRC. She remembered heated discussions between her parents about how much time and money her father devoted to his charity. Even after her mother died, Franklin Weber made his law practice and the DRC his top priorities, with Adena coming in a distant third. Since his death, she'd neglected her own life to keep his firm and charity running smoothly. How dare anyone question her dedication or leadership?

As for John Tabor's accusation, she'd get to the bottom of that one soon enough. The center had been slammed, providing shelter to the overflow from Urban Ministry after the early onset of cold weather. They'd done their best, but sometimes they just didn't have enough room, yet as Oliver had said, they always suggested another place for them to go.

Linen ended the article with a quote from city councilman Sterling Harbinger. "I think the city should set up an oversight committee to look into the center before they give them another dime of the taxpayers' money."

Adena's hands shook as she clenched the edges of the paper, and tears splattered onto the page. Her father had saved and sacrificed to establish a place for the homeless, and she wouldn't let anyone taint his work or dilute the center's effectiveness. Her father's words came to her as clearly as if he were standing in the room. "Honey, in times of adversity our family makes a plan, works it, and fixes the problem."

The first step on her fix-the-problem list was to contact the city council, donors, and other stakeholders who were probably reading this article and wondering if Harbinger had a valid point. With early damage control, she might be able to allay their fears before the political tide turned against her completely. But she didn't have the luxury of time. Her cell phone rang and she recognized the mayor's number. "Great. Just great."

"Good morning, Mayor. How are you today?" She stalled with niceties as she formulated a strategy on the fly.

"How am I? If you'd seen the morning paper, you wouldn't be asking such an asinine question." Mayor Freda Tremble's name had become something of a derogatory mantra among her detractors, and this morning Adena understood why. The woman's voice practically vibrated with nervous energy.

"Yes, I've seen it, but I'm sure there's just been a misunderstanding. Any problems that existed were addressed months ago. We're running like a well-oiled machine now."

"A misunderstanding?" Her voice rose an octave and quivered. "And turning people away on a freezing-cold night? If you could see the list of messages on my desk from DRC donors and citizens, you wouldn't call it a misunderstanding. People are seriously concerned about how their money is being spent. Can you blame them? Ever since your father..." The mayor's voice trailed off into a nervous cough, and Adena winced at the implication of her statement.

"Mayor, I assure you the DRC is being managed with exactly the same high standards my father demanded throughout his tenure. The center is part of his legacy, and I won't allow anyone to sully it or his name."

"Of course. I didn't mean to imply otherwise, but I need assurances for the donors and other stakeholders that their money and the city's funds are being spent wisely. Can you put something together and get back to me as soon as possible?"

How was she supposed to find immediate answers to nonexistent issues or ones that had already been resolved? "I certainly will, Mayor." She hung up and read the article again, making notes as she went. Could she have been so blinded by grief and her desire to make sure the center survived that she'd missed some obvious problems? Or was someone trying to destroy the center's reputation and her father's as well?

❖

A car alarm and thick exhaust fumes startled Colby from her nap. Had her parents left the windows open? She flipped over and fluffed her pillow, but the rough edges fought back. Not soft. Not home. Images of a night gone wrong returned. She looked around, confusion slowly giving way to realization. She should be excited about her undercover opportunity, but instead she felt isolated and nervous about diving into this new environment.

A cacophony of train horns, emergency sirens, and the compressive boom and hiss of commercial air conditioners had continually interrupted the little rest she'd gotten. She didn't function well without proper sleep. Her body throbbed from tossing and turning on the hard ground, and when she sat up, her bruised ribs made it hard to breathe.

Homeless and alone. Before yesterday, she would've considered either of those conditions unlikely. Today they were her reality. She wasn't sure which terrified her more. Was she afraid of the professional trial she was about to face or the personal challenge of doing it alone? It couldn't be worse than Iraq. *Aim High.* She repeated the motto for encouragement. Like she'd done with the air force, she'd signed on for this and had to make the best of it.

She rolled up her sleeping bag, tied it to her backpack, and slung it over her shoulders. The western sky was still dark, but shop windows across the street reflected the orange glow of sunrise. She checked to make sure no pedestrians or police cars were around before stepping onto the sidewalk. At least she didn't have to worry about taking a shower or fixing her hair.

She stopped at the corner of Bellemeade and Elm streets to get the lay of the land. High-rise office buildings in front and to the left of her, the parking deck she'd used for cover to her right, and a park catty-corner were within immediate view. She headed for the park and slid her belongings under a bench before taking a seat. A shiny building of metal and glass fronted the park, and to the left a clock tower flashed the time and temperature, six thirty, breakfast time.

Her stomach growled as she thought about her mother cooking bacon and eggs in their comfy old kitchen with the woodstove ablaze in the corner. Eating wasn't as simple as walking into the kitchen and foraging through the refrigerator or stopping by a fast-food joint anymore. She choked down the tightness in her throat and pressed a hand against her empty stomach.

Digging her phone from her boot, she dialed her parents. "Mom, it's me."

"Colby, darling, where are you? We were worried sick. Honey, come here. It's Colby." Her mother put her on speaker. "Talk to us. Are you okay?"

"Hi, Dad. I'm fine. I'm on an undercover assignment out of state. It came up really last minute, and I didn't have a chance to tell you before I left. I won't be home for a while."

"I don't like this. Sounds like the military all over again, secret missions with no contact." Her father's voice was lower than usual, and she imagined the horrible images running through his mind.

"Neither do I." Her mother's voice trembled. "That type of work is dangerous."

She hadn't considered this assignment might revive unpleasant memories of her time in Iraq for her mom and dredge up painful flashbacks for her father. If she told them she was living rough, with no backup, they'd only worry more. "I'm sorry, Mom. I'll be careful. The experience will be good for my career. I won't be able to check in every day. Would you please tell Kali that I'll call her when I can?"

"Of course, dear, but can't you at least tell us where you are?"

"Sorry, Mom, but we can email. I'll be able to pick up messages."

"Well, stay alert and keep your head down." Her father's advice harkened back to his days in the army, and she choked up remembering some of the experiences he'd shared. He'd suffered so much physical and emotional trauma, but instead of discouraging her dreams, he was encouraging her and letting her know he trusted her judgment. Classic Dad. She loved his unassuming nature and willingness to let her find her own way. She was going to miss their

Saturdays alone in his workshop creating some wooden masterpiece for a client.

"I will, and try not to worry about me. I love you both." She waited for them to hang up and blinked back tears. They'd worry no matter what she said, and that made her both happy and sad. She'd be one of the lucky ones in a homeless community.

Wiping her eyes with the back of her hand, she scanned her surroundings to make sure no one was within hearing distance before dialing her contact.

"Yeah?"

"Frankie?"

"Who wants to know?" The woman's irritated words overshadowed her soft tone.

"I'm Colby Vincent and—"

"Is this an emergency?"

"No."

"Are you in danger?"

"No."

"Injured?"

"No, I just—"

"You just what? Were lonely? Needed to talk? This is only your first day. I'm not a babysitter. I'll contact you when I can. In the meantime, don't blow up my phone with your sad-and-lonely messages." The call ended.

"Thanks for nothing." Colby slid the phone back inside her boot and checked the area again. Center City Park, as the colorful green flags on the streetlights indicated, covered a city block and resembled outdoor rooms bounded by raised planters and granite benches. Two pergolas and a pavilion provided shade for the hot summers she'd heard about in the South. A lawn branched out in front of the pavilion, and another small grassy area showed the wear of frequent activity. Crescent-shaped water stairs culminated in a central pool with a spouting fountain. The bench she'd chosen was one of several nestled among trees and bushes that in the spring would bloom and obscure their occupants from passersby.

As she watched, the city came to life. Business-suited workers filed into the high-rises, and loiterers settled around the perimeter of the park. A woman on the Friendly Avenue sidewalk perched on the edge of a planter and tucked her heaving garbage bag out of sight behind a bush. On the opposite side of the pavilion, an unkempt man settled onto a bench and opened a book but constantly scanned his environment instead of the pages. Colby was in the right place. All she had to do now was wait, not a well-developed trait.

She'd run several agents at once in undercover operations and always managed to do it without breaking a sweat. Sitting around a park all day watching for drug deals or waiting for homeless people to lead her to something useful was as interesting as swatting flies at a picnic. And forget about extracurricular activities to pass the time. Who would want a smelly, bald, unemployed woman even for a one-night stand? She'd have lots of downtime for introspection and planning her future. What could be more miserable?

"You new?" A tall young man wearing a lime-green work shirt walked toward her. A patch on his left pocket read CITY OF GREENSBORO, the name Eric embroidered on the right.

"Did I do something wrong?" The man and woman she'd seen earlier moved to the sidewalk off the park property as the employee approached her.

Eric sat down beside her on the bench. "Not really. Just thought I'd give you a few pointers since I haven't seen you before." His rounded face was almost cherubic, and his smile lit bright-blue eyes.

"I'd appreciate it. This isn't New York City, but it's still challenging since I don't know anything about it."

"You're from New York?" His eyes widened and he slowly scratched his head. "Why in the world would you come here?"

"It wasn't exactly a choice. I got robbed and dumped here. Now I'm stuck until I can figure out a way to get back."

"Well, my name's Eric." He waved his hand in front of him. "And this is my kingdom. Not really, but I work most days, sometimes evenings, keeping the park in order. Opening time is seven and closing at eleven. No trespassing after hours. There's a restroom around the side of the pavilion and a drink machine in back. No dipping, wading, or washing in the pools or fountain. Animals have to be on a leash and can't drink from or wade in the water features. You have to pick up after your dog too. No alcoholic beverages except with an event permit, and possession or use of any controlled substance in the park is not allowed. Littering is prohibited. No storing or leaving personal belongings unattended. Anything left unattended will be destroyed." He took a deep breath.

"Thank you for—"

"And firearms, motorized vehicles, remote-controlled cars, boats and planes, loud radios and boom boxes aren't allowed."

She started to thank him again, but he held up his hand. What more could there possibly be to prohibit in a park this small?

"Smoking, defacing park property, bicycling, skateboarding or rollerblading, building fires, barbecuing or outdoor cooking, disturbing the peace, panhandling or selling products, removing items from trash receptacles, gambling, sleeping, engaging in illegal activities, and distributing or posting flyers are also not allowed." He gave her a quick nod as if satisfied with his recitation.

"How long did it take you to learn all that, Eric?"

"Quite a while. It's a mouthful, but you get the drift. Just about everything is prohibited except short-term sitting, eating, and looking. If you need a reminder, I can get you a printed copy of the rules. Unfortunately, our society tends to criminalize homelessness, so be careful."

"I think I'm good, but maybe you could help me with something else."

He leaned back and entwined his fingers behind his head. "Shoot."

"Where would I find a map of the downtown area?"

"No problem. One block east." He pointed to the left. "And two south to the train depot. They've got bus and train schedules too, and a small coffee shop. Anything else?"

"Library?"

He inclined his chin toward the restaurant across the street. "Take that alley to the domed building. You need a library card to use the computers and check out books, but it doesn't cost anything." He looked up at the clock tower, stood, and stretched his skinny frame. "Opening time. I have to remove the chains across the entrances and put out the chairs and umbrellas."

"One more question. Where can I get a shower, preferably free?"

"I was hoping you'd ask." He pinched his nose but winked at the same time. "You're not bad yet. Daytime Resource Center, just down the street from the depot, on the left. If you have questions later, I'm in and out all day. Good luck."

"Thanks, Eric." He lumbered off like a man in no particular hurry to begin his day. She was impressed with his overall knowledge of the area, his willingness to spend time explaining everything to her, and his Southern hospitality. She'd try not to break his litany of rules.

Her first priority was a toilet, then a map and something to eat. She grabbed her backpack and scooted around the side of the pavilion to the restroom. The space was large for a toilet, clean, and even had a thermostat, but no paper towels. It would be a good place to sleep at night if she could pick the lock and sneak in. She splashed water on her face and freshened up before heading to the depot for a map.

The J. Douglas Galyon Depot, at the T-intersection of Church and Washington streets, was a striking building with Ionic columns and three-story arched entry. It was no Grand Central Station in size or activity, but the architecture was indicative of the early twentieth century and had been meticulously renovated. Inside, the vaulted ceilings and substantial benches made the space feel expansive. A mural displaying the service area of the Southern Railway system in the 1920s decorated the ticketing area. Colby stood at the entry staring like a child in a huge cathedral for the first time.

While the space was beautiful, it wasn't very user friendly for non-travelers. The waiting room was plastered with signs, FOR TICKETED PASSENGERS ONLY, and the restrooms had a secured keypad entry system. Colby collected a city map and train schedule before checking out the small coffee shop. She really wanted one of the pastries, but decided to wait until she finished exploring and could sit and enjoy the treat. When the ticket agent started eyeballing her, she headed back up Church Street toward the library.

"Good morning, honey." The middle-aged attendant gave her a wide smile, and Colby actually felt welcome in the large space. "How can I help you?"

"I'd like a card, please. I understand they're..." Why was it so hard to ask for something free? It just felt wrong, like she was taking something from someone who needed it more than she did.

"Free? Of course. Everybody should have access to knowledge. Don't you agree?"

"Absolutely. Thank you." Colby provided the necessary information and then accepted the library card with a smile. She explored the two floors of the facility and found secluded spaces where she could contact her parents and sign into her DEA account. On the way out, she picked up two leaflets that gave the bus schedules around town.

Hunkering down on the curb outside the library, Colby unfolded the downtown map and studied it. Market Street was the north-south divider and Elm Street the east-west line. Her shelter last night had been the Bellemeade Street parking deck between Elm and Greene streets, marked by a large P on the map. She could find that again with no problem. The depot was only two and a half blocks from where she sat on Church Street, and if she remembered properly, the homeless camp she'd been thrown out of was only a short walk from there. The streets formed a series of squares that made getting around relatively easy. She'd never realized how slowly time passed when she had nothing to do.

"Hey, you, bald girl, what're you doing here?"

"What?" She looked up at an unsmiling police officer. "Sorry, sir." She'd only made it a day and a half before violating the no-cops rule of street survival. She slowly stood, careful not to make any sudden moves. He looked young and inexperienced, and she didn't want to startle or provoke him.

"You're new around here. I know my area."

She glanced at his nametag. Officer Reynolds looked about sixteen, and he probably hadn't been in the area long either, based on his accent. "Yes, sir, just a couple of days now."

"Let me see some ID." He held out his hand, and she carefully slid her card from her back pocket. "Colby Vincent from New York City. What brings you to Greensboro?"

"A bit of bad luck." She knew what police officers looked for on routine stops, so she kept her answers informative but not too specific and always respectful. "I'm looking for work and the quickest way back, not that I don't like your nice town, but it's not home." She gave just the right amount of eye contact and kept her expression neutral as he checked her name for warrants. She felt strangely comfortable in the officer's presence. They were similar—protectors—who spoke the same language and stood for a code of conduct, like soldiers.

He handed back her ID and gave her a final once-over. "Okay, Ms. Vincent. Stay out of trouble. I'll be watching."

"Thank you, Officer. Have a nice day." She was conflicted about their interaction. While it was comforting to think someone might be looking out for her, his attention could potentially jeopardize her case. She continued scanning the map until the officer was out of sight in the opposite direction. On the legend, she found a coffee shop right across the street from Center City Park. While constantly scanning for homeless folks or possible drug activity, she made her way to what would serve as breakfast and possibly lunch.

The quaint European style café, Dolce Aroma, was built into a lower corner of the parking garage and had a seating area on the sidewalk. When she entered, a white-haired lady greeted her with a heavily accented good morning, pointing to the menu board behind her. Colby studied the offerings and the pastries in the display case. She was desperate for a mocha latte and a piece of the sticky sweet baklava but needed to watch her money and eat something more substantial. "I'll have a small black coffee and a blueberry bagel with cream cheese, please."

"Very good." The lady prepared the coffee in a paper cup and carefully placed the lid on it. "Sugar and cream is over there." She nodded toward a small cart to the left of the counter. She placed the bagel on a paper plate, rang up Colby's order, and returned her change from the twenty. "You like baklava?"

Colby glanced from the change in her hand to the treat. "I guess not, but thanks."

"This one is free. I must throw it away soon. It grows stale." She opened the case and retrieved the pastry in a piece of parchment and placed it beside the bagel on Colby's plate. "Please, enjoy."

She didn't hesitate. "Thank you so much." She took her treasures to one of the outside tables and dropped her backpack against the wall out of the path of foot traffic. Across the street, the two homeless people she'd seen earlier eyed her suspiciously as she ate. Were they afraid she would threaten their turf or take some kindness intended for them?

As a cop, she'd honed her observation skills, but how much more astute would she have to be to survive the streets on a daily basis? At least a cop could go home at night for a respite from danger, but the homeless lived it twenty-four seven with fewer resources. The tension of survival was constant. Taking the last bite of her bagel, she realized she'd eaten both pastries without making a conscious choice. She should've saved one for later, been more frugal, but hunger had won the battle before she knew she was in one.

She watched the two across the street study her and decided it was better if she kept her distance. She might give off some kind of cop vibe, and she couldn't afford that. Like any other legend in a new assignment, she had to bide her time and ease into the local scene. Another day or two of acclimation and she'd be ready to mingle with the natives and perhaps visit the Daytime Resource Center.

CHAPTER THREE

For the fourth day, Colby woke stiff and disoriented under the garage ramp. A group of feral cats fighting and fucking all night had made sleep impossible. As she emerged from beneath the concrete slab, a passerby eyed her. People were starting to take notice, so she'd have to find another place to sleep soon. And today was definitely the day she needed to visit the DRC for a much-needed shower. The French whore's baths she'd been taking in the park restroom were no longer effective. And it was time to dive into this assignment.

"Poor little cherry, boo-hoo-hoo. Don't even know what to do."

Colby recognized the high-pitched voice of the woman from the depot her first night. She looked even scarier than she sounded in a Hello Kitty sweatshirt, pink tights, and a matching plastic roller bag. Her hair stuck up, thousands of blond cactus needles, and her eyes were so blue and wide she looked as if she'd been scared. She rambled and waved her hands, keeping time to some internal rhythm. With a nice hairstyle and different clothes, she could've passed for another worker filing into the city for an eight-to-five job, except for the crazy look in her eyes.

"Go away." Colby regretted the comment when the woman's gaze shifted to the ground. "I'm sorry." How could anyone survive on the streets without regular food, shelter, and medicine, not to mention significant human contact? This woman was apparently managing while also struggling with mental issues. She should probably admire her resilience, not make assumptions based on her appearance.

"Boy or girl, can't really say, but you better come this way." The woman inclined her head for Colby to follow. Sooner or later she'd have to decide whether to continue as a lone wolf or join the community, and the former wouldn't help with her assignment. She trailed behind just in case they ended up somewhere helpful. She didn't have anywhere else to be, and the last four days of idle wandering were getting old.

Miss Kitty retraced Colby's path from her first night, through downtown, past the train depot, and under the bridge to a building set back from the street. A line of people snaked from the door of the single-story structure in a zigzag through the small parking lot.

"I looked for you like some ole fool. You made me late, the coffee's cool. I may not eat another day. And if I don't, your ass will pay." Miss Kitty squealed through clenched teeth that were surprisingly well kept for a homeless person.

"Sorry." Kitty's eyes widened as Colby felt a hand settle on her shoulder.

"I see you've met Sing Song."

She turned, and the man who'd exiled her from the homeless camp pointed to her companion. "Sing Song?"

"That's what we call her. You *have* heard her."

She nodded, afraid the more she talked the more trouble she'd be in.

"I'm Cowboy, by the way." He held out his hand.

Perfect. She accepted his greeting. Why was he being so friendly now? "Colby."

"The FNG. I could tell the other night."

She hadn't been called the fucking new guy since her initial assignment in Iraq. She had a feeling some of the same restrictions applied.

"Didn't mean to be rude the other night, but we've got rules. You'll learn pretty fast. Today is all that matters. Take care of yourself because it's damn sure nobody else will. Don't take anybody else's sleeping spot. And don't attract attention. Homed people think we're invisible. Stay that way." Cowboy emphasized each statement as if her life depended on it.

He sounded like an audio book of unhelpful slogans. She was in a different kind of organization here, fighting a different battle, but it felt familiar. Every culture had its mores. She wondered again how military men dedicated to service and honor ended up in the middle of a drug investigation.

"I'll do my best. What's this place, Cowboy?" She'd already read about the DRC but had so far only observed. She needed to sound like the new kid who didn't know anything.

"DRC. Daytime Resource Center. It's *our* place. They've got showers, job training, laundry facilities, counseling, phones and computers, lots of other stuff."

"Coffee. Just let there be coffee."

Cowboy eyeballed her hard. "You a girl? Hard to tell with no hair and those clothes."

"Yeah. Why?"

"You need to find a woman to hang with out here. It's safer. And not that one," he said, nodding toward Sing Song. "She's crazy and draws too much attention."

"What am I supposed to do, take applications?" No one had even spoken to her except Cowboy and Sing Song, if you considered her rhyming verses actual conversation.

"And a smart-ass too. What was your SC in the air force? Barracks queen?"

Colby bristled at the insult. Barracks queens slept with anybody in the camp. She'd never been that lonely or desperate, but didn't judge women who were. War was hell on men, but more so on women because everybody expected or wanted you to fail. "My specialist code was information technology." Her four-year stint had been intense, but she'd escaped relatively intact compared to most of her fellow airmen. "You?"

"Army treadhead, tank driver, until we rolled over an IED. Next stop disability and discharge. I'd planned on a career in the army. Now look at me." He tapped against the lower part of his leg and produced a metallic ding. "When you're out, nobody cares, especially not the government." Cowboy stared toward the DRC and fell silent as they inched forward.

While they'd been talking, Sing Song had nudged her way up the line, most folks giving way to her rants and arm flapping. Like society at large, the homeless community seemed to neither understand nor tolerate the mentally challenged in their midst. Colby suddenly felt ashamed for being so critical of her earlier.

"Could I have your attention, please?" A tall African-American woman with a soldier's bearing stood beside another woman at the entrance of the DRC and waved her hands.

"Uh-oh, this can't be good." Cowboy slapped his hat against the side of his leg.

"The day room is almost full, and we're already overbooked for beds and chairs tonight. If you're new or need to see the doctor, come up front." Few moved from the line. "Come on, people. I see some of you every morning and evening. Let the new folks in."

The line thinned, and Cowboy pushed Colby toward the front. "Get up there. Have that eye checked, and if the doc offers you a script for pain, take it."

"But—"

"Don't argue with me, airman. Take the damn meds and find out what the center's got to offer. They'll make you sign in. Don't panic. Miss Adena and Flo are the good guys."

Colby moved toward the door, and as she got closer, she dug into her backpack and fished out the small tube of toothpaste. She squeezed a dab on her finger and rubbed it on her teeth like she'd done as a kid on camping trips. A bottle of water would be heaven, but she licked and swallowed until her mouth felt semi-refreshed.

"Good morning. I'm Adena." The dark-haired woman welcomed everyone as they entered, holding each person's attention for a second of individual recognition. Her presence seemed to calm the restlessness in the room, and several people lingered near her. "If you'll take a seat at the tables against the wall, those ladies will handle your sign-in and intake." Adena turned back to the line, and when Colby met her stare, the nerves she'd been experiencing all morning vanished. Adena's left brow arched over golden-brown eyes as they swept Colby.

"The doctor needs to check your eye. Are you hurt anywhere else?" The low, silvery tone of her voice dimpled Colby's skin.

"Ribs." Without thinking, Colby pulled up her shirt. "Only hurts when I breathe."

Adena reached out but stopped just short of touching her side. Colby sucked in a mouthful of air. "Ahhh…like that."

"I'm so sorry. How did it happen?"

"Would you believe I woke up like this a few days ago?"

Adena's manicured eyebrow curved higher toward her salt-and-pepper hairline.

"Seriously, I don't remember how it happened, but it's not bad. I can almost see out of my eye now." She smiled, trying to reroute the sensations tingling in her middle. For a second she imagined that the involuntary arch of Adena's brow signaled mutual attraction. Colby hadn't responded this pleasurably to her girlfriend in months and immediately felt a pang of guilt for not being honest with Kali.

Adena pulled back and straightened her collar, seemingly unaffected by their interaction. The white silk blouse and tapered wool pants labeled her as volunteer or administrator, definitely not guest. When Colby finally looked back at Adena's face, her smile relayed total confidence. This woman knew who she was and where she belonged.

"Move on. You're blocking the door." Flo's voice cracked like a drill sergeant, snapping her out of the trance Adena had cast.

"Head over that way, please." Shaking her head slightly at Flo, Adena pointed to the opposite wall, but one of the ladies at the sign-in area raised her hands. Every seat was occupied. Adena looked at her watch and directed Colby to a card table in the main room. "Wait over there. I'll help you shortly."

Colby settled between a heavyset African-American woman who clung possessively to a grocery cart overflowing with clothes and a middle-aged man with a marine buzz cut. Neither spoke, and she was grateful as she cataloged the routines around her. After a few minutes, Adena walked toward her. Colby nervously brushed at sleep wrinkles in her clothes and combed a hand over her shaved head. *So much for flicking my strawberry-blond hair for effect.*

Adena greeted her with the same expression she'd used earlier, confident and sexy as hell. Her short black hair feathered toward her face in layered waves, and Colby wanted to reach up and brush it away from her beautiful face. She studied the arc of Adena's mouth and traced the natural upward curve that accentuated luscious lips. How she'd love to—

"Are you ready?" Adena stood over her, eyes boldly scanning her as if already forming a first impression.

"Oh yes. I mean, sorry. I was daydreaming."

"Clearly." The word slid from her mouth with a sexy intonation that evoked the most enjoyable chills. "First-time guests have an intake form, just a few questions." She handed Colby a sheet of paper and a pen. "If you have any problems, ask."

"I can come back later. It looks like you're busy this morning. Other people may need help more than I do." Adena stared at her, and Colby felt like the clichéd specimen under a microscope. "Did I say something wrong?"

Adena shook her head. "First-timers aren't usually willing to give up their place. Thanks for your concern, but we'll try to see everyone. The form, please."

"Do you run this place yourself? Everyone defers to you, and you seem very good at the hands-on role."

"Not even close. You know what they say: 'It takes a village.'"

"You're doing a good thing, providing a place for them—us. Thank you."

Adena gave her another strange look as Colby turned her attention to the paperwork. She provided as much information as possible without revealing her real purpose. Without a home, she didn't fill in many of the spaces. She admitted a twinge of disappointment at not being able to share the truth with Adena. She didn't want to be just another homeless person to her.

Just another homeless person? God, she sounded so privileged and judgmental. She was no better than anyone else here. Maybe this assignment was exactly what she needed to reinforce the lessons of her childhood. She signed the paper and slid it too forcefully across the desk, upset with her inability to immediately adapt and empathize.

Adena's intense stare lingered on her until silence hung between them. Had she seen something beneath Colby's façade? If she wasn't careful her attitude would expose her as a fraud before her work began.

"Let's see what we have." As Adena scanned the registration, her brows bunched together. "Colby Vincent. No offense but—"

"Why is that phrase always followed by something totally offensive?"

"Sorry. I'm trying to be delicate. Male or female? Your appearance and that husky voice are deceiving, which could be an asset in your current circumstances."

"The shaved head doesn't help. The guys thought it was funny, but I'm all woman."

Adena's smile widened for a second before she caught her bottom lip between her teeth and schooled her expression. "You need to be careful out there, Colby. The streets aren't safe, especially for a young, attractive woman. Find somebody to watch your back."

Was Adena flirting or merely trying to be helpful? Colby was about to toss out one of her flirty comebacks but stopped. Leave it to her to meet someone interesting at the most inopportune time. "Thanks for the advice."

"Do you have identification? We usually make a copy to keep on file."

Colby pulled the slightly altered driver's license from her back pocket, grateful that she'd gotten into the habit of carrying it just in case. If the cop hadn't noticed anything suspicious about the card, it should pass Adena's inspection. The information was accurate, except her address, an apartment complex on the opposite side of town from her parents' home.

While Adena made a copy, she faced the wall but rattled off information that sounded like part of a prepared speech. "We offer skill assessment, some job training, interview pointers, and we have a computer lab for job searches and resume preparation. If any of that interests you, let one of us know. Our housing specialist can discuss short- and long-term options with you as well. The main goal here is to get you back into a full-time job and permanent housing as soon as possible and to support you during the transition. The longer you're displaced, the harder it will be to rejoin the mainstream."

"I could really use laundry facilities and a shower. I totally reek."

"Sorry. I get carried away with the long-term goal sometimes and lose sight of the more immediate needs." Adena pointed to another room. "The showers are next to the washer and dryer, but there's a sign-up sheet and the last load is at one. Do you need anything else?"

"Actually, this probably isn't your job, but I'd kill for a cup of coffee."

"Of course." Adena wiggled a finger at one of the volunteers. Within seconds, he appeared with coffee, cream, and sweetener.

"Anything else, Miss Adena?" The man stared, obviously as infatuated as Colby had been moments before.

"Will you join me for a cup?" Colby realized too late that she'd overstepped.

Without Colby noticing, Flo had walked up behind her. "This ain't a damn coffee shop. Does it look like we've got time for drinks and small talk?"

"Flo, there's no need to be rude," Adena said. "No, thank you, Colby. One of the staff or volunteers will assist you with orientation if you'd like. And don't forget to have Doctor Raymond check your eye and ribs in the clinic. Good day, Ms. Vincent, and good luck."

Adena forced herself not to run from the room, more specifically from Colby Vincent. She walked normally until she reached the office bathroom and locked the door behind her. Colby's shaved head had caught Adena's eye as she waited in line, but something more primal held her attention. Was it her androgynous body, her powerful air of independence, or those absinthe-green eyes gleaming with possibility, totally unaware of what lay ahead? She was newly homeless, as evidenced by her relatively clean clothes and willingness to offer her place to another. Adena tried to help people like Colby before they lost the ability and the will to live and thrive. But she'd never been so completely blindsided by a guest. Not here.

She'd experienced instant chemistry with women before, but this one stirred more than an itchy desire for pleasure. The closer Colby got to her, the more her skin tingled and flushed. When Colby raised her shirt, Adena's pulse raced and her usually steady breathing quickened. She'd barely stopped her hand from skimming the bruised flesh along Colby's ribcage. Her palms felt sticky as she imagined the color of Colby's hair and running her fingers through it. Her responses to this woman made no sense. She should've handed Colby off to another staffer, but everyone was busy.

Adena functioned efficiently because she adhered to rules. One was inviolate. She did not sleep with clients from her law practice or guests from the DRC. Until today, the latter had seemed inconceivable. Even if Colby eventually resurrected her life and moved on, preying on women who came to them for assistance was both unethical and untenable. She'd been outraged several years ago when a volunteer had behaved so despicably. Adena was the gold standard for proper conduct, not the exception to it.

She'd never reacted physically to a client, but Colby Vincent seemed different from the typical homeless person. Adena shook her head at her image in the mirror. "You of all people should know there are no *typical* homeless people. And sexual attraction is a physiological response, not a mandate to act. You haven't broken any rules yet. See that you don't."

She splashed water on her face and focused on her upcoming meeting with Oliver instead of the feeling that she'd slipped off kilter. Since she was a child, she'd sensed significant events in her life before they happened—her mother's sudden death when Adena was ten; her father's murder last year—but today something had definitely rattled her without warning. Maybe she was just tired, overworked, and stressed about that bloody article Linen had written.

She exited the restroom and almost bumped into Flo going in. "That baldy is going to be a problem, Adena. You know I can smell trouble."

Florence Chamberlin had been the director of the DRC for only a year, but she ran it like clockwork. Nothing fazed her. The center would probably have folded after her father's death without Flo because Adena had been unable to set foot in the place for months. Now she came by on her way to her law office and after work to help out, but Flo was the driving force behind the center's success. "I hope you're wrong, because she really looks out of place."

"That's what I'm talking about. She doesn't belong here and that means trouble. Mark my words." Flo sliced her index finger through the air in the shape of an X.

"If anyone can handle her, it's you. I'll be in the office with Ollie if you need me. By the way, have you had a chance to look for that name I asked about?"

"John Tabor. Yeah, I checked, but he's not in our system."

"Really?"

Flo shook her head.

"That's strange. Why would Linen have interviewed him?"

"I just said he wasn't in the computer. We only got that system nine months ago. He could've been a one-time walk-in who never got transferred."

"You could be right, but check our log-in books anyway. Keep it quiet though. I don't want our guests upset. They're probably already afraid we're going to be shut down."

"Just FYI, most of our guests want to beat the crap out of Martin Linen for that article, bringing up the past and all that pain for you. Several have volunteered to give us glowing recommendations, if you want."

"Tha...thank you." Adena ducked her head as her vision blurred. "They're very kind. I'm so proud of our people and the work we've done here. Thanks, Flo. We'll talk later."

When Adena opened the private office door, her law partner, Oliver Worthington, was settling into a leather wingback chair in front of her father's antique desk. Out of respect, he never sat behind the desk, and she appreciated the gesture.

She flashed to a memory of her father leafing through law books, preparing for trial at that desk and a ten-year-old Adena perched on the edge reading comics. After her mother died, most of the time she'd spent with her father was either at the charity he and Oliver founded, in his law office, or in the back row of a courtroom watching him try a case. He'd promised more time together, but it never materialized. Eventually, he too was gone.

Oliver rose and pecked her on both cheeks. "Are you all right, Adena? You look flushed."

"I'm fine, Ollie. It's been a hectic morning."

"Then my timing is perfect."

She took a chair beside him and waited. When he was ready to broach the topic he'd tiptoed around since her father's death, he'd come out with it. Ollie was a patient man. Her, not so much. "Any time now. I do have DRC guests and a law practice that need attention."

He chuckled. "There's my goddaughter." He gave her a fatherly smile, genuine and nonjudgmental.

"How can I help?"

"Actually, I want to help you, if you'll let me. I'd like to take over the resource center." She started to interrupt, but he gave her one of his I'm-not-finished stares that she used to get during law school when they argued cases. "I know. It's part of your father's legacy. We started it together, supported it until we obtained charity status, and nurtured it into a cornerstone of homeless services for the community. This place means as much to me as it did to him. I just think you've got too much on your plate right now. And with the recent article in the paper, maybe a change would help for a while."

"I can handle it. Besides, I need to find out Councilman Harbinger's agenda. He could really hurt us if more of the council jumps on his bandwagon at budget time."

"I think the leadership concerns were about our former director, as I told Linen. Best to just let it blow over, Adena."

"That's not an option. I appreciate you handling the interview, but we can't afford to have anything affect us financially. John Tabor has questioned the equity of one of our basic services. Our economic future depends on answers. Now the mayor wants a report."

"Adena, you have to choose your battles wisely."

Pressure built in her chest, but she kept her voice calm as she spoke. "I will always fight to defend my father's legacy, and I'll do it alone if necessary."

"We all need help occasionally, and that's what I'm trying to do. I haven't approached you before because we were both grieving, and still are. But we have to look forward. The practice has slowed since your father's…death."

"Murder. He was murdered, Oliver."

"And that's another thing. I understand you want answers, but you can't keep hounding the police department. They're doing the best they can."

"Are they?" She stood and paced, hands clenched at her sides, forcing her voice to remain steady. "It's been a year since he was killed in *this* parking lot after work. Is the police department so incompetent they can't find the killer of one of the city's most prominent men? My father will *not* become another forgotten victim."

"I've spoken to the chief several times, and the detectives are pretty sure the suspect is a homeless person, possibly a transient."

"I don't accept that. It's too convenient. I'm not convinced they're really trying."

"Adena, come sit down, please. I didn't mean to upset you. I'd just like to relieve your workload for a while so you can focus on whatever is most important to you, whether that's remodeling your home, trying cases, volunteering, or vacationing. If you're uncomfortable turning over the DRC permanently, we can have a trial period. You're here first thing in the morning and until after check-in at night and trying your cases during the day. It's not healthy."

Oliver was trying to help, and it wouldn't do any good to lash out at him. She collapsed in her chair again as some of her irritation quieted. "I know, Ollie. I wasn't sure I could continue to work here at all after he died, but this was his baby, his dream. I can't let him down."

"Of course not, but you need to take better care of yourself. Enjoy life. Date occasionally. I wouldn't expect you to totally give up the center. Just leave the financial and fundraising aspects to me. Flo and I would probably have a riot on our hands if you dropped out completely."

"You've already taken most of Dad's legal clients, which was a tremendous load."

"Keeps me out of trouble."

"I'd probably be more inclined to turn over the practice. Something about philanthropic work appeals to me."

"We can talk about that down the road, but in the meantime will you at least consider my offer?"

The thought of relinquishing her father's work to Ollie felt like failure. She'd vowed to keep his firm and his charity healthy and viable, regardless of the sacrifice. She had to get to the bottom of his death and that newspaper article before she released the reins even slightly. And besides, she didn't really have a life outside of work. Dating was time-consuming and long-term relationships overrated. Her parents' love hadn't been able to protect her mother from a brain aneurism or her father from a murderer's knife. Permanence was an illusion. "I'll consider it, Ollie, but don't rush me."

CHAPTER FOUR

By the time Colby showered, threw her clothes in the washer, and met with the doctor, it was almost ten in the morning. He'd declared her ribs only bruised and handed her a roguish patch to wear over her eye for a few days. She spotted Flo near the front door scanning the room like a prison guard, and Cowboy at the computers with a nerdy-looking guy.

He looked up as she approached and waved her over. "Hey, it's Blackbeard. All right?"

"Yeah, mostly bruised."

"You get the script?"

She waved the square of paper. "What am I supposed to do with it? I don't even know where the drugstore is."

"Hang on to it. There's always somebody going for meds."

Agent Curtis had briefed her and Leon on the little they knew of the diversion scam, but Cowboy's comment sounded more like friendly advice than anything nefarious. She folded the prescription and stuffed it into the pocket of her backpack. "What's everybody still doing here?"

"Haven't had orientation?"

She shook her head.

"Probably need to do that, just so you know what you can get."

"Can't you tell me?"

"Didn't take you to raise, airman." Cowboy tipped his hat and turned back to the computer guy, who'd reduced the screen he'd been working on when she approached.

"Can you at least tell me where I can hang out without being harassed?"

"Hang here, take a nice long walk, or Center City Park. Walk down Washington Street to the first traffic light. Turn right and go to Friendly Avenue. The park's on your left. Can't miss it. Just remember—"

"Don't attract attention. What about dinner and somewhere to sleep?"

"Grab a Little Green Book from Carolyn, Doc Everett's nurse, before you go. It has all the meal places in town. Try First Presbyterian up Elm tonight for dinner and Urban Ministry on West Lee Street to sleep. Get there early."

Like she had any idea where either was. She retrieved her clothes from the dryer, picked up her copy of the blessed food book, and snagged a couple of apples on the way out.

"Hey, new girl," Flo said as she passed. "What you doing here?"

The question took her by surprise. "Isn't it obvious?"

"Don't get smart with me, newbie." Flo stepped closer, eye-to-eye with Colby's five-foot-ten frame.

"Sorry, I'm just trying to get some help, like everybody else." Colby had the uncomfortable feeling she wasn't fooling Flo.

"Not buying it. I'm watching you, so don't cause any trouble. Adena and the DRC don't need any more problems, especially right now."

"Yes, ma'am." What had tweaked Flo's added scrutiny, and what did she mean about the DRC not needing more problems *right now*? And why was everybody *watching* her? Colby vowed to be more cautious, especially around Flo and Adena. Both women were sharp and had keyed in to the fact that maybe she wasn't as she appeared. Pretending to be homeless wasn't just about showing up at the center, hanging out on the street, and foraging for food. Everyone in this world seemed suspicious of everyone else. Nobody got a pass.

Colby headed back toward the park, feeling clean and refreshed, and reflecting on her current situation. She'd never been completely free without the demands of family, girlfriend, or job. The training, deployments, and specific missions of the air force had kept her occupied. The loose-ends aspect of this assignment made her uneasy. She appreciated the structure and stability of connections and purpose. She had to identify some goals, or the amorphous nature of this job and the solitude could overwhelm her.

She straddled a thigh-high bird sculpture in the park, dropped her backpack, and enjoyed the sun as it chased away the cold that lingered from the night before. Looking around the park and nearby streets, she decided this area was too populated and well patrolled to be a drug hotbed, but it was definitely the homeless mecca. She had to find the place where the two collided. So far, she hadn't noticed anything suspicious. Maybe she'd been distracted trying to adapt to the loneliness and isolation of her legend.

She pulled the phone from her boot and dialed her parents. "Hi, Mom. How are you?"

"Colby, darling. It's so good to hear your voice. It's been days and I'm not used to that. Are you all right?"

"Fine, but I can't talk long." She really just wanted to hear her mother's voice, to know she was loved and missed. "I wanted to check on you and Dad."

"Always worried about somebody else. We raised a good daughter. We're fine, honey, but we miss you whizzing through all the time. Are things okay with the job?"

Colby's heart swelled at her mother's words. She missed talking about her day with her parents and troubleshooting cases with her dad. Nothing compared to the unconditional love of parents. "Not much progress, but I think this one will be slow to develop. Anyway, got to go, Mom. Tell Dad hello for me, and I'll call again when I can. Please don't worry. I love you."

As she closed the phone, a shadow appeared on the ground next to hers. She turned and Adena was standing behind her, a curvy outline against the eastern sky. "Hello, Miss Adena."

"Just Adena, please." She pointed. "The eye patch makes an interesting statement."

"I told the doctor it wasn't necessary, but he insisted."

"Either of your injuries could've been serious. Would you like to share how they really happened? Anything you tell me will be kept in confidence."

"You certainly are persistent, but I really don't remember. You realize you can't save everyone, right?" Colby winced at the low, intimate tone of her voice. Talking to her mother had left her vulnerable, and vulnerability could get her killed on the street.

The sparkle in Adena's eyes deepened. "I'm just concerned. Sorry if I overstepped."

"I should apologize for being presumptuous. I don't know you. Forgive me?"

"No need." Adena motioned to a bench near the bird sculpture. "Sit for a moment?"

"Don't like birds?"

"Let's just say I'm not used to straddling one at ten o'clock in the morning." Her expression softened, the warm brown of her eyes turning darker.

"Stop," Colby said.

"Stop what?"

"Looking at me like that."

"How exactly?" Adena asked.

"Like you can see into my soul." A woman who maintained eye contact while delivering a sexually charged line was a major turn-on. A tendril of arousal crept up Colby's spine, and she forced herself to breathe steadily as Adena took a seat on the bench. "I should probably let your comment pass, but I'm not that virtuous, and you left yourself wide open. So, what *are* you used to straddling at ten o'clock in the morning?" She grinned and appreciatively scanned the suit jacket that completed Adena's earlier ensemble. She looked delicious.

"A fine line between legality and justice in a courtroom."

"You're an attorney too?" Adena's cool demeanor made sense, but her unwavering stare hinted at something else. The combination was seductive, a promise of passion just beneath the surface.

"Among other things, but let's talk about you. I didn't mean to eavesdrop, but I overheard part of your phone call. You obviously have someone you love. Why don't you go back? Is it worse than being homeless?"

Colby warmed at Adena's obvious concern for her welfare and almost told her the truth. "My parents, but they're not an option right now."

"Any other family or friends you can ask for help?"

"Not really. I've pretty much burned all those bridges or I wouldn't be here, right?" Her experience in New York had shown most people wouldn't choose a life on the street if other options were available. Hopelessness fueled the cycle of homelessness.

"Then at least promise me you'll look for housing and a job soon. I can help...I mean the DRC can help. I don't want to see you stuck in this life, beaten up again or worse."

Her eyes held Colby in thrall, urging, almost pleading. "You're doing it again, staring at me like I'm the only person in the world. No wonder people are all over you at the center."

Adena ignored her observation. "You're different, Colby." For the first time, Adena broke eye contact, as if she'd said something inappropriate. "Talk to some of the folks on the street. You'll see it's not as easy as it may seem."

"You care about me." The realization caught Colby off guard. She hadn't meant to say it aloud, but Adena's compassion had made her feel special, and she'd momentarily slipped out of character. She'd felt something when they met but only imagined Adena had as well. "I'm sorry. I shouldn't have said that, any of it."

Adena stood and hoisted the strap of her briefcase onto her shoulder. "I care about all our guests. Please think about what I've said." She walked toward Elm Street without looking back.

As she watched Adena disappear around the corner, Colby buried her head in her hands. She was five days into her first undercover assignment, and the only progress she'd made was thinking about Adena constantly since meeting her. She'd been flirty, suggestive, and downright overt about her attraction. Almost everything she'd said to the woman was out of bounds. She'd never behaved so badly.

❖

Adena shifted her briefcase from shoulder to shoulder, uncomfortable with its weight and the conversation she'd just had with Colby. She hadn't expected to see Colby as she cut through the park on her normal route to her office. She'd fixed her eyes on the direction she intended to go but wound up standing behind Colby eavesdropping on her phone call. She rationalized that the more she knew about Colby, the better her chance of easing her back into the mainstream.

When she'd heard Colby say, "Please don't worry. I love you," she'd been compelled to approach her. If there was someone who could help Colby, she needed to encourage her to reach out. But the warmth she'd witnessed on the phone had faded, and Colby was as evasive about her injuries as she'd been at the center. Then she'd been surprised again when Colby had spoken so freely about her parents. This woman was a contradiction, a puzzle she didn't have the time or energy to piece together. She'd invested in guests before and been disappointed when her efforts only enabled a hopeless case. Maybe Flo was right. With everything else on her agenda, she didn't need another distracting project.

She walked into her law office, shoving thoughts of Colby Vincent aside and preparing to defend the underrepresented. "Any messages, Chris?"

Christine Mitchell, her receptionist and doer of all things necessary, slowly rose from behind the chest-high counter. Her close-cropped black hair appeared first, followed by an eyebrow ring over deep-blue eyes, a tiny diamond stud in the left side of her nose, and finally an incongruous welcoming smile. Chris was over fifty but never copped to her true age, saying it was irrelevant if properly camouflaged.

"Your first two clients cancelled, which is no great loss since neither pays. Looks like you have what's left of the morning free."

"You should've texted me."

"Why? So you could spend more time with other people who also don't pay for your time? We might as well put *pro bono* before attorney at law on the sign out front. I thought a break would do you good, maybe lunch?" Sometimes her young-at-heart assistant couldn't resist mothering her.

"Just because your kids have flown the coop doesn't mean you can—"

"Blah, blah, blah. Yeah, I know. You're doing such a great job taking care of yourself. Call Lois. Have a martini. It's not like your two o'clock would notice."

"Chris!"

"Don't worry. Nobody's here. In other news, I get lonely with just my Internet porn. You should hire me an assistant so we could watch together."

"I'll get right on that." She grabbed her messages and retreated to her office. The alphabetized books on the shelves, tidy seating area, and computer on an otherwise clear desktop gave the outward appearance of calm and control, belying the turmoil following her father's death. She still looked for him first thing when she walked into the office, picked up the phone often to consult him on legal questions, and walked toward his office at the end of the day to check on dinner plans. Her debilitating grief had dwindled, but everything still felt off, unsettled.

She'd joined the firm to spend time with him, prove her worth, and feel like a priority in his life. Now the work was the only thing holding her together. Her personal life had faltered like a stuttering old movie reel. She couldn't enjoy anything until her father's killer was captured and brought to justice. And now his legacy was being questioned. Pushing the stack of messages to one side, she picked up the phone and dialed the newspaper office.

"*Greensboro Daily Record.* How may I direct your call?"

"I'd like to speak with Martin Linen, please."

"I'm sorry. He's on another line. Could I take a message?"

"I've left messages for two days. I'll hold. It's important." She tapped her nails on the desk as irritating elevator music blared in her ears. Her temperature rose with each second that passed, and she fanned herself with an empty file folder. Finally the blessed click as a live person engaged the line.

"This is Martin Linen." His chipper voice was clear and confident over the background noises of a busy newsroom.

"Mr. Linen, I'm Adena, the—"

"I know who you are, ma'am. How can I help you today?"

His attempt to sound nonchalant made her wish she'd paid more attention to the etiquette classes at boarding school. "How can you help? Your question is several days too late, I'd say. I'm calling regarding the article you wrote about the Daytime Resource Center." She tried to keep her tone light and agreeable, but with each word of explanation she felt more annoyed. She hated that he could affect her so.

"Ah, yes, the Resource Center. Would you like to make a statement now? You weren't available the day of my visit."

"I'd like to discuss your sources on that article because I believe someone is trying to malign the center and its staff."

"As an attorney, I'm sure you understand the First Amendment privilege, which protects my right to refuse to disclose confidential sources of information."

"I'm also aware there are two sides to every story. I'm sure WGRC television would be happy to run a more in-depth feature, complete with testimonials of people the center has actually helped."

"If you're displeased with the story, you can talk to my editor."

"Speak with someone who signed off before the story came out? I think not. Mr. Linen, the DRC has always been run with the utmost integrity and stewardship of the city's tax dollars. I take issue with anyone who implies otherwise or that we abandon people who need our help."

"Is it true the city and your donors are threatening to withdraw funding?"

"I assure you, Mr. Linen, the DRC will survive if I have to fund it myself. It meant that much to my father, and it means that much to me. Good day." She hung up the phone so hard that Chris poked her head around the door.

"You all right?"

"That damn Martin Linen makes me—"

"Hotter than a pissant in a wool sack?"

She stared at Chris for a second and then burst out laughing. "I wouldn't put it that way, but yes."

"Isn't he the one who reported on your father's death?"

She nodded. "And he quoted others who speculated that Dad's death may have been related to the work he did with the homeless community."

Chris shook her head and pursed her lips in her trademark way that said she really didn't understand people. "I'm sorry, Boss. That sucks."

"Yes, it does." Adena took a few minutes to calm down before reaching for the phone again. She'd put the mayor off for three days. "Good morning, Mayor. Sorry I haven't gotten back to you before, but I don't really have anything new to report."

"Well, that just won't do. I have to be able to defend the center if it's to survive."

"I understand. I've talked with Martin Linen, but he refuses to reveal where he got his information." She didn't mention that she couldn't find the name of one of his sources in the DRC records. That could be interpreted as just another indication of their incompetence. "But I give you my word I'll get to the bottom of this."

"See that you do, Adena, and soon. I'm not sure how much longer I can postpone a meeting with the city council and the other stakeholders."

"Thank you, and I appreciate your support." Why did she feel like the forces that were supposed to help and support her were the very ones trying to bring her down? If Flo couldn't find John Tabor in the DRC logbook, she wasn't sure where to look next.

An hour later, she grabbed her coat and headed toward the front door. "Chris, would you call Lois and see if she's available for lunch, please?"

"She's in 2C today and will meet you in the hallway behind the courtroom."

"Aren't you just too clever?"

"Sometimes. Would you bring me an order of bacon-cheese spuds and fried pickles?"

"Seriously? Pot. Kettle. Don't mention my less-than-healthy eating habits again."

Chris saluted. "Roger that, Counselor."

As Adena walked the few blocks to the courthouse, she left her coat open, enjoying the brisk air that announced winter's approach. She loved the way her skin prickled and came alive with every gust of wind or drop of chilly rain. Summer was heavy and oppressive, so stifling she often avoided outdoor activities completely. Winter demanded action to survive and she embraced its advance. But the knowledge that the homeless didn't have an option except to endure the brutal temperatures tempered her enjoyment. Her cheeks were just starting to feel the wind's chilly sting when she reached the courthouse steps.

She paused to enjoy the juxtaposition of the 1920s neo-classical, revival-style courthouse made of North Carolina granite to her right and the more modern 1974 concrete-and-glass one she was preparing to enter. She remembered following her father down the halls of the older judicial building, her black patent-leather shoes tapping across the marble floors, envisioning the day she'd traverse the halls on her own as an attorney.

After going through security, she made her way to the second floor, stopping occasionally to chat with colleagues. She was waiting in the hallway outside Lois's courtroom when Detective David Carrick exited. He briefly caught her eye and turned in the opposite direction.

"Detective, a moment, please." She tried to catch up, but he dodged a bailiff and jury filing out of another chamber. "Detective." He moved surprisingly quickly through the corridor, but she had no difficulty keeping track of his tall frame in the crowd.

Carrick finally stopped at the elevator. "Adena. What can I do for you?"

"Stop avoiding me, for starters. I want what every victim's family wants, justice."

His handsome features scrunched tighter around his dark brows and mustache. "I'm doing everything possible."

"I want to know who killed my father. If that's impossible then perhaps you need to change professions." Carrick's face flushed, and she realized what she'd said. Her accusation of incompetence was totally unfair. She'd checked Carrick's credentials when he received her father's case, and he was an extremely competent investigator. "I'm sorry, David. I didn't mean to insult you. I'm just very frustrated."

He nodded, accepting her apology. "I *will* find him." He touched her arm briefly before stepping onto the elevator.

She tried to draw comfort from the certainty in Carrick's last statement. She'd also learned he was a man who spoke only when he had something significant to say. She stood, lost in thought, with the recess crowd surging around her until she heard Lois call her name.

"Let's go to my chambers." Lois cupped her elbow and guided her toward the office.

When the door closed, Adena wrapped her arms around Lois's waist and held on. "I can't bear not knowing any longer. I'm on a virtual treadmill running to the DRC, the office, court, home, and chasing detectives…and now this annoying reporter is raising questions. Am I losing my mind?"

"You'll be fine, Adena. Murder investigations take time, and so does your grief. Be kinder to yourself, darling."

She inhaled Lois's flowery perfume and recalled bedsheets covered with her scent. Adena clung to her, grasping for something stable. She could almost taste the bittersweet memories of their lovemaking. They'd satisfied and comforted each other for months and then gently turned each other loose when their time was over. She wanted to cry because nothing was permanent. Her father's admonition that emotional outbursts never solved anything came to mind, and she pulled away from Lois. "Yes, I'll be fine."

"I'm familiar with that tone. It's your 'I'm telling you I'll be fine but I don't believe it myself' voice. But you will get through the pain and figure it all out." Lois tugged at the snaps of her black judge's robe. "Let me shed this shroud and we'll go to lunch. I'm starving."

"You're always starving for something."

"And that's one of the things you liked about me."

Lois never mentioned love, at least not with her. They'd been lovers for almost nine months, her longest attachment to another woman. When Lois had met OTC, out-of-town counselor, as Adena called her, she'd immediately fallen into lust. Love was debatable.

Lois unsnapped her black robe, revealing full breasts tastefully accentuated by a red V-neck cashmere sweater. Her black slacks hugged sculpted thighs and buttocks that Adena recalled vividly.

Lois always wore her long blond hair up in a chignon for work, but Adena preferred it loose across her shoulders.

"You're not the only one who remembers." Lois's blue eyes met hers.

"Sorry. I was staring."

"And lusting a little, I think." Lois smiled the way she did when she was being understanding but apologetic. "You know if I were planning to step out, it would be with you."

"It better be. And just for the record, I'm glad you're not stepping out. You and OTC give me hope for the future."

Lois swatted her playfully with her coat as they headed for the door. "Could you please stop calling her OTC? You make her sound like something I picked up in a drugstore."

"You did pick her up over the counter—bench, same difference. Flirting in open court. Shame on you, Judge Adler." They stepped into the brisk air and Lois pulled her coat tighter. "And what's her name again? Is it *honey, baby, darling,* or *Oh God?*" She imitated lusty moans. "You really should be more original. I remember some of those names while we were—"

"You're not helping. It's six hours until I see her. And her name is Beverly."

"Perfect. Lois and Beverly sitting in a tree—"

Lois feigned pushing her down the courthouse steps. "What are you, twelve? If you don't stop immediately, I'll hold you in contempt."

In addition to satisfactory sex, she and Lois had made each other laugh, and Adena craved that right now. After her conversations with Martin Linen, David Carrick, and especially Colby Vincent today, she needed lots of laughter.

"So, what do you think?" Lois asked.

"Huh?"

"You totally spaced out." She searched Adena's face and gave her a knowing smile. "You were thinking about a woman. Still me?"

Adena's face grew warm.

Lois's mouth dropped open and she stopped walking. "*Not* me. Tell. Everything."

"Let's go. There's nothing to tell." But Adena could feel her face almost glowing red. She raced across the street and held the door open to Stumble Stilkins, Lois's favorite lunch spot. They knew the owner, the food was always good, and they appreciated the table arrangement that afforded privacy to diners discussing legal cases or illicit affairs.

Lois glanced at her over the top of her menu but kept quiet until the waitress took their orders and left. When she started to speak, Adena tried to divert the conversation to another topic. "I had a meeting with Ollie this morning and a phone conversation with Martin Linen, both very interesting."

"Table that. I want to hear about this woman."

Adena struggled with the idea of discussing Colby as a *woman*. As long as she defined her as a DRC guest, anything personal she might have felt was irrelevant. Defining Colby as a case was her best defense, but she'd always treated the guests as individuals. No wonder she was conflicted. "There is no woman."

"I'm calling bullshit. Your left eyebrow's doing that twitchy thing. Spill."

"Really, it's nothing, a new client. She's a bit of a contradiction and she's...attractive. Can't I appreciate aesthetic beauty now and then?"

"Sure, but she intrigues you. I see it in those brown bedroom eyes. Admit it."

"No." She rubbed her forehead, trying to conceal her tell and the heat creeping across her face again.

"Something about this woman got to you. Where did you meet her?"

Adena stabbed the lime wedge floating in her Diet Coke with her straw. "The DRC." She didn't look up, knowing the railroad tracks between Lois's eyes that signaled disapproval would be pronounced. "Totally inappropriate to notice that she's a ten on the hot-o-meter." She hoped the joke would convince Lois she wasn't serious. When Lois didn't speak, she finally glanced up, and her blue eyes were wide, her jaw slack.

"You're attracted to a *homeless* woman you met at the DRC?"

"When you say it like that, it sounds practically vulgar. I just noticed she's cute."

"It *is* vulgar. I know your father's death has been hard on you, but this stretches the boundaries of normal behavior. You realize this is impossible, right? You've never mixed business with pleasure. What could you possibly have in common? Forget it. Immediately. I bet Flo's having a conniption."

"Flo is very protective of me and the center, but we don't have personal conversations." Lois knew she was withholding. If she told Lois she was more attracted to Colby than she'd ever been to another woman, Lois would probably think she'd lost touch with reality. But after everything they'd shared, Adena owed her the truth. Emotional honesty had to be a two-way street. "Oh, Lois, I *am* attracted to her, but I have no intention of pursuing my feelings."

"Good, and thanks for admitting it. We all have physical and emotional needs, and God knows you don't cop to yours often, but we have to satisfy those needs with someone appropriate. This person is *so* not appropriate."

"You're right, and I'm embarrassed that I can't control my feelings. You know me, Lois. I'm not a person who snubs convention. I'm very rule bound. It's just nice to notice an attractive woman again. I don't know why it had to be her. Can you understand? We haven't been together in over a year."

"And you haven't slept with anyone else?"

Adena shook her head.

Lois patted her hand. "I'm sorry. Of course I understand, but I'm just looking out for you. We need to get you laid, ASAP."

For Lois, the subject was closed. Adena wished she could say the same, but Colby was a splinter that could fester and destroy her reputation and everything her father had left in her care.

"You should come to dinner with us tonight. Bev would love to get to know you better, and it would do you good."

"Can't."

"Too busy prepping cases? Tucking in the homeless? You need a social outlet, Adena. What if we stop by your place on our way from dinner?"

Adena immediately looked up and met Lois's eyes. "What?"

"I wish you could see your face right now. You look like you're in shock. I temporarily forgot. No one comes to your place."

"That's not true." When Lois glared at her, she asked, "Is it?"

"Duh."

She tried to remember the last time she'd invited anyone to her house, while she lived at home or since she'd moved...nothing. Was she really so disconnected? A feeling of emptiness settled in her chest. "I'm renovating."

"I love you, Adena, but you've never been exactly open with your home or your life. It's who you are."

"Sorry. I'm just not ready." When Lois started to argue further, she shook her head.

"Fine. I can take a not-too-subtle hint. This is me changing the subject. So, you met with Ollie this morning? What's he up to these days?"

Lois was a problem-solving machine in the courtroom and in life. Adena admired her logic and efficiency and wished she could channel some of it in her situation with Colby. "He wants to manage the DRC, give me time to adjust and focus on whatever I'd like."

"Great idea, especially in light of Linen's article and what you've just told me. You might actually have time for a social life, and then you wouldn't be lusting after homeless women."

"Lois—"

"I know." She held up her hands in surrender.

When their orders arrived, Adena pretended to be hungry and took a bite. As she looked at the other half of her sandwich, she wondered if Colby had lunch. She'd helped hundreds of homeless people, but no one had infiltrated her thoughts as silently and completely as Colby Vincent. Was it a sign that Colby needed special help? Or was it the signal for her to let Ollie manage the DRC?

One option guaranteed contact with Colby, and the other almost ensured they wouldn't see each other again. Her choice should be simple. So why was she struggling?

CHAPTER FIVE

Colby juggled using two apples and a kid's tennis ball she'd found for the entertainment of a small group of onlookers in the afternoon shadow of the Center Pointe building. Having a patch over one eye screwed with her depth perception, but she managed to keep the three items airborne most of the time. She'd spread a T-shirt on the ground and dropped some seed money in hopes of landing enough to buy a burger. Her stomach growled again. She hadn't eaten since lunch the day before and was starting to feel shaky. She glanced toward her backpack, lost concentration, and her act fell apart.

"Ahhh." Most of the onlookers walked away, some leaving a dollar or loose change, while the kids screamed for another show. She felt like a failure begging for coins. Most people who passed didn't make eye contact, pretending she didn't exist or too uncomfortable to admit she did. Only children or the elderly, too young or too wise to judge, actually looked at her. She never realized how much it hurt to be invisible, not to be acknowledged as a human being who mattered. When Cowboy entered the far side of the park and shook his head, she took a bow and wrapped up her meager collection.

"What the hell you doing?" Cowboy's gray eyes flashed angrily.

She couldn't understand why he'd be upset with her for making the most of her time. "Juggling. I used to go with my parents to the circus every year, and I loved the jugglers. Taught myself when I was eight. Pretty good, huh?" Those simple times had been her favorite growing up, and she'd felt a bit of that happiness return while performing for the kids.

"If you want to get busted for panhandling, it's great." He rubbed just below his knee as if his prosthesis was causing pain.

"Arrested? Really?" Eric had mentioned no panhandling in the park, but she'd assumed a warning would precede arrest. Besides, she had to eat.

"Yeah, really. And another no-no is any kind of contact with kids. I already told you about attracting attention, but that's the worst. For every person watching you, there's probably another one not happy about you hanging out in the park all day. And another handful will think you're a child pervert and call the police. Leave the kids be."

"I didn't think about that." If she were a parent, she wouldn't want her kids in close proximity to questionable characters either. And maybe that was wrong. Maybe adults would be more compassionate if they'd been encouraged as children to interact with and learn from folks different from themselves. "But it's boring with nothing to do all day, and I'm hungry."

"You need to find work."

"And how do I do that? Got any contacts?"

"Maybe," Cowboy said. "I'll get back to you. In the meantime, keep your head down and try to follow the damn rules."

He ran hot and cold, helpful one minute and dismissive the next. She worried about depending on his advice too heavily regardless of how much she wanted someone to trust. In her experience, inconsistency was a big red flag.

He limped away, and she stuffed her shirt into her pack, counting her money as she followed. "I might have enough for a hotel. Where's the closest one?"

"You won't find anything within walking distance that you can afford. Besides, you need to save your money for food. It ain't cheap, and even if you get on SNAP, you can't buy certain things that you'll need."

"What the hell is SNAP?"

"You really are a street virgin, aren't you? SNAP is Supplemental Nutrition Assistance Program from the government."

"I don't want to be on SNAP. I want a real job," Colby said.

"Yeah, like that's going to happen. When you've been out here long enough, you'll take whatever you can get from anywhere. And when you do, you can't buy any kind of paper products, deodorant, soap, laundry detergent, or restaurant food with government assistance. And women can't buy those female products they need every month either."

Colby hadn't thought about that aspect of living on the street. What would she do without money? She'd stretched the twenty dollars Agent Curtis had left her as far as she could, managing to put some extra time on her phone, but it was long gone. She shoved the change into her jeans pocket and fell in behind Cowboy. "Where you going?"

"Urban Ministry for a hot and a cot."

She waited for him to tell her to get lost, and when he didn't, she followed at a safe distance. As they walked south on Elm Street, the men she'd seen at the camp the first night joined in, always after a nod to Cowboy. The closer the other guys got, the less Cowboy spoke to her. He reminded her of the training instructor she'd had in boot camp. He'd been as easy to get along with as a cactus, but occasionally he'd find her alone, and often at her lowest, and give her a pep talk. The next day he'd be a hard-ass again.

She got the impression Cowboy was the informal leader of this group, most of whom still carried themselves with the bearing of military men. Could being accepted be as easy as just following the pack and doing what Cowboy said? One of her father's favorite sayings came to mind: "Nothing is ever as easy as it seems, and if it looks like it is, watch your back."

Greensboro Urban Ministry resembled a church with its redbrick façade and white steeple-like front. Some of the guys grumbled about the evening meal being served with a side of religion, but if that was the price for hot food and shelter for the night, she'd pretend to listen. As they got closer, her hope for creature comforts faded. The line stretched across the front of the building.

"Will we get to eat?" she asked.

"They run out sometimes, and you can forget sleeping here tonight," Cowboy said. "Best look for another place."

"Think I'll pass on the sermon then. See you guys later." She nodded to the others and started walking again. As much as she wanted to fit in, she needed to eat and find a safe place for the night. She'd seen a Hardee's on her downtown map, and right now a burger and fries sounded better than a roomful of smelly men and a dose of Jesus. And a little alone time in a warm space would give her a chance to review the facts about her case. So far she hadn't seen anything that resembled a drug ring or even a simple drug buy.

Hardee's was the only restaurant she'd been in recently that didn't have a customers-only, no-loitering, no-backpack, or nobody-that-looks-like-you policy, so she felt reasonably comfortable being there for a while. After scrubbing her hands in the bathroom and getting her order, she sat at a booth facing the two entrances from Market and Edgeworth Streets.

She usually savored the meals her mother prepared morsel by tasty morsel, but with the burger and fries in front of her, she lost control. Her hunger and the uncertainty of when she'd eat again outranked culinary appreciation. She wanted to eat slowly and let the food settle and fill her emptiness. Instead, she stuffed her mouth with the savory fries and chewed quickly. *So good.* She picked the onions off her half-pound bacon-cheeseburger and took a bite. The smoked bacon and cheese flavors combined with rich Angus beef, and she moaned aloud. In too few bites, her tray was empty and she was still unsatisfied. She licked the salt off her fingers from the last fry and then ate the onions she didn't like. Suddenly she had a new appreciation for how anyone could sell drugs—hunger was a powerful motivator.

She cleared her tray and began a methodical review of the basics of a prescription-drug diversion operation: individuals obtained scripts from a doctor, or group of doctors, and presented the prescriptions at various drugstores or pain centers to be filled. The pills were sold to a dealer who peddled them on the street to individuals or other dealers. The person obtaining the prescription made very little in the transaction, the majority of profit going to the dealers and kickbacks to the doctor.

The most sought-after medications on the street were opioid analgesics because of their high potency and lack of fillers. The favorites of dealers and addicts were Roxycodone, a brand name of oxycodone, called blues or Roxy, and OxyContin. Each sold on the street for a dollar per milligram. An organization with ten recruits at thirty pills each could gross about nine thousand dollars a day. Profits rivaled the cocaine business, and dealers weren't pursued as aggressively as coke peddlers. These pill mills had recently become pervasive in the U.S.

Agent Curtis had also mentioned three people possibly connected to the scam: Worthington, Winston, and Weber. W-cubed, she called them. Worthington and Weber were supposedly directly linked to the DRC, while Winston's connection wasn't yet clear. She hadn't heard of either yet, but the homeless didn't seem keen on using real names. These three could be anyone she'd run into so far.

Was Cowboy involved in the operation? He'd suggested she get a prescription from the DRC doctor when she didn't really need one, but only mentioned trips to a drugstore, nothing specific. If she asked questions too soon, she'd arouse suspicion and alienate herself from the rest of the group. The waiting part of the job hadn't been so bad when she ran the operation, but now *she* was the legend and couldn't make moves too quickly. At least the agents she'd handled had places to live and food. Maybe she should've thought this assignment through more carefully before volunteering.

When the manager of Hardee's turned off the outside lights, Colby hurried to the bathroom and brushed her teeth before heading out to find somewhere to sleep. She knew only two places, and she'd frequented the parking ramp too often. Maybe she'd head back to the camp. At least they'd had a fire. She was grateful it wasn't raining again, but the wind cut through her ragged jeans, and she walked faster to generate heat.

"Little honey boo-hoo out in the street. What kind of monster will she meet?" Sing Song darted from between the buildings, screeching and flailing her arms.

Colby jumped, swinging her backpack in front of her for protection. "Are you trying to give me a heart attack?"

"Going to the ramp or going to the camp? Where will you sleep? Nowhere's cheap." She fell in behind Colby. "I'll come with you. We make two."

Colby wanted to shoo her away, but for some reason she couldn't snub the odd-looking character who seemed totally deranged but harmless. "Come on, Sing Song." She waved for her to catch up. "Do you have a real name?"

"Call me Sing Song. Can't be wrong."

Colby smiled as Sing Song mumbled and occasionally broke into a silly made-up verse.

When they approached the overpass where the camp was, she smelled marijuana and heard laughter and cursing. In only five days on the street, she'd come to anticipate the bewildering and unrestrained atmosphere permeating homeless life. Even the innocuous could be dangerous, and this scene was anything but safe. Sing Song tried to pull her back toward the street. The group vibrated with frenetic energy reminiscent of walking into a crack house or driving down Route Irish in Baghdad. She stopped at the perimeter of the circle, but Cowboy motioned her to the center of the camp where several men huddled around a small fire.

"Want you to meet the guys." Cowboy pointed to each person as he introduced him. "Wolf, Coyote, JR for Jackrabbit, Badger, Raven, and that runty-looking guy in the back is Bug. You two might get along. He's a computer geek. Welcome to the club, Eagle."

"What is this? A menagerie?" Colby scanned the group. The guys seemed friendly enough, but she'd learned the hard way not to trust appearances. She recognized the geeky guy as the one Cowboy had been talking to at the computer in the DRC earlier.

"Nicknames. Since we don't really exist to most folks, it's just easier. Everybody here has served in some branch of the military and fought a rich man's war. And we've all been dumped like garbage. Forgotten by the service, the government, and our families."

"So why am I Eagle?" she asked, not really up for a sermon about man's apathy toward man. She'd seen the effects of war on friends and family up close.

Cowboy nodded to one of the guys, and Wolf rose on thick legs and towered over her by at least three inches. Black hair reflected the firelight, and a full beard and bushy eyebrows conjured images of a deadly wolf. An indentation on the left side of his forehead reminded her of similar injuries she'd seen from IEDs.

"That peach fuzz sprouting on your bald head glows in the sunlight, but Golden Eagle's too long. And you were in the air force. Go with it. Have a seat and a smoke."

She dropped her bedroll and sat near the edge of the circle but passed on the joint when they offered it to her. "I'm good with secondhand smoke. That shit fucks with my head." The last time she'd smoked marijuana, she'd hallucinated and been crazy paranoid. She wasn't eager to try it again.

"You sure?" Bug offered it to her again. "You're not a narc, are you?"

"No. I just don't like to be fucked up. Marijuana has that paranoid effect on some people. If you've got anything else, I'll try it." She bluffed, hoping nobody did. She tried to make her eyes flat, bored so they wouldn't see her relief when each shook his head.

For two hours everybody except Cowboy shared their military battle and discharge stories while they smoked. Wolf and Coyote became more animated and agitated as the others seemed to mellow. She'd learned from the drinking games in the DFAC, or military dining facility, to make her exit when the guys got rowdy.

"I think I'll head out." She stood to go, but Cowboy signaled Wolf again. He jumped in front of her.

His dark eyes blazed, and she stepped back. "What's wrong, Eagle. You wanna fly? We've got a surprise for you."

"Run, girlie, run. Do not stay. These boys are mean. They do not play," Sing Song yelled as she bolted toward the street and disappeared around the corner, her pink roller bag flipping over and over behind her. The outburst sent tingles of edged fear up Colby's spine.

"That one is a stone nut job," Wolf said, giving Sing Song a dismissive wave.

"So you really are a girl?" Coyote asked. He was lean but muscular, not as tall as Wolf and with blond hair. "This is going to be more fun than I thought."

She backed away, her knees wobbly as adrenaline surged. "Look, I don't want any trouble. If you don't want me here, I'll leave."

"Oh, we want you here." Wolf grabbed her wrists and pulled her against him. "I got something for you." The bulge in his crotch pressed against her, and she tried to back away. "If you're going to live on the street, you have to protect yourself."

"Cowboy?" She looked toward the man she'd begun to consider a friend, but he sat cross-legged at the head of the circle watching. *What the fuck? Why didn't I consider this possibility?* "Come on, guys. Really? Don't do this. We're all soldiers. Act like it." Then she remembered some of her comrades in Iraq who hadn't behaved honorably toward women either.

Wolf looked toward Cowboy and, when he nodded, threw her to the ground. "Yeah, so help a soldier out, girlie."

He pinned her shoulders against the damp ground with his knees and unzipped his pants. She stopped struggling, as her energy drained like blood from the wounded. As she stared into Wolf's cold, angry eyes, all the dangers of Iraq returned. She was going to die at the hands of a fellow soldier on home soil, because she'd die before she'd let him rape her.

The chanting voices of the other men kindled her anger. *Hell, no! This will not happen.* When Wolf reached into his pants, she bucked her hips against him, and he toppled over. She slammed her foot into his chest. He spun sideways, and she kicked him in the back, her foot striking something hard in his waistband. While he struggled to regain his breath, she jumped to her feet, pivoting side to side.

She snatched the patch off her left eye and threw it to the ground. If she stood any chance of surviving, she needed her peripheral vision. Coyote circled her in a boxer's stance. She dropped low and swept his feet from under him in a roundhouse kick. Bouncing on the balls of her feet, she waited for the next attacker. She was grateful no one else in the group moved.

Wolf rose slowly, zipped his pants, and lunged toward her. She used his momentum against him and sidestepped, then kicked the side of his knee, bringing him down again. If she could keep one of them out of play, she might stand a chance.

Coyote came at her swinging both fists. His right connected with her left eye, and she stumbled backward. Blood clouded her vision, and the tender flesh around her eye began to swell immediately. He caught her with a left uppercut to the chin, and her head snapped back. The deep, thick sound of flesh pounding flesh and causing damage made her nauseous. She choked down bile and kicked blindly, connecting solidly with something. *They're going to overpower me.* The horror brought a potent surge of adrenaline that kept her moving.

Wolf charged her again. She dodged one blow, but a second to the gut robbed her of air. She gasped but aimed a quick jab at his nose to create distance. He wailed and stepped back, and then she kicked him between the legs so hard the vibration ran all the way through her. She jumped and sent another roundhouse to his chest. He dropped to the ground like a rag doll. *Don't get up. Please don't get up.*

When she whipped around, Coyote was already too close. He dove on her back and brought her down, landing on top of her. Her breath gushed out with a painful moan as the unfamiliar feeling of defeat consumed her. A bitter taste filled her mouth as she imagined what would happen next. *I'm going to die.*

Wolf kicked her in the ribs twice and knelt beside her. "Now, where were we?" He reached to unzip his pants again.

Cowboy yelled, "Enough."

"But I'm just getting started." Wolf dragged her to her knees. "She owes me now."

"I said enough." Cowboy waved his hand like a referee, and Wolf and Coyote backed off.

Colby crouched on her knees and pulled for breath, scanning the crowd for another attack. Her left eye was swollen shut again, her ribs ached, and the rest of her felt like a deflated punching bag. When she was able to stand, she faced Cowboy. "What the fuck?

If this is your idea of a welcome party, I'm out." She dragged her backpack toward the street, unable to lift it.

"Hey, wait up, Eagle. We were just having a little fun," Cowboy called.

"Fun? Really? You should be ashamed to call yourself soldiers." She didn't look up until she passed the depot and Sing Song rushed out to the sidewalk, falling in step beside her.

"You okay?" For a second she sounded almost normal, almost sympathetic. "That shit was wrong, but I couldn't stay. I wouldn't be no help no way."

Colby wanted to be upset with her, but Sing Song was right. She would've been more of a hindrance if she'd been there. "It's okay. Let's find somewhere to sleep."

Sing Song danced beside her and broke into a tune that reminded her of the Lone Ranger. "To the ramp, to the ramp, to the ramp, ramp, ramp."

"Sure. I'm too tired to look for something new." Though the other woman had done nothing to earn her trust, Colby felt she'd be safe with her, or at least not overtly harmed.

As they walked, Colby wondered about the fight. What was Cowboy trying to prove? He seemed so helpful at times but brutally controlling at others. For a second she'd flashed back to her early days in Iraq when she'd fought off another soldier who professed to be her friend while the team leader watched. She'd survived Iraq with a knife wound to her side and a single piece of shrapnel to her upper thigh from terrorists. She couldn't stomach the thought of adding to her scar collection from fellow soldiers at home. The enemy wasn't always who you expected.

Adena had stopped on the street near Center City Park on her way home from work, torn between watching Colby juggle for a group of children and offering her legal advice about panhandling. Colby's tall body stretched as she reached up, exposing glimpses of bruised flesh between the small sweatshirt and her low-cut jeans.

Only occasionally did her attempts to entertain seem painful. She'd been smiling, totally engrossed in the repetitive action while Adena watched her move. Colby seemed to be having as much fun as she was giving. Their brief exchange had replayed in her mind all the way home.

"When's the last time you laughed or had a good time?" Colby asked.

Adena stepped back, creating some space between them. She took a couple of deep breaths before looking into those inquisitive green eyes again. "What? I'm really not comfortable—"

"I can see you're not comfortable talking about having fun. What about actually having fun? Does that make you uncomfortable too?"

"Life isn't just about having fun, Colby, and you've already had your first lesson."

"Touché, but it shouldn't be all work and no play either. Trust me, Counselor."

How long *had* it been since she'd done something frivolous, taken time off, seen a movie, or been to a play, anything enjoyable? She struggled for the answer but actually couldn't remember, probably not a good sign. Deciding to save the lecture about panhandling for another time, she'd continued toward home.

She'd cut through Fisher Park, enjoying the crunch of fallen leaves as she walked. Her family had picnicked here when she was a child. Her mother loved the flowers and the cool canopy of trees, and her father appreciated the vitality of being so close to the city center. It was one of only a few happy memories of their family together without worries. But the place also held deep sadness. Her mother's last outing was in this park. Adena had learned of her father's murder while having a late dinner here. And she and Lois had broken up on a walk around the perimeter. One place filled with so much history, so much love and loss.

Her father had encouraged her to buy a home of her own and had taken time from his busy schedule to help her find the perfect location near Fisher Park. Had he finally grown tired of her caretaking attempts, or was he feeling guilty for never being at home with her? She'd been inside the family residence only twice since he died, but she couldn't bring herself to dispose of his things, much less sell the place.

Now she stood on Hendrix Street staring at her two-story Dutch Colonial house with gambrel roof, double front doorway, and wide porch. The scent of fresh cuttings signaled that Joe, landscaper and DRC regular, had just manicured the lawn for the final time this season. As she slid her key into the lock, she wished the inside of her home were as welcoming as the exterior.

She'd bought the house two weeks before her father's death and started extensive renovations. Now unfinished cabinets and flooring made the kitchen unusable. The few pieces of furniture she had were draped with plastic sheets topped by a thick layer of dust. A leather recliner parked in front of a small television was the only habitable spot in the living room. She'd existed in the disarray for almost a year, unable to muster enough motivation to finish the projects. If her orderly office represented her public persona, her home certainly exemplified the chaos and emptiness she felt privately.

She navigated the boxes and construction materials through the hallway to her bedroom. An air mattress on the floor, a microwave and coffee kettle on a corner table, and a functional sink and shower provided the essentials. But what else did she really need? She used to think homeless people were different from everyone else, but home and money could disappear overnight and through no fault of one's own. Homelessness could happen to anyone, even her.

Adena peeled off her department-store wool trousers, jacket, and polyester blouse—the physical wrapping that held her façade together during the day. Each item fell to the floor in a pile with the other clothes from the week, and she stepped over them on her way to the shower. "Clothes make the man, or woman," her father had said, but she'd never fully embraced the adage. She made a note to do laundry soon because part of her wardrobe was at her law office and a few changes were at the DRC. She slept at both places more often than at home.

She slid under the hot shower spray and leaned against the tiled wall. As the water enveloped her, she relaxed under the heated stream. She exhaled deeply and choked back a sob at the end, but then started to cry—for another day with no answers about her father, for a new group of homeless people, for living in squalor when she had the means to do better, and for an intriguing woman the universe had dangled in front of her but made impossible for her to touch.

When her tears stopped, she was sitting on the shower floor shivering under a spray of cold water. She turned off the tap, wrapped a bath sheet around her, and collapsed on the air mattress. Before she tumbled into sleep, Colby Vincent's reassuring words down a phone line flashed through her mind.

"Please don't worry. I love you."

CHAPTER SIX

Colby and Sing Song were the first ones in line at the DRC the next morning. Her roomie had woken her with a rhyme about leaving their ramp hotel before the real people came. She'd barely been able to roll over, the reminders of last night's fight evidenced in even the slightest movement. Her pulse raced at the thought of seeing Adena, but she'd have to dodge questions about her fresh injuries.

When the DRC door swung open, Adena stopped abruptly and focused on Colby's left eye. "Not again." She stepped aside, and Colby and Sing Song headed toward the showers.

"See. Told you. Trouble." Flo shook her head and gave Colby a serious I-told-you-not-to-fuck-up look.

"Colby, wait. Come with me." Adena guided her toward the small clinic. "I'll be in the exam room when the doctor arrives. Please send him in." She held the door open and waited until Colby was seated on the table.

The room shrank around her as Adena closed the door and moved toward her. She wore a dark pinstriped suit with a coppery-colored top that brought out gold flecks in her eyes. She looked gorgeous. The strands of gray in her black hair hadn't been as noticeable yesterday. Or maybe she'd been too focused on her eyes and that mouth. Dark circles and tiny streaks of red marred those deep pools of brown today. She'd been crying, recently. "Are you okay?"

"Am *I* okay? Look at you. What happened? And don't insult my intelligence by telling me you woke up like this again. Sing Song doesn't strike me as the violent type."

Colby wanted to be honest with Adena but wasn't sure whom she could trust yet. Even this stunning woman might, perish the thought, be involved in her drug case. Adena seemed truly concerned about her wellbeing, and Colby needed a friend, or something more. No time to indulge her hormones. Maybe she could tell Adena most of the truth. Nope. Distraction time. "Yeah, about Sing Song, does she get help for her…condition, whatever that is?"

"No diverting, Ms. Vincent. Besides, I can't talk about other guests." Adena lightly skimmed the swollen ridge beneath Colby's eye and flinched. "Who did this?" She captured Colby's hands and turned them, inspecting the bruises encircling her wrists and the raw flesh across her knuckles.

Adena's hands were warm, their connection electrifying, and Colby relaxed into her first compassionate touch in days. Her parents' hugs and the touch of her lover belonged to the past, and she missed them desperately. Just to stretch across her parents' sofa and know she was safe or to curl up to Kali's back and sleep with both eyes closed would be heaven.

"Colby, look at me." Adena moved closer and placed a finger under Colby's chin. "Did someone…rape you?"

"God, no! I'd die first." The concern on Adena's face made her insides ache. She hated being the cause. "I got into a fight… and lost. It's a hazard of being on the streets." She wanted to tell her everything, if only to keep Adena close enough to smell the fresh scents of her bath soap and shampoo.

"Will you answer *my* question? Are you okay? You look…sad, like you've been crying."

Adena stepped back and started rearranging chairs in the exam room. "I'm fine, and this is really not an appropriate conversation. One last time, would you please tell me how this happened?"

Before Colby had to skirt her question again, the door opened and Doctor Raymond entered. "What do we have today, Ms.

Vincent?" He stopped when he noticed Adena. "I'm sorry, Adena. I didn't realize you were in here."

"I was…just leaving."

"Could you stay for a few minutes while I examine Ms. Vincent. Carolyn is a bit late."

"If Colby doesn't mind."

Her skin tingled just having Adena in the room, and while she didn't want her to leave, she absolutely didn't want her to see the other injuries from her fight. Adena would probably think she was a common street thug, or worse. "I don't mind."

Doctor Raymond checked her pupil responses, pulse, and blood pressure before examining the obvious bruises and scrapes on her body. "Would you raise your T-shirt, please? I'd like to check your ribs."

She grasped the hem of her shirt but couldn't pull it up far enough. "Sorry."

Adena reached toward her. "May I?" Colby nodded, and Adena slowly edged the shirt up and stretched the fabric out to free her arms one at a time.

She felt the heat from Adena's skin and prayed for one accidental touch as she carefully raised the fabric away from her body. Closing her eyes, she imagined Adena's actions leading to more intimate touching instead of the shock and questions about to come.

When Adena pulled the shirt off, she gasped. "What the hell?" Her brown eyes sparked and the muscles along her jaw clenched.

"Adena, please." Doctor Raymond urged her back and bent to inspect the bruising across Colby's sides, along her stomach, and between her now-bare breasts. "This is all new, as are the cuts over your eye and under your chin, the bruises on your wrists, and scrapes on your knuckles. Street fight, if I had to guess. Hope the other guy looks worse. Does it hurt to breathe?" She shook her head. "Can you see out of your left eye?" She nodded. "Where's your patch?"

"Lost it."

Adena mumbled something from the corner, but Colby didn't look at her.

"Do you need another one?"

"No thanks. I'll be fine."

Adena walked toward the door. "I'll be outside, if you need me, Doctor."

"Wait. Please," Colby said. "I might need help getting dressed." Adena stopped but didn't turn around, her shoulders rising and falling as if she was struggling for breath.

"Okay, Colby. It doesn't look like anything is seriously damaged. I'll give you some stronger pain meds." She started to tell him she didn't need anymore, but he pulled out his prescription pad and scribbled on it. "Let me know if you have any complications." He nodded to Adena and exited, leaving the room feeling considerably cooler.

She wanted to ask Adena to help with her shirt, but her nipples were still puckered from their last encounter, and she could feel her anxiety from across the room. She shouldn't be so attracted to this woman. The timing was entirely wrong, personally and professionally. She needed to officially end her relationship with Kali and close this case before she even thought about Adena romantically, but her emotions weren't listening to reason. Silence stretched between them, Adena still facing the door, until Colby couldn't take it. She reached for her T-shirt, but a shard of pain ripped through her bruised side. "Crap."

Adena was at her side instantly. "Be still." She caressed Colby's bruises with her eyes, and when her gaze shifted to her bare breasts, Colby's body warmed. Adena's breath hitched as she scanned Colby's torso and locked eyes with her. "Why?"

She swallowed hard, unable to find her voice. Her skin felt as if Adena had touched her, leaving fingerprints as clearly as the knuckle bruises on her sides. Could Adena see the effect she was having on her? Did she feel it too? "Huh?"

"Why won't you tell me what happened? Let me help you?" Her voice was soft and compelling. "I want to."

Her final statement was almost a plea, and it burrowed deep into Colby's chest, urging her to share. "I want you to, but it was just a street brawl. Please don't think badly of me."

The vulnerability on Adena's face vanished, and she seemed to shut down. "Do you have a death wish? Are you selling yourself and he got rough?"

"No."

"Do you just love to fight?"

Colby struggled to find an answer that would satisfy Adena without revealing too much but failed. "No, but some things are worth fighting for."

Adena stretched Colby's T-shirt over her head and, just as tenderly as she'd removed it, pulled it back down over her heated skin. "I would tell you to take care of yourself, but that seems like wasted breath." She walked out the door, closing it softly behind her. Colby felt the sting of Adena's disappointment as she grabbed her gear and headed to the shower.

Sing Song was humming in her high-pitched voice and scrubbing her body with a bar of blue soap. "If you want to keep the bugs away, you better shave that bush today."

Colby's thoughts were still on Adena. "What?"

"Ticks and lice and things that crawl, like those moist dark places, y'all."

"Do you have any idea how gross that sounds?" Having a shaved head had taught her that more hair was definitely better in cold weather. Besides, she'd done the bushwhacking thing once on a dare, sprouted a patch of red bumps, and itched for days. The stubble was a Brillo pad between her legs, and her girlfriend said it felt like licking a cat's tongue. "I'm not shaving my bush, especially not in the winter."

"Don't be square. Shave that hair." Sing Song stepped out of the shower and dressed while Colby did the opposite. "Holy fuck. You look—yuck." She pointed to Colby's bruises. "Hang with Sing Song. Can't go wrong. Meet me in the park at four. Can't sleep at the ramp no more."

As Sing Song rolled her belongings into a ball and left, Colby enjoyed a cool shower to quell lingering thoughts of Adena and to stimulate ways to get her investigation rolling. The latest beating was a good excuse to have one of her prescriptions filled. She had to start somewhere, and after last night it looked like Cowboy was out as a resource. By the time she dressed and reached the day room, Cowboy and his crew were just coming in.

Adena was heading directly for Wolf, his nose swollen and red with a cut across the bridge. She stood toe-to-toe with the hulking man, whose eyes held the same anger Colby had experienced firsthand. "Did you do this?" She pointed toward Colby.

She loved that Adena felt so protective of her, but she had to stop her before she blew her cover without even knowing it. "Adena, stop." But it was too late.

Wolf didn't back down. "Why would you say that?" He glared at her over Adena's shoulder, and she shook her head, trying to let him know she hadn't ratted him out.

"You look like you've been in a fight, fresh injuries. You know the rule about fighting. If you had anything to do with her—"

"Hey, take this down a notch." Flo stepped between Adena and Wolf, her stature almost matching his. Her voice carried authority that neither of them seemed prepared to challenge. "What's going on?"

Cowboy took off his hat and said, "Ma'am, he was with me last night." His tone was deferential and he even bowed his head. Colby had never seen Cowboy yield to anyone.

"Yeah," Wolf said, "I had too much to drink and fell over. Hurt like hell too."

Cowboy's intervention seemed to take the fight out of Adena. She raked her fingers through her hair and nodded. "Very well. Sorry if I overreacted."

"It's okay, ma'am," Wolf said, but the tightness around his mouth said it wasn't.

"So, we done here?" Flo asked.

Cowboy gestured toward his friends. "I'll take care of these boys, Miss Adena. Don't worry. I won't disappoint you."

Seeming satisfied with Cowboy's assurance, Adena and Flo turned to her, and Colby said, "And I probably will."

"You can depend on her like an amputated limb." Flo stalked off in the opposite direction, and Adena continued to stare at her as if she hadn't heard properly.

Colby hadn't meant to be so blunt, but she wanted to warn Adena. She didn't deserve any fallout from Colby's temporary presence in her world or from her investigation.

Wolf followed Cowboy toward the showers and, as he passed, winked at Colby. What the hell? An ass-whipping at night and a wink in the morning. She was getting whiplash from the erratic behavior of this group. She should've expected some degree of instability when dealing with the homeless, but Wolf gave her a different vibe altogether, more volatile.

On her way out, she stopped by the clinic and asked Carolyn, Dr. Raymond's nurse, about drugstore locations. The attractive middle-aged woman was cooing to someone on her cell phone but handed her a list and waved her off. Colby nodded and walked toward Washington Street.

Cowboy and his band of muddled men had made it clear how they felt about her, so she'd give them lots of room. Besides, she needed to show she could manage on her own and work her way into the drug culture. As she headed for Center City Park, she reminded herself that she'd actually asked for this assignment.

❖

Adena walked slowly to her office, trying to understand how she'd completely lost her cool and accosted a DRC guest. She wasn't a violent or confrontational person, yet she'd jumped to defend someone who seemed content to let the real perpetrator go free. Why should she care if Colby didn't? If Flo hadn't stepped in, would she have continued to accuse Wolf of assaulting Colby?

The image of Colby's injuries had been too fresh and her desire to help too strong. The thought of anyone abusing Colby angered her, and she flinched at the depth of her concern. What was going on with her? She was definitely drawn to Colby, but she'd better off steering clear like Flo said.

She checked in with Chris before heading to the courthouse. "Anything urgent?"

"You mean other than my desperate need for a date? I'll take anything, male, female, as long as it has a pulse and I can ride it to—"

"Chris, please. Spare me the details of a riveting but highly unprofessional discussion of your sex life. Is there anything work related I need to know?"

"Nope. Your two pro-bono clients will meet you in the courtroom. And two more came by asking for *free* help. If it wasn't for the paying clients you turned over to Oliver, we could declare bankruptcy. Just saying."

"Thanks for that, Chris." Her assistant had a knack for stating the facts without filtering. Most of the time she loved her for that, but today she didn't need to be reminded her law practice, along with her personal life, needed serious attention.

When she walked into Judge Adler's courtroom, the docket call was underway. She and the clerks had developed an arrangement about her indigent clients. They scheduled all her pro-bono cases together, let her know when they were on, and she took them out for lunch once a month. Smiling at Lois, she took a seat beside her clients. The cases should last only a few minutes if nothing more pressing was on. When the bailiffs herded in a group of inmates Greensboro PD had arrested for armed robbery, a low mumble of frustration from those waiting to be heard rumbled through the room.

She reviewed the notes on her two cases, checked her calendar for the rest of the week, and looked for a time to meet with Ollie about the business. She didn't want to think about her exchange with Colby in the exam room. Just seeing her first when she'd opened the DRC had been a shock, but her fresh injuries had stirred something deep and protective inside Adena. Why did she care about someone so evasive and cavalier about her own safety?

The image of Colby's nude torso flashed through her mind, and she warmed as if seeing it for the first time. Smooth, pale skin stained with ugly purple bruises. High, tight breasts marred by a bull's-eye injury in the center. Dark nipples puckered and begging to be sucked. Adena slid her hand down the side of her neck. Her pulse pounded wildly beneath her fingers.

When she'd stared into Colby's green eyes, she'd seen something struggling to escape. Colby wanted to confide in her but wouldn't or couldn't. And the off-handed comment about disappointing her this morning seemed like a warning. What was going on with Colby and how could she reach her? She was a contradiction that defied understanding.

And why had Colby's questions about having fun made her so defensive? Had her career become her life? Her father always said, "Hard work eventually leads to happiness." Did it? Maybe not everything he'd said was gospel, like his advice about expensive clothes. Was it time to re-evaluate her priorities? She felt a pang of guilt for questioning her father's teachings, but he'd also encouraged her to think for herself and live her own life. Maybe she'd consider *that* advice more seriously in the future.

"*Counselor?*" Judge Adler called from the bench. It wasn't the first time. Everyone was staring at her.

"Sorry, ma'am."

"Approach the bench, please."

Adena walked to the front of the courtroom and nodded in deference to her friend's position. "Your Honor."

Lois lowered her voice. "Daydreaming in court, Counselor?"

She felt her cheeks flush. "Guilty. I apologize."

"We'll discuss that later." She stepped away from the bench as Lois leaned back in her chair. "In the meantime, you have business with the court?"

"Yes, ma'am. Two clients for panhandling."

Lois looked into the audience and back at her. "Pro bono?"

Adena nodded.

"And I assume you're paying the court costs?"

She nodded again.

"Does your bank account ever run out?"

"I'm starting to wonder," she mumbled to herself. "They're homeless and just trying to survive, ma'am."

"Of course they are." Lois addressed the clerk. "In the cases of Joe and Fred, names as provided by counsel, cost of court and twenty hours' community service to be carried out at the Daytime Resource Center under the supervision of counsel."

"Thank you, Judge." Adena escorted her clients from the room and explained once again the laws pertaining to panhandlers and buskers on city streets and public areas. They probably knew the ordinances as well as she did, but she considered it part of her civic duty to make sure. "Try to stay out of trouble, guys." They both shook her hand and blended into the crowded hallway. She always felt conflicted after one of these cases, gratified to offer legal assistance to those who needed it but annoyed that such laws still criminalized the homeless and less fortunate.

As she walked down the courthouse steps, someone called to her. When she turned, Detective Carrick was approaching. "Good morning, David." The detective's usually clean-shaven face was shaded by several days' growth. His eyes were bloodshot and his wrinkled clothes smelled of continued wear. "Keeping late hours?"

"I have something for you." He handed her a black-and-white photograph. "This was taken from a CCTV camera near the area where your father was attacked. Not sure if it's going to be much help."

She glanced at the grainy image that could've been any white male. He wore dark clothing, and a cigarette hung from the corner of his mouth. "Enhancements?"

"We've tried everything. That's as good as it gets."

"Why am I just seeing this now?"

Carrick scuffed a shoe against one of the steps and didn't look at her. "I'm embarrassed to admit it was overlooked in the digital evidence. I thought the crime-scene tech checked, and he thought I did. No excuse, but that's what happened."

She was stunned by the oversight and started to tell him so, but his pained expression suggested he'd suffered enough. A man with his reputation took pride in his work. She was certain he'd never make the same mistake again. "I guess it happens."

"I've been working the streets trying to identify the guy. I'm not sure if he's a suspect or just a person of interest at this point. The folks you deal with are out all the time. Maybe they can help. Just ask around, but don't put yourself in danger."

As she held the photo, her hand trembled. She'd questioned Carrick's dedication to the case, but maybe she'd misjudged him.

He didn't have to share this with her. "Thank you. I'll let you know if I find anything."

He left her standing on the steps holding a photo that could've been anyone. The image was grainy, a white male, but little else definitive. The man's clothing was nondescript, dark with no identifying characteristics. Her heart thundered as she focused on the only recognizable part of the picture, the back door of the DRC inches from where her father's body had been found. She grabbed the step railing as the painful memory returned.

"Are you sure you want to see this, ma'am?" Detective Carrick guided her around the side of the DRC building toward the back garden area. "It's pretty gruesome."

"He's my father. I have to see..." Her legs threatened to crumble, each step an advance toward a place she didn't want to go. As she approached the group of uniformed officers, detectives, and crime-scene specialists, they turned away. On the ground in the center of the circle lay a figure covered with protective sheeting. Carrick nodded to the detective closest to the body, and he pulled back the covering.

Adena's stomach heaved. Her father's body was peppered with injuries, blood coagulated around him, and his clothes were stained brownish-red. His fingers were slashed with defensive wounds around his gold wedding ring and watch on his left hand. She forced herself to look at his face—a blank mask. The ground gave way, and she collapsed.

"Adena, you okay?" The husky voice registered before the realization that someone was guiding her to sit on the courthouse steps. Colby knelt in front of her, green eyes boring into her.

"I'm...fine." The warmth from Colby's hands on her arms made her almost believe she was telling the truth.

"You're so pale. I was afraid you'd pass out."

Her father's case was in the forefront of her mind every day, keeping her focused and moving forward. She took a few seconds to steady her breathing and then rose. "I'm really fine, just distracted."

Colby stood very close, as if poised to catch her if she faltered. "The last time I saw a look like that I'd just told my parents I'd joined the air force. They were both in shock. My father's skin paled, probably remembering his own experience in the army and hoping he could persuade me to change my mind. My mother's mouth opened and closed, but nothing came out. They were in denial until the day I left for boot camp, and I could still see that same shocked expression in their eyes."

Colby's candor surprised Adena. She almost forgot her own issues as she listened to the heartfelt revelation.

Colby lightly cupped her elbow. "You don't have to say anything, but I'm a good listener. Maybe I should walk with you a bit, just to make sure you're okay." She smiled, and a light dusting of freckles across her nose became more pronounced.

The morning sun created a halo of blondish-red hair sprouting from Colby's shaved head. She wanted to touch the angelically soft-looking sprigs, to feel something at least symbolically new and fresh, but she was too emotionally drained.

"What's wrong, Adena? I know I'm not really in a position to help anybody, but sometimes just talking will make you feel better."

Adena wanted to accept the strength Colby offered, to explore the possibilities of that smile and the unexplainable feelings it evoked, but common sense prevailed. "Thank you for your concern, but no."

Colby pressed her hand gently against Adena's back and stared into her eyes. "Just remember I'm here if you change your mind."

As Adena walked away, Colby stuffed her hands into her jeans pockets and stared after her wistfully. With the faded bomber jacket and ripped jeans hanging below her hips, she looked very much homeless and lost. Adena's job was to help her, not exploit her. She shouldn't even be considering Colby a possible friend or confidante, not that she wasn't worthy, because she was. Her father would've been appalled.

She cancelled the rest of her workday and went directly home after talking with Detective Carrick. There she changed into a worn pair of jeans, sweatshirt, and an old pea coat she'd picked up at

Goodwill. With the photograph in hand, she paced her empty living room, willing the image to reveal something worthwhile. She'd been stuck in a loop for months, living around her father's death, unable to get a foothold on the why of it all. She needed answers and closure so she could move forward with her life, whatever that was.

Maybe someone in the homeless community knew this man. She headed downtown, daylight slowly giving way to dusk. Her first stop was the tent camp closest to the train station. As she walked up, two of the men she recognized from the DRC rose, brushed the dirt off their pants, and came toward her.

"Miss Adena, what you doing out here alone at night?" one of them asked.

"I need help, guys." She pulled the photo out of her coat pocket, and they passed it around. "If you know this man or think he looks familiar, please tell me. There's a reward."

The other man took a second look and handed the picture back. "We don't need a reward, Miss Adena. We want to help you, but this is a bad shot. Don't give us much to go on."

"I know, but thank you for looking just the same." She tucked the glossy paper back in her coat pocket and turned to leave.

"Be careful out here," the first man said. "Want me to walk with you a bit?"

The kindness and generosity of people with so little often surprised Adena in her work with the homeless. "I appreciate it, but I'll be fine. I'm heading home shortly. Thank you all."

Every stop meant more wasted time. No one had seen the man in the photograph or knew John Tabor, who'd spoken to the reporter. The suspect and Tabor were either out-of-towners, weren't homeless, or did a great job of hiding in plain sight. Or maybe the photo of the suspect was just too unclear to be helpful. She fought back tears.

By the time she reached the DRC, people taking shelter from the cold had claimed all the cots and warming chairs. She worked from the outside in, showing the photograph to everyone discreetly and promising anonymity if they provided information. Nothing. She'd started to give up for the night when Cowboy came out of the shower room. He nodded, and she inclined her head toward the office.

"Evening, ma'am." Once inside the office, he took off his cowboy hat and assumed a military stance. She wondered again how such proud men coped with their current circumstances after distinguished careers of service.

"How are you, Cowboy? How's the leg?" She'd watched him transform a ragtag group of vets into a cohesive group resembling a family, often utilizing some rigorous methods. A few of his recruits had moved on, but many were long-term guests.

"'Bout the same, ma'am. Good days and bad."

She handed him the picture. "Have you seen this man?"

Cowboy glanced down and quickly looked away. "No, ma'am."

"Are you sure? Take a good look." She held the paper closer, but again Cowboy gave it only a cursory glance.

"I'm sure. Pretty bad picture."

She sighed. "Yeah, it is, but I keep hoping. Have you heard the name John Tabor before?"

"No ma'am. Can't say I have. Is this about your father?"

She nodded and brushed away a tear as she dropped the photo on her desk. "Thanks."

"Night, Miss Adena." He pulled his hat low on his forehead and, as he turned, added. "Maybe you should let the police handle this. I'd hate to see you get hurt."

"Thanks, Cowboy, but some things you have to do yourself. If you hear anything, please let me know."

She picked up the photo and some other paperwork for home and headed toward the exit. Just outside her office in the clinic waiting area was a bank of telephones the guests used to contact friends and family and make appointments for job interviews. As she passed, she heard Colby's distinctively throaty voice and slowed. She'd eavesdropped on her before in the hopes of helping her, but this time Colby's pleading tone compelled her to listen when she knew she shouldn't.

"Kali, I'm sorry, but we've both known this wasn't working for months." Colby paused, listening to the other party before continuing. "You like the *idea* of us, our parents' friendship, their causes, a comfortable existence. We've been trying for two years."

Adena felt guilty but couldn't force herself to move away. She was violating Colby's privacy, acting unprofessionally, and just being rude. She still couldn't leave.

"It's not enough," Colby said. "I want chemistry, passion, and a heart connection."

The words hammered into Adena's chest with the conviction of her own desires. "Chemistry, passion, and a heart connection."

"I'm sorry, but I don't feel that with us," Colby said. "Please forgive me. Kali, wait. Don't hang up angry. I'm not sure when I can call again. Kali—"

Adena peered around the corner. Colby held the phone against her forehead, light reflecting off tears on her cheek. She'd gotten a glimpse of an unguarded Colby Vincent on the courthouse steps earlier today and again just now, superseding her first impressions. Adena wanted to console her, but she'd have to admit she'd violated rules of the center and of common decency. Why was every encounter with this woman a challenge? She needed fresh air.

The only way out the front was past Colby, and she couldn't face her right now. She walked to the rear exit but stopped, unable to push the lock bar. She hadn't used this door since her father's death or even visited the gardens this spring and summer. Could she walk past the spot where his body had lain without breaking down? She stood, gripping the lock, struggling with which direction to choose. Finally, she went back to her office and stretched out on the sagging sofa in the corner.

CHAPTER SEVEN

Colby nodded to a middle-aged attendant with large glasses and thrift-shop clothes as she entered the library.

"You going to be long, hon?" The staff got upset if the homeless monopolized the chairs and computers for long periods of time.

"No, ma'am. Just need to check email." She scanned the room. Most of the regulars had already gone so she should get some leeway. She'd told her mom to email but forgot she didn't have a smartphone to respond immediately. Time to check in before her father had one of his army buddies track her down.

"Okay. You should be fine today."

As Colby waited on the slow connection, she thought about lounging in her recliner at home with a hot cup of coffee, feet up, and tablet snuggled in her lap. She could kill hours emailing friends and checking Facebook posts while munching on the snack of her choice. After ten days of living rough, she'd worked, foraged, or begged for simple things she used to feel entitled to. Now she was grateful for nice weather, somewhere warm to sleep, a coin donated by a stranger, a free shower, and especially a hot meal. She didn't take anything for granted on the streets. Why had she before?

She appreciated her parents and the life they'd provided, but would she go back and live as if this experience never happened? Even before this assignment, she'd started to question her lifestyle—devoting herself to her career and dating occasionally. Her relationship with Kali was never going to be a forever situation. She wanted to share the kind of love her parents enjoyed with a partner of her own. Adena's image filled her mind, and she wondered what she wished for. It wouldn't be anything like her.

She signed into her email account and her mailbox pinged with unread messages, one a day from her parents and several daily from Kali. The tone of her mother's messages grew more urgent until she threatened to file a missing-person's report. She envisioned her mother pacing their spacious kitchen, wringing her hands, and waiting for a phone call that never came.

She typed quickly.

Dear Mom and Dad,

I'm so sorry for not getting in touch sooner. I'm fine, but I do miss hanging out with you and just talking. Don't worry about me. I promise to do a better job of keeping in touch and don't call the police or army (Dad). ☺ *Please forgive me and know that I think of you every day.*

Love you both,

P.S. FYI, I broke up with Kali. It wasn't working for me. Help her if you can.

Kali's messages ran the emotional gamut from angry to begging for a second chance. Colby had tried to leave before, but Kali could be very persuasive, especially in bed. Now she wouldn't give in to Kali even if she weakened. She'd made the right decision, and eventually Kali would realize it too. She kept her response brief.

Kali,

I'm sorry if I hurt you. Find someone who makes you truly happy.

C

Before she ended her session, Colby opened her work account and read an email from Leon, who was just checking on her. She sent a brief reply and mentioned speaking with her contact, but not the less-than-welcoming response she'd received.

After closing her account, Colby put on her coat and exited the library. As she walked, she dialed Frankie's number. "Hey, I'm laying low, nothing to report really. Just wanted you to know I'm still alive. Later." She'd kept closer tabs on her agents in New York. Leaving a legend twisting in the wind was just asking for trouble. Maybe they did things differently in the South.

"Well, look who we have here."

Colby dropped her phone back in her boot and pretended to be adjusting her socks before she faced Cowboy.

"Where you been, Eagle?"

Her body hummed with a warning flood of adrenaline. She scanned the area for his posse. "Around." She was no longer comfortable with Cowboy. He'd proved his true colors.

"You looking for your police friend? I saw you getting chummy with that beat cop the other day."

"Right." She kept walking, putting distance between them.

"I thought you'd found a place or a boyfriend to keep you warm at night, but I can tell by your smell you haven't."

She continued down Church Street, hoping he'd get the clue and leave. He didn't need to know she'd spent the past four days washing up in fast-food restaurants, avoiding him and his roving zoo. She wasn't afraid, just being cautious as she made her own way. Sing Song had appeared and vanished like a magician, offering rhyming pearls of wisdom, but she wasn't a reliable companion.

"You upset with me?"

She stopped and squared off with him. "Why should I be? Oh, wait. I remember. You let your guys beat the crap out of me and almost rape me."

"It wasn't personal."

"Seriously? You don't get more personal than rape. I don't want any more trouble, Cowboy. Just leave me alone." If he wasn't involved in the drug operation, she really didn't need him or his friends, and so far she had no clear indication that he was.

"Let me make it up to you. There's a big show at the Cone Denim Entertainment Center tonight. Have a shower, change clothes, and come by at ten. We're all going, my treat."

"No thanks."

"Come on. It'll be fun. The guys miss you."

"They miss using me as a punching bag."

"It won't be like that again. I promise."

"I don't know." It seemed strange that a group of homeless people would spend money to go to a show, but what did she really know about being homeless? She was just playing at it.

"Go with us. Besides, I might have some work for you." He patted her shoulder and walked away. "See you tonight."

Adena greeted folks at the DRC for the fourth day and looked for Colby. Had she finally taken her advice and gone back home or to the girlfriend she'd broken up with over the phone? She hated knowing those tidbits of Colby's life, but hated more not knowing if she was safe. Though they'd had limited contact, she felt an affinity for Colby she couldn't deny.

"Have you seen the new girl?" She asked every person who passed through the doors.

"You're better off not knowing," Flo said.

"Please, Flo."

"Just trying to help. And if you keep sleeping in the office, I'm going to charge you hotel rates. We could use the cash."

"Did I ever tell you what a pain you are sometimes?"

"Backing off." She raised her hands and did a moonwalk toward the dayroom.

"Wait," Adena called. "Did you find anything about that Tabor guy yet?"

"Nope. I've searched back three years. If he was ever here, the record has disappeared."

"Great." Disappeared, just like Colby. Adena had seen a compassionate side of Colby in her concern for Sing Song, in the way she'd spoken to her parents and girlfriend on the phone, and in the comfort she'd offered her on the courthouse steps. Colby was different, and Adena couldn't stop trying to figure out how and why.

"Has the new bald girl been to your camp lately?" she asked two of the guys as they signed in at the front desk. They shook their heads and a sick feeling settled in her gut. People didn't just appear and disappear. She tried to argue her own logic, because homeless folks did exactly that and often for no apparent reason. She couldn't do anything unless Colby wanted help. When the last person in line entered, Adena retreated to the office.

She needed to think about Ollie's offer to take over the DRC operation. Pulling up the financials on the computer, she scanned last year's figures. Since her father's death, she hadn't paid much attention to the day-to-day operations, leaving the details to Flo. The center normally ran close to the financial edge, but the past few weeks of serving as an emergency night shelter during the cold snap had pushed them way over budget.

Donations and the small stipend from the city were consistent with previous years but couldn't cover the demand. Ollie excelled at serving as the public face of the center and fund-raising among the city's elite. Maybe he should take the helm for a while, at least until the recent bad publicity blew over. He was as invested in the DRC as her father had been, and she didn't have the time or energy to devote to a large public appeal, which inevitably came with political discourse.

She stared at the portrait of her father on the wall. He'd instilled in her a strong work ethic along with an understanding of the importance of giving back. Growing up, she'd thought he neglected family for his career, but as an adult she realized his commitment to both had been absolute. He believed a profession that provided financial stability and status *was* the best way to care for his family, and she'd adopted his philosophy. If she worked hard, she'd be successful and even happy, eventually. And maybe if she repeated the mantra often, she'd really believe it.

She checked her appointments and caseload with Chris before deciding to stay at the DRC for the day. With the added burden of providing forty cots and a warming room as an emergency shelter, Flo could use an extra pair of hands. She laundered sheets between loads for guests, made beds, and restocked towels and toiletries in the showers, anything to keep from thinking about what could've happened to Colby. By the end of the day she'd convinced Flo to have dinner with her and to overlook her sleeping in the DRC office another night.

❖

Colby waited by the train depot until Adena and Flo left for dinner, then ducked into the DRC for a quick shower. She wasn't in the mood to answer questions about where she'd been or where she was going, no matter how well intended. Tucking her backpack and oversized coat into a locker, she rifled through the clothes rack for something nicer for the evening. After a pack of peanut-butter crackers and an apple for dinner, she met Cowboy and the others in front of the Cone Denim Entertainment Center on Elm Street.

"Glad you came, Eagle," Cowboy said.

"Yeah." Wolf added. "No hard feelings?" He offered his hand and Colby took it.

"No hard feelings, but if you touch me again, I'll fucking kill you." She held his hand and made eye contact with him, Coyote, JR, Badger, Raven, and Bug before letting go. Her father had taught her, and the air force reinforced, when in danger never show fear. "Got it?" Each man nodded. "Now let's have some fun, since it's on Cowboy."

They let out a collective whoop while Cowboy pulled a wad of cash from his coat and paid the entry fees. Soldiers didn't get that much money from retirement or disability benefits. She'd followed the other guys around at night enough to determine they weren't dealing drugs or spending large sums of cash. Cowboy definitely had another source of income, and she couldn't wait to find out what.

The evening's entertainment was a country-western band complete with two-step dancing. She made the rounds with the guys, demonstrating a subtle scoot-a-boot move, restoring good faith, and cementing her place in the group. Every time she returned from a dance, fresh drinks were on the table, but she paced herself. Some of the guys were loud and boisterous, and one of the bouncers was eyeballing them.

Bug pulled out an e-cigarette, screwed a new cartridge into the battery, and pushed the button. "Hey, let's smoke the peace pipe. We've had a rough patch, so I think we should bury the hatchet." When the tip lit up and vapor escaped from the end, he took a drag and passed it left. "Here's to new beginnings." Each guy took a hit until it got to her.

"Told you before, I'm not a smoker." She tried to pass the metal cigarette.

"You have to take a hit with us," JR said, "as a show of good faith."

"I appreciate it, but I was the girl in high school who could only handle one puff of a blunt. All I wanted was a laugh, a snack, and a nap."

"But this isn't just any e-cig. We're not smoking. We're vaping budder, man."

"That shit is powerful." The recent trend of vaping hash oil had hit New York just before she left. It wasn't considered especially dangerous, but it had a much higher percentage of THC than marijuana. She stared at the device and weighed her options.

"It won't hurt you. It's my own personal concoction," Bug said, his face morphing into a silly grin. "Trust a fellow geek."

What if this was another test she had to pass before they'd let her into the inner circle? Legends occasionally used drugs to prove themselves while undercover, so she wouldn't be violating protocol. "Are you sure this shit won't mess me up, because if it does—"

"I know. You'll fucking kill us. Right?" Wolf grabbed her shoulder. "It's just a relaxer. Nothing heavy, Eagle."

Colby nodded and inhaled a small puff. She felt the burn all the way down. Her breath caught and her lungs felt sticky. "Can't breathe." She coughed and held her throat, pulling for air.

"Short breaths," Bug said. "Let the panic pass, then you'll like it."

She took a few gasps of acidic air and her lungs eventually stopped burning, but her heart pounded. "Got to get out of here." She tried to stand and tripped over her chair.

"Hey, you can't smoke that shit in here." One of the bouncers pointed toward the door.

"Fuck off, man," Coyote said and took another puff. "It's just an e-cig."

"Out." The bouncer wasn't giving up.

Cowboy waved the guy back. "Come on, fellas, let's go. We've worn out our welcome." They started for the door with JR and Badger holding her arms while the bouncer followed.

"Back off, asshole," Raven said.

"Yeah or I'll slit you a new one." Coyote reached in the back of his waistband and pulled out a hunting knife just as they got outside. "Now, talk shit." He flipped the knife back and forth in his hands before lunging at the bouncer.

Colby's head was buzzing from whatever she'd inhaled. Her heart hammered, her breathing was erratic, but everyone moved in slow motion. She tried to back against the cool brick building, but a group of people rushed out of the club and shoved her to the ground. Now Coyote and Wolf both held knives and danced menacingly around the bouncer. Coyote charged the man again, but he sidestepped. People exiting the club and men with knives surrounded her, but she couldn't stand. Blinding streetlights. Screaming. Flashing lights and sirens. Someone pulled her arms, and she fought back. Then she was tasered.

Chapter Eight

"Vincent. Colby Vincent." Her name echoed down a long tunnel, barely audible. She was buried under a scratchy covering with a strong disinfectant smell. Her limbs felt thick and clumsy when she tried to move. Not freezing, but not toasty warm. Inside. Muffled voices bounced off bare walls. "Vincent, goddamn it. Wake up."

"Shush, don't yell." Her own voice rumbled painfully through her head.

"You got bail."

"Bail?" She opened her eyes and stared at bars across the entrance of the small cubicle. "I'm in jail?"

The deputy shook his head. "No, smart-ass, you're at the Ritz. If you want to keep your luxury suite, I'll tell your lawyer to leave."

"I don't have a lawyer. I didn't call anybody."

The heavy bars slid sideways with enough noise to chatter her teeth. "Fortunately for you, your lawyer has friends in low places. Let's go."

She tried to stand but tilted sideways and grabbed the wall. "What happened?"

"You're asking me? Officer Reynolds said probably an overdose, but he had to taser your ass because you were flopping around like a dying chicken. Doc said you'd sleep it off."

She remembered Reynolds from their first encounter outside the library. Being arrested by him was not a good second impression.

The deputy nudged her into the hall and directed her until she reached what looked like a checkout desk. Another brown-suited officer slid a form toward her, along with her cell phone in a plastic bag. "Sign here and you're free to go. Your court date is on the paper. If you fail to show up, bail will be revoked and the money paid to secure it will be forfeited."

Who'd paid her bond? She hadn't been coherent enough to call Frankie, her parents didn't know where she was, and Leon wouldn't interfere if he did know. She made an illegible mark and waited while the deputy keyed the exit to the lobby. When the door opened, she shielded her eyes as the bright sun shot pain through her skull.

"Are you all right?"

Adena's sultry voice was a welcome but embarrassing greeting. She slowly opened her eyes. "How did you know? Who called?"

"Let's get out of here." Adena's tone was quiet and reassuring, but her beautifully curved lips showed no signs of pleasure. "Can you manage a walk?"

"Would probably help. Where're we going?"

Adena took her elbow and guided her carefully down the jail steps. "I thought you might like some breakfast. Hungry?"

"I think so, but it's hard to tell right now. Everything's fuzzy." She waited for the inevitable questions about what happened and how she ended up in jail, but they didn't come. Adena seemed content to walk beside her quietly, occasionally steadying her wobbly gait. The brisk morning air cleared her drug-shrouded brain, and in the clearing, she fabricated a story she hoped would satisfy Adena's curiosity.

When they reached the Smith Street Diner, the smells of frying bacon and freshly brewed coffee hit her when they opened the door, reminding her of home. She was suddenly starving. She practically inhaled her first cup of coffee and raised her hand for more.

The waitress took their orders and placed a basket of fresh biscuits on the table. She practiced the table manners her parents had taught her and waited for Adena to start, but when she didn't immediately reach for the fist-sized delicacies, Colby grabbed one. Splitting the biscuit open, she slathered butter on both halves and, without waiting for it to melt, took a bite. The taste of salted butter and freshly baked flour mingled in her mouth. "Mmm, so good."

When she looked up and saw Adena focusing on her mouth, she stopped in mid-chew. "Stop it. I'm trying to eat."

"And you're doing a marvelous job." Her voice was husky and her cheeks flushed.

Colby was torn between her hunger to kiss Adena or eat her meal—what a horrible choice. Another injustice of being homeless. How could anyone have a relationship when her first priority had to be nourishment? She'd survived on cheese or peanut-butter crackers for days, so real food was a luxury. When the waitress placed a steaming plate of eggs, hash browns, and bacon in front of her, the feeling was almost orgasmic.

"My mother makes biscuits for every meal because my dad loves them, but hers are flat, nothing like these huge monsters. She squishes them down with her first three fingers and makes indentions on top. She says we get to have a little piece of her at every meal." Colby's throat closed and she placed the biscuit back on her plate.

"You miss them."

She nodded. This would be a perfect moment to share part of her life with Adena. She already knew Colby wasn't being honest. But if she told the truth, she'd risk the case and perhaps her job. She had to put her feelings on hold. In the meantime, she'd be as truthful as possible. "There's just the three of us, so we were close. I've always lived at home, never had my own place, yet."

"I'm sure they miss you too." Adena placed her hand over Colby's on the table. The gesture felt natural and Adena's compassion genuine.

"One night this week I huddled beside a church's heating unit to keep warm and just cried. Not for things. I miss the people and feelings—a quiet breakfast with my parents, laughter with coworkers, closeness of friends, and...sex. I never imagined how much I'd miss emotional intimacy." Adena's eyes held hers, and when she licked her lips, Colby swallowed hard.

How would it feel to press her lips against the softness of Adena's mouth, to gather her in her arms and inch toward her until there was no space left? Her body tingled. None of that mattered. It couldn't. She reluctantly withdrew her hand. Adena's touch was too comfortable, and she was close to revealing too much. "But things change." As the truth tried to claw its way out, she buried her feelings. She forced herself to eat, the food suddenly not as appetizing. "You have any special memories of your mom?"

"No, not really."

"Seriously?"

Adena fiddled with the handle of her coffee cup and didn't look up. "My mother died of a brain aneurism when I was ten. The few memories I have aren't very clear."

"Oh my God, I'm so sorry." Colby imagined a slide show of family highlights without her mother at the center, and the images froze. She placed her hand over her heart. "So sorry. Did you and your father get along?"

"I didn't think so when I was young. After my mom died, he was always busy. I never felt like a priority. I'm not sure he knew exactly what to do with a pre-teen." Adena's eyes glistened. She captured her bottom lip in her teeth but not before Colby saw a slight tremor. "When I was older and took an interest in the law, we bonded more and ultimately joined career paths. And then he was killed."

Suddenly Adena's independence and reluctance to accept help made sense. She was afraid of abandonment and of being second choice again.

"So is that why—"

"Can we talk about something else, please?" Adena asked. "It's inappropriate to discuss personal issues with a DRC guest."

"You mean *your* personal issues."

Adena seemed to consider her question and her face flushed. "I guess you're right, but it's my job to explore your past so I can help with your future." She scanned the room behind Colby but didn't meet her gaze again until the pink left her cheeks.

"Whatever you say, Counselor. I won't push. Maybe one day you'll look at me as something besides a DRC guest." This was the first time Adena had opened up to her emotionally, and Colby was reluctant to move on. But something told her if she hoped to get closer to Adena, it would be a slow and patient process, like this case.

"I don't see how that—"

"Please," Colby said, holding up her hand. "Let a girl dream. So, you're probably wondering about last night."

Adena shrugged. "If and when you're ready to talk, you will. But I'd appreciate it if you'd do two things for me."

"I'll try."

"If you decide to tell me anything, please let it be the truth. I can handle a lot of things, but I'm not good with lies."

A part of Colby shut down. She'd always been open and honest in personal relationships, but she'd never been in a professional situation where deception was not only necessary for success but also mandatory for survival. "I told you I'd probably disappoint you." The light in Adena's eyes dimmed. She'd hoped for more. "And the second thing?"

Adena picked at her food for several seconds and finally lowered her fork. "Whatever drugs or violence you're into, please don't bring it to the DRC. Both are grounds for a permanent ban. But more importantly, that place is part of my father's legacy, and I couldn't bear to have anything happen to it. A reporter recently raised questions about our work, so that's all I can handle right now."

"Have you had problems at the center before, with drugs and violence?"

"Not that I'm aware of, but it's possible things go on behind my back. I certainly hope not." Her forehead wrinkled and her mouth pursed into a tight grimace. She'd answered honestly.

"Why do you put so much time into the DRC, Adena? Is it just your father's legacy or something deeper?"

Adena stared into her plate without answering for several seconds. When she spoke, her normally confident voice was tinged with uncertainty. "I'm not sure anymore. He used to quote a Bible verse. "From everyone who has been given much, much will be required. Maybe the message of the words stuck with me, or maybe my father's living example is what made the impression. Who knows?"

Adena's eyes filled with tears and she pulled a heavy breath.

Colby wanted to comfort her, to tell her it would be all right. Instead she settled for the only truth she could offer. "I promise I won't be the one who brings drugs or violence to your doorstep." Her answer didn't change Adena's expression, maybe because it sounded as unconvincing to her as it had to Colby. She hoped she could live up to her promise. Adena cared deeply about her father's work, and she didn't want to be the one to compromise or destroy it.

"I appreciate that," Adena said.

Colby finished her eggs and bacon and swabbed the plate with the remnants of the last biscuit. "By the way, how did you know I was in jail?"

"Officer Reynolds called. He volunteers at the center."

"You paid my bail out of your own pocket?"

"I have a fund for my pro-bono work. When you show up for court, I get it back."

"Must be a large fund. You seem to do a lot pro bono. Do you ever get paid?" Colby was kidding, but Adena's grimace said she'd hit a nerve. "I'm sorry. The folks on the street just talk about how hard you work and how much good you do for the community."

"That's nice to hear." Adena waved for the check and counted out the money to pay. "We'll talk before your case comes up."

"Sounds good. Guess I better get going." She wasn't anxious for Adena to ask more questions. "Thank you for bailing me out and for breakfast."

Colby ran from the Smith Street Diner as if distance could separate her feelings from reality. *Adena.* She mumbled as she headed back to the DRC to shower and collect her belongings. This case sucked because she had no real leads, but she did have feelings for Adena.

"And I should probably call Frankie. Damn." She fished her phone out of her boot and hit speed dial. When she got a message, she said, "Just wanted to let you know I got arrested last night for disorderly conduct, not sure how since I was unconscious, but that's another story. The lady from the DRC bailed me out. Nothing new on the case. I'll call back when I have more." When she looked up the street, Cowboy was limping toward her, but she didn't stop. Every time she turned around, he was there, almost like he was stalking her or watching her for some reason.

"Hey, wait up." She wasn't in the mood for more games. "Don't be like that, Eagle." She heard his irregular gait hurrying to catch up.

She spun around so quickly that he stepped back and wobbled at the edge of the curb. "*Don't be like that*? Really? First your groupies tried to rape me, then beat the crap out of me, and last night they gave me enough drugs to sedate a horse, and now you want to play nice?"

"If Wolf wanted to kill you, we wouldn't be talking. And Bug feels real bad about the smoke. I've told him to stop tinkering with that shit, but he won't listen."

"Good for you. Leave me alone." She purposely walked faster so he couldn't follow.

"You passed." He called after her. "It was all a test."

She clenched her fists at her sides and breathed through the anger. She'd had her head shaved, been drugged twice, taken two beatings, gotten tasered by the police, disappointed a woman she desperately wanted to impress, and been locked up during this investigation with nothing to show for it.

She turned back toward Cowboy but didn't move any closer. "A test of what? The ability to protect myself? Courage under fire? Been there, done that in Iraq. I don't want or need a refresher course, and I certainly don't need to prove myself to you."

"Loyalty," Cowboy said, finally catching up to her. "I needed to know you could keep your mouth shut and not involve the police."

"As if they would do anything."

"And it was sort of a job interview."

Colby walked away again, trying to appear disinterested, but her gut told her this was her first break in the case. "No thanks. I fell for the let's-make-up trick last time. I'm a fast learner. Give your job to somebody else."

"I want you."

"Should've thought about that before." She was really pushing her luck but felt confident he'd take the bait.

"Are you interested or not?" Cowboy stopped and scratched his gray beard. He was obviously uncomfortable asking for anything. She wasn't one of his flunkies, yet, so he handled her with slightly more respect.

"Depends on the job…and whether or not I can expect any more tests like last night."

"That's it. You're in, if you want to be." He tugged the brim of his hat lower on his forehead. "Well?"

"You haven't told me what the job is yet. At this point I'm not inclined to trust you." Part of her wanted to hear him say he was running a drug ring, but another part wanted him to be more careful. The game was on and she expected to be challenged. So far she'd only practiced patience and endurance.

"I'd rather show you. Be at the corner of Lee and Eugene streets in the morning at eight, showered and looking nice. Bring your prescriptions and photo ID."

"Where are we going?"

"You'll see." He lumbered away, no doubt fully expecting her to show. He had no idea just how much she was looking forward to the trip.

CHAPTER NINE

As Adena walked through Fisher Park on her way home, she thought again about her talk with Colby in the diner the day before. The current between them had been intense, more emotional than sexual, but with definite undertones. Something about Colby's telling of her experience beside the church, the loneliness that made her weak, struck a familiar chord in Adena. She'd stared into her coffee cup after Colby left as if the dark liquid held magical answers to their connection.

She'd been awake since the five o'clock phone call from Officer Reynolds advising her Colby was in jail. He indicated there wasn't enough evidence to connect her to the fight or knife assault on one of the bouncers at the Cone Denim Entertainment Center. Colby had apparently been too stoned to provide much information, so they'd let her sleep it off. Adena had tried downplaying it, but Flo caught her again.

Flo answered the call, cranky as she wrestled her way out of a cot in the office. She handed the phone to Adena and waited until she hung up. "It's that girl, right? The bald one you're always worried about. Fighting, knife assault, drugs? Really? You want to get involved with that? Why?"

"Flo, it's too early and I'm too tired to argue. Can we go back to sleep?"

"You mean before you dash off to rescue this girl. What's so different about her?"

Adena rolled over on the couch with her back to Flo. It didn't help.

"I'm talking to you."

"I haven't done anything special for her." She tried to sound convincing, but she couldn't lie to Flo. "I don't know why I'm trying so hard with this one. I wish I could figure it out."

"Fine. Just wanted to hear you admit it."

God, how I wish I could figure it out. Colby's story of her mother's baking had reminded Adena of what she'd missed as a child. She'd seen a deeper, softer side of Colby that she'd truly enjoyed. She'd opened up to Colby about her family—a first for her. The sharing had been freeing as emotions rushed to the surface. And then Colby had rushed out of the diner.

Maybe Flo was right and Colby wasn't the kind of person who'd benefit from second or third chances. What if her parents had kicked her out after numerous interventions because of her propensity for drugs and violence? Colby obviously still loved her parents, but if they couldn't help her, what chance did she have of making a difference?

At the corner of Elm and Hendrix Streets her thoughts drifted to the other unsolved mystery in her life. She remembered a small homeless camp near her house that she hadn't visited the night she made rounds with the suspect's picture. After changing clothes and stuffing her carry bag with a few items, she headed in that direction.

She walked across the bridge over the railroad tracks and into a small park at the dead end of Hendrix Street. Not many people knew this place existed, but a few itinerant folks called it home. The families in the area knew about the squatters but didn't bother them and vice versa. They respected each other's boundaries, and the park was always left clean and ready for day visitors before the nomads left in the morning.

"Annette, you here?" Adena called out to the elderly African-American woman who usually parked her teeming shopping cart in the park overnight.

"Who wants to know?" Annette used her don't-mess-with-me voice, trying to ward off potential danger.

"It's Adena. I'm alone. Can we talk?"

"You bring anything?"

Everything was a negotiation with the homeless—food, money, or a place to sleep for information. Seemed like a fair trade, as she'd often been surprised by how much some of her guests heard. People tended to talk around them, as if they didn't exist. "Of course." She dug into the small bag she'd slung over her shoulder and pulled out a sandwich. "How about ham?"

"Hand it over." Annette was alone, sitting on the ground with one leg resting on the bottom tray of her cart. She never relinquished contact with her possessions and became quite combative if challenged, as Adena had learned during their first meeting at the DRC.

She stood a respectable distance away and offered the sandwich. "How's it going?"

"Does it appear that I'm thriving? For someone so intelligent, you can be really asinine sometimes. No disrespect intended."

"Sorry." Adena was momentarily taken aback. She'd forgotten Annette had been a college professor before mental illness, unemployment, and an apathetic family changed the course of her life. She'd been honored when Annette chose to share part of her former life story with her. She'd tried several times to help Annette get reestablished, but the former professor had been unable to sustain a structured life. Annette had finally declared herself a nutcase and a teacher to the travelers. People expected nothing and gave her a wide berth.

"What brings you out tonight, Counselor?"

She pulled the photo from her bag and handed it to Annette. "I need help."

"Well, hallelujah. It's about time you asked for something for a change. Let me see what you've got." She took the image, held it up to the streetlight, and squinted. "Hmmm, not much to go on is there? What's this about?"

"My father..." Her voice failed.

"I understand." She patted Adena's hand and returned her attention to the picture. "The coat isn't typical street wear, not a hoodie or heavy winter type, maybe leather? Look." She pointed to the shoulder area. "See how that shines under the light? Could be either leather or ski-jacket material, but it doesn't really look billowy enough. Know what I mean?"

Adena stared at the photograph, hoping to see something she hadn't noticed before, but even with Annette's encouragement, it looked the same. "Maybe. I don't know. Thanks though." She slid the photo into her bag and retrieved another item. "I brought you something else." She handed a worn copy of *Rebecca* to Annette and watched her face transform.

"I *love* this book. I've probably read it a hundred times but was thinking yesterday how I missed it. Where did you find this?"

"In my father's library, and I couldn't imagine anyone who would appreciate it more than you. The print might be too small. Next time you're at the DRC, have Doctor Raymond check your vision. You were squinting when you looked at the picture."

"Thank you, Adena. And don't worry. I'm fine. You'd squint in this light too."

"Have him check just the same, for me?"

Annette nodded.

"By the way, have you ever heard of a guy named John Tabor?"

"No. He homeless?"

"I'm not sure what or who he is yet."

"Stop chasing ghosts. Nothing good will come of it." She rose, gave Adena a hug, and stuffed the book into the top of a large canvas bag spilling over the side of the shopping cart. "And you know what I mean. You could get yourself hurt out here."

"Thanks for your help." Adena waved and started back across the railroad bridge, hope fading that she'd ever identify the person in the photo. She'd gone halfway when she noticed a man coming toward her. He was white with tape over his nose like a ballplayer and a toboggan pulled low on his forehead. She didn't recognize him as a client at the DRC, but she nodded and kept walking. When she got home, she'd examine the photo and check Annette's observations. Maybe—

She was grabbed from behind and felt something cold against the side of her neck. "W—what do you want?" A vision of her father's bloody body flashed through her mind. *Please, no.*

"I want you to stop asking questions, bitch." The man's voice was raspy and his breath smelled of cigarettes. "Leave it alone if you want to live." She tried to turn, to look at her attacker pressed too closely against her. "Stop struggling or I'll slit your throat right here."

She scanned the area for something to defend herself with but saw only trash. Panic rose, strangling her attempts to scream. *I shouldn't be here. I'm going to die on this bridge.* She looked toward Church Street and saw two figures approaching in the darkness. Suddenly one of them screamed "Stranger danger. Stranger danger," and waved her arms frantically. She recognized Sing Song's squeaky voice and prayed she wouldn't get involved.

"Run, Sing Song. Run," she called. And she did, in the opposite direction, but her companion barreled toward them.

"Get your hands off her." Colby's voice registered, and Adena felt her muscles relax slightly then seize again as Colby rushed toward them, into another fight.

"No, Colby. He's got a knife." *Please don't let anything happen to her.*

As if she hadn't heard the warning, Colby dropped to the ground and kicked her attacker's feet. When Adena felt his grip loosen, she spun out of his arms, her momentum propelling her into the side of the wire cage that canopied over the bridge.

She turned to help, but Colby was scuffling on the ground with the man. Light bounced off metal as the attacker raised his arm. She lunged for the knife but fell short. *God, please!* Adena shivered as the blade came down into Colby's body. "No!"

The man ran off, his entire face now covered by the ski mask, yelling, "Remember what I said, bitch. Next time it'll be you."

She raced to Colby, cradled her head against her chest, and rocked. The image of the masked man stabbing Colby replayed repeatedly in her mind. "Can you hear me?" No reply. Colby's eyes were closed, her breathing deep and labored. "Please. Can you hear me?" She fumbled for her cell phone.

"Sure. He didn't stab me in the ears."

Adena started, the response not at all expected. "You must be all right if you can still be a wiseass. Are you hurt?"

"Yeah, but not badly. Are *you* okay?"

"I'm fine. You're the one bleeding. What were you thinking, Colby? You could've been killed." As the adrenaline dissipated, she felt weak and shaky.

"I saw the knife at your neck and reacted. I told you, some things are worth fighting for."

"I'm calling 911." Her hand trembled as she tried to dial.

"No, Adena, please don't. It's nothing. Where's Sing Song? Is she all right?"

"I told her to run, and she listened for a change. I think you need to see a doctor, and we need to file a police report."

"No police." Colby slowly rolled away from her and stood, holding her hand against her left side, blood oozing through her fingers.

"Then you're coming to my house so I can make sure you don't bleed to death. No arguments. It's right across the street." She pointed toward her home and immediately felt a wave of panic. Was she really going to let someone see her residential catastrophe?

Colby nodded, picked up her backpack, and followed without further argument.

"And just for the record, I'm an officer of the court and this needs to be reported. That guy may have been involved in my—"

"In what?"

Adena ignored the question as she unlocked her front door and ushered Colby inside. "Sit in that chair while I find my first-aid supplies." She pointed to the only useable piece of furniture but realized Colby hadn't crossed the threshold. "What's wrong?"

"Do you actually live here, or are we breaking and entering a construction zone?" Colby scanned the interior of the house with the same look of disbelief she experienced every time she came home.

"This *is* my house. Whether or not I actually *live* here is debatable. Come sit." Adena moved on automatic pilot, located her first-aid kit in a moving box under the bathroom sink, checked the contents, and grabbed a bath towel. The images of her father's body were still too fresh, and the thought of another corpse materializing in her life was too disturbing to consider. *Think, and don't do anything stupid.*

When she returned to the living room, Colby had removed her oversized coat and blood-soaked T-shirt and was pressing it against her side. She was bare-chested, and Adena forced herself not to stare as she knelt in front of her.

"Let me look at your injury." She'd been doing that a lot lately, but this time Colby's wound could be very serious. Her hands trembled as she gently raised the blood-soaked fabric. The cut was still bleeding but didn't appear too deep. Thank goodness for her leather jacket. "This will sting a little." As she cleaned and inspected the injury, she glanced at a jagged scar across Colby's right side, one that had obviously needed stitches. Her vision blurred as she imagined what this woman had been through. "How'd you get that one?"

"Hand-to-hand combat in Iraq. We were struggling over a gun, but I didn't realize he had a knife as well."

"Do you think about these things before you rush in?" She sounded harsh, but the attack and having someone in her home had left her unsettled. She was desperate to understand the mentality of someone who intentionally put herself in danger time and again.

"I always think. But I choose to take action when most wouldn't. My parents taught me to be responsible and look out for others. Guess it stuck."

Colby's eyes had a faraway look as she stared into the distance, and Adena was touched by the sincerity of her tone. "You love them very much. I hear it in your voice."

"Yeah. I'm an only child, and we always did things together. It's been an adjustment being so alone without any support. I had no idea."

"Then I don't understand how they could let you—"

"Adena, please. It is what it is."

And just what is *it?* Shut down again and it stung more than a little this time. Why was Colby so open in some areas and so guarded in others? Colby's first instinct tonight had been to help, disregarding her own welfare. Was that how she'd been injured in the previous two incidents, protecting someone else? Not every soldier was a hero, not even during wartime, much less after they returned home. What made this woman tick? How did she end up homeless? She wanted to know more about Colby. It was time to stop pretending she wasn't interested.

"I think it's clean." Colby nodded toward Adena's repetitive wiping of her injury.

"Sorry. I don't think you need stitches for this one." She applied a couple of Steri-strips to be safe and covered them with a wider bandage. When she finished, she looked up, her focus on those perfect mouth-sized breasts.

"You're giving me that look again," Colby said.

"What look?"

"The hungry one."

She finally met Colby's eyes and immediately wished she hadn't. Fire burned hot and deep in this woman, and it showed on her moist lips, in her hooded stare, and in the way her chest rose and fell with each excited breath. "I'm sorry." She didn't know where the words came from, but she'd never been less sorry to be so close and so drawn to another woman.

"Don't be sorry. Just answer one question?"

"W—what?" Adena's nerves felt raw as she recalled her father's lectures about professionalism and Lois's admonishments about inappropriate behavior. She tried to ignore them. "What's the question?"

"You feel this, don't you? This attraction? Because if you don't, I'm really losing touch with reality."

The question was so unexpected she simply nodded. If she didn't say the word, maybe her admission would be easier to deny.

"But we can't act on it...right?" Colby hesitated as if hoping for another option.

Now she had to say the words. She couldn't mislead Colby or herself into thinking they actually had a chance. "No. We can't." She wanted Colby to object almost as much as she wanted to touch her.

"I wouldn't want to put you in a bad position professionally." Colby glanced down at her body. "But you have to admit, this is getting to be a habit. Better be more careful."

"Yeah. Let me get you another shirt." She reached for Colby's backpack.

"I was talking about getting hurt. The naked part's fine with me." Colby's green eyes turned dark and heat radiated from her. "I'm not shy."

Adena rifled through the pack and pulled out a red thong. Her face burned when Colby chuckled. "I can see that." She dug in again, retrieved a white T-shirt, and handed it to Colby.

"Might need a little help. Unless..." Colby glanced between her breasts and Adena.

Could Colby see what she was trying to hide? Attraction didn't begin to cover her feelings. The woman made her ache for things she shouldn't have. When Colby grinned and licked her lips, Adena's mouth went dry.

"I don't understand you, at all. You're evasive about most things but blatantly direct with your sexuality. I'm not sure what to say."

Colby ran her hand up Adena's arm and stroked the side of her face. "Yes would be a really good start."

For a second she rested her cheek against Colby's hand, absorbing the warmth of human contact she missed so much. Her pulse quickened, her nipples pressed painfully against the fabric of her bra, and her crotch grew damp. "I..." *You want this. No one will know.* "I'll know."

"Sorry?" Colby had inched forward on the chair, her legs on either side of Adena.

"I can't do this." She picked up the first-aid supplies and rushed to her bedroom. Closing the door behind her, she slumped against it and pulled for breath. "What's wrong with me?" She made a mental list of all the reasons she couldn't and wouldn't get involved with Colby. She reviewed them again and gave her body time to cool. She could be professional. She had to be.

When she returned to the living room, Colby had managed to put on her very small T-shirt. A Hooters logo stretched across her chest and stopped inches above the waistband of her low-slung jeans. Every facet of this woman enticed and tormented her, even the seemingly neutral things—how comfortable she seemed with her body, how easily she juggled tennis balls to entertain children in the park, her unconscious habit of swiping her hand across her shaved head. Adena looked away but stood in the center of the room, nowhere to go. The kitchen was a construction zone and there were no other chairs. She felt like the guest and Colby the comfortable homeowner.

"Guess I'll leave," Colby said. "Thanks for the first-aid and bandages. Sorry if I upset you. I shouldn't have been so forward."

"Thanks for the rescue."

Colby started toward the door.

"Why don't you stay?" At Colby's questioning expression, she added, "That guy could still be out there, and you don't need another fight right now. At least you'll have a roof over your head. I don't have a bed to offer, but you'll be dry and warm. Just for the night." She was rambling because her nerves were igniting like sparklers at a holiday parade.

"You sure? I don't want you to be uncomfortable."

"I'm fine. Really. You can roll out your sleeping bag here in the living room, but you'll have to leave early in the morning."

"That works for me. I have an appointment anyway. Thanks."

"The guest bathroom is down the hall on the right. Nothing fancy, but it's functional. Feel free to shower." She meant to walk away but couldn't take her eyes off Colby or forget the things she'd said.

"You feel this, don't you? This attraction? Because if you don't, I'm really losing touch with reality."

What would it be like to touch and be touched by Colby? She tried to say a cordial good night but ran from the room instead.

CHAPTER TEN

Colby woke to the smell of sawdust and wondered if she'd fallen asleep in her father's workshop, but the aroma of coffee was out of place. She rolled over, and a stream of sunlight slashed across her naked chest, warm and arousing like touching Adena's face last night—Adena's house.

This was the last place she should be until this case was over, especially since Adena admitted she felt the attraction between them. She hadn't imagined their connection, but Adena made it clear they couldn't pursue it. Thank goodness one of them was thinking clearly. Her desire to move this investigation along grew more urgent.

Turning slightly, she saw Adena, fully dressed in another tailored business suit, carrying two cups of coffee toward her. Her shoulders were back, her head high, and she walked with purpose until their eyes met. Then she stutter-stepped, and coffee sloshed over the sides of the cups. Her skin tingled when she saw the way she affected this poised and confident woman.

Colby impulsively sat up, and her sleeping bag fell to her waist.

"Will you *please* stop doing that? Don't you own a bra?" Adena looked away while Colby reached for her skimpy T-shirt and tugged it over her head.

"Don't really see the need. Sorry. I like to sleep in the nude."

"I hope you don't do that on the street. It's not safe." She handed her one of the cups and sat in the recliner across from her. "Cream and two sugars, right?"

"You remembered." She should probably feel guilty for embarrassing Adena, but she couldn't muster the false sentiment. "Thought I'd be okay sleeping *au naturel* here. Felt good to be almost normal again. Who knew you'd be skulking around to catch another glimpse." She tried to sound teasing, but Adena looked genuinely shocked. "Kidding."

"I put a few things together for you." Adena indicated a small pile of clothes beside her backpack. "That T-shirt won't be very warm. Pick the things you want and leave the rest."

The thought of Adena's clothing next to her skin made her warm and wet. "Thank you." Adena's face was flushed like it had been last night when they'd touched. Colby needed to concentrate on something else. "If you decide to finish your renovations, I could help. My father taught me how to work with my hands." The image of touching Adena replayed again. "I mean, woodworking."

"Really?" Her tone held a hint of surprise.

"Just because I'm homeless doesn't mean I'm unskilled."

"I'm sorry. You just don't seem the type to be into woodworking."

"What type do I seem to be, Counselor?" She enjoyed teasing Adena too much, watching her squirm uncomfortably.

"I'm not sure. You're not exactly forthcoming." Adena sipped her coffee and looked around the room, out the front window, everywhere but at her.

"Can I ask you a question?"

"I'm not sure. The one last night was a zinger."

"This one isn't about that."

Adena nodded.

"You mentioned the guy who attacked you last night might've been involved in something else. What?"

Adena's fingers tightened around her coffee cup just enough for Colby to notice. "I'm...It's..."

Tiny lines around her mouth deepened into a painful grimace. She was struggling with confiding in her, and who could blame her? They'd just met, knew nothing about each other, and were on opposite ends of a very long social continuum.

"I apologize if that's too personal. I've obviously upset you."

Adena tried to smile but her eyes were haunted. She placed her cup on the floor beside her and worried the hem of her shirt until she'd twisted a corner around her finger. "You'll hear it soon enough if you hang around the DRC. My father was...killed by a man with a knife a year ago. The police haven't found him yet."

Colby inched toward her and took her hands. "How horrible. I'm so sorry." She let the silence linger until Adena appeared ready to continue. "What does that have to do with last night? Was it the same man? Is he after you now?" If Adena said yes, Colby would break legend and tell her the truth. Some things *were* worth fighting for, and Adena was already one of those things for Colby.

"I've been showing a picture around some of the tent camps and asking questions, trying to put names with faces. He warned me off. It might have nothing to do with my father."

"Seriously?" Colby bit back a response about taking this man to jail and getting the truth out of him. Her allegiances blurred. "You could've been killed as well."

"If it hadn't been for you." Adena closed her eyes, and when she opened them, they were soft and teary. "It's been difficult not knowing the truth. I can't move forward until I do. Can you understand that?"

She squeezed Adena's hands until she looked at her again. "Sort of. My father was in the army and came back with dreadful PTSD. He used to say he wished he'd died, because his life stalled in a spiral of flashbacks and horrific memories. My mom and I were useless, unsure how to help, afraid we'd set him off, and more afraid he'd give up. It's not the same as someone dying, but it was very much a place of fear and uncertainty. I get that."

They sat in silence for several minutes, Adena staring at their joined hands and Colby desperately trying to find something more encouraging to say. She was torn between wanting to help Adena and wanting to keep her safe.

Her feelings for Adena weren't clear, but one thing was certain: she didn't want her hurt while tracking her father's killer. Colby kept her voice steady as she said, "What you're doing is dangerous. Please let the police handle it."

Adena recoiled, stood suddenly, and thrust her shoulders back. "You sound like everybody else. If the police *were* doing their job, I wouldn't have to. I don't know why I expected you to understand. You're just a…a…"

"A what, Adena? A homeless street urchin with a penchant for violence?" She regretted her outburst immediately, but having Adena think she was insensitive because of her homeless status hurt more than it should have.

"I would never say anything like that." She picked up her briefcase, grabbed her coat, and headed for the door. "Lock up on your way out."

"Adena, I'm sorry. I'm just concerned. I probably shouldn't be, but I care what happens to you, and you're dealing with a dangerous situation."

Adena rested her head against the doorframe for several seconds. When she spoke again her voice was barely audible. "I appreciate your concern, and I apologize for overreacting, but my father's murder is with me every day and will be until it's solved." She took a deep breath and finally turned to face Colby. "Feel free to stay as long as you'd like. I should probably give you my number in case you get into more trouble." She reached into her bag, scribbled on the back of a business card, and handed it to her. "My mobile number is there as well."

"Thanks." Colby took the card and read the inscribed name, *Weber and Worthington, Attorneys at Law.* Her hand trembled, and the card nearly fell from her fingers. She rubbed her thumb over the raised lettering, hoping she'd read wrong. She swallowed hard so she could speak. "Wait. Your last name is…?"

"Weber. Is that a problem?"

She didn't want it to be, but what if Adena was the Weber involved in her drug case? Was that the reason she didn't worry about her pro-bono expenses? Is that why she worked so closely with the homeless community, to exploit them for her illegal operation? She scanned Adena's wavy black hair, golden-brown eyes, perfectly shaped mouth, and remembered the brief connections they'd shared. Looks could be deceiving, and attraction often created a huge blind spot. Adena couldn't be a criminal. Could she? There had to be other Webers in Greensboro.

"Colby? Are you all right? You obviously didn't have the DRC orientation. My family's name is all over the literature and the website. My father, Franklin Weber, and his law partner, Oliver Worthington, started the Daytime Resource Center."

Colby flipped the card over and over in her hand, unable to formulate a response. In her legend as a homeless woman, Adena's surname made no difference, but as a DEA agent it could be a lead in her case. Worthington and Weber identified. Winston was still an unsub. "I...no, I didn't go to orientation, but I should have. I'm sorry, Adena."

"Sorry for what?"

"Everything." She was sorry for not being better informed about the players before going undercover, sorry for not asking more questions in the homeless community, sorry for worrying and disappointing Adena, sorry she was so attracted to her, but mostly she was sorry she might have to arrest Adena Weber or a member of her family. The prospect nauseated her.

"You're a strange woman, Colby Vincent. I have to run. And again, I'm sorry."

Colby stared at the thick antique door after it closed, hoping Adena would return so she could ask her outright if she was involved in the drug case, knowing that she wouldn't. Her coffee grew cold but still no Adena. Her attraction to Adena now felt like an unwelcome burden. She'd have to stay away from her until she knew the truth.

As she walked through the kitchen, regret replaced yearning. The sink was missing, cabinets ripped from the walls, and holes waited for appliances. Was the disarray fallout from the death of Adena's father? Had they been so close that his passing had severed her connection to the house? Had she misjudged Adena's professional confidence, unable to see reasons for her pain? Now she might never be able to uncover those secrets.

She tried to put herself in Adena's place. Maybe she'd felt safe asking about her father's case in the homeless camps at night because she knew most of the occupants from the DRC, not from any drug connection. Maybe she thought she'd get more cooperation than the police would. What would she do if *her* father had been murdered and the suspect wasn't caught? The thought sent shivers through her. She'd be doing the same thing Adena was. How did that compassionate and loyal side of Adena mesh with the possibility that she might be a drug dealer?

For the first time in her career, Colby had to make a judgment call about a suspect based only on her own knowledge and intuition, not on filtered information passed through another agent. Her head told her one thing, but her gut was leading her in another direction. Could she rely on a decision tainted by emotion?

Colby brushed aside her doubts and wrote a note of apology she hoped would convey how truly sorry she was for upsetting Adena and left it on the recliner. After a quick shower, she packed her belongings, chose a couple of thick sweatshirts from the clothes Adena had left, and unplugged her cell phone from the wall. As she started to leave, the phone vibrated and she stepped back inside to talk.

"It's Frankie. How's it hanging, sport?" Her soft, concerned voice was out of character from the first time they spoke. Colby was reminded again how much she missed regular contact with her family and friends. They were the touchstones that kept her grounded and focused on what mattered in life.

"Harder than I thought it'd be. If you ever repeat that, I'll deny it."

"Well, it is your first time in legend."

"I'd hoped it wasn't so obvious." Colby wanted to think she was handling herself well, but a memory of her flirty behavior with Adena made her feel guilty.

"All first-timers have the same issues with acclimation, fearing discovery, not knowing who to trust, not having any interaction with family or friends, and getting involved with the wrong person just for intimate contact. Do I need to go on?"

"Please don't. I'm meeting some of the guys this morning, not sure what's happening, but Cowboy mentioned a job. This could be my entry into the operation, if this group is involved. The invitation came with a couple of pretty painful tests."

"Yeah. I got your message about being arrested. I'll take care of that. You all right?"

"Just part of the process. Anything else I need to know? I don't want my inexperience to jeopardize the case."

"As you get info, call and leave your notes on my phone. I'll let it go to voice mail, pick up the messages later, and file your reports. We can't risk you making physical notes or leaving them on your phone. Text me a 9-1-1 if you need to talk."

"Guess I better get some more minutes on this phone."

"You need me to float you a loan?"

"I'll let you know. Maybe I won't need it soon."

"Making any friends?" Frankie sounded pure cop, teasing in the twisted way that implied friends weren't likely in her situation.

"If you call a crazy woman a friend, I guess so." She should've told Frankie about Adena, but she probably already knew she was a Weber. Why hadn't she or Ted Curtis mentioned *that* fact? Maybe Adena was already a suspect and Curtis had withheld that information, part of his "fresh eyes" approach, because Adena's family was influential in the community. In order to indict her, he'd need solid evidence. Whatever the reasons, Colby had to know more before she jumped to any conclusions.

"Don't knock it. Sometimes crazy is perfect on the street. Folks don't fuck with loonies. Anyway, stay safe and keep in touch."

Colby put the phone back in her boot and headed toward Elm Street with only thirty minutes to make it to the pickup location. Her hamburger from last night was long gone, but she didn't have time to get anything. When she arrived at the corner of Eugene and Lee, some of the guys were climbing into a gray van in the gas station lot across the street. Wolf motioned for her to hurry.

"We were about to leave your slow-poke ass." He swatted her on the shoulder as she climbed into the packed vehicle.

She nodded to the homeless guys and looked at three new men, trying to memorize their faces for later identification. "Where's Cowboy?" She felt a bit uncomfortable as the only woman in a van with ten guys, including the driver. The odds of her fighting them all off weren't good. She jostled for a seat near the door just in case.

"He don't do runs." She glanced in the rearview mirror and caught the snaggletooth grin of their white chauffeur. He pulled on a cigarette until his mouth puckered like an asshole, then blew the smoke out the window. Most of it wafted back inside. Between him and three other guys who were pulling on the death sticks, the enclosed space smelled like an ashtray. "Don't I know you?" He still stared at her in the mirror.

"I don't think so. I'm new in town."

"Know I've seen you somewhere. It'll come to me."

"That's Dodge," Wolf pointed toward the men she hadn't seen before, "Stretch, and Runt. They help us out sometimes when we need runners."

Stretch grinned, sucked his teeth, and eyeballed her like a meal. "You bring entertainment, Wolf? Ain't heard nothing about no bitch joining us."

"Well, that's 'cause you don't know everything."

Colby grunted a noncommittal greeting while the two men stared each other down. Didn't any of these people have real names? "Helps us with what? Is somebody going to tell me what we're doing?"

"You bring your scripts?" Coyote asked.

She nodded.

"What they for?"

"Roxycodone 30mg."

"You're in pain, right?" Wolf sounded like he was coaching her.

"Yeah."

"That's all you got to say. We're going to a clinic to fill scripts, but only get one today and save the other for later. We give the meds to Sheriff," he said, nodding to the driver. "And he gives us cash for the run. Got it?"

"Yeah." She barely contained the urge to pump her fists. Game on. "And what happens to the meds?"

"Need-to-know, girlie," Sheriff said. "Need-to-know."

So far one cog in the wheel was better than nothing. She glanced at the three new guys again, assessing their slumped shoulders, unkempt hair, and overall unhealthy appearance. "You fellows military too?"

Stretch blew a puff of cigarette smoke toward her. "Fuck that shit, bitch."

He occasionally eyeballed the homeless guys, but nobody talked during the ride, leading Colby to believe their alliance hadn't always been an amicable one. Bad blood and past grievances were often effective weapons to use against co-conspirators.

When the van stopped, everybody except Sheriff filed into a small clinic in the corner of a shopping center on the outskirts of town. She checked for a street name and other identifying characteristics of the area. The pill bottle would have the name of the place, but she wanted to be thorough.

As each guy walked up to the pharmacy counter, she watched and listened as he went through the process. Present the script and photo ID, complain about pain, and get the medicine. This was the easy part. She needed to know what happened next. Did Sheriff sell the drugs on the street himself, or did he sell in bulk to another dealer? Individual sales were risky, an unreliable source of income, and were disruptive to a dealer's life. Junkies called at all hours. If Sheriff sold to another dealer, the cut would be more and the risk considerably less.

"Next." The young lady called from the prescription counter.

Wolf nudged her in the back, and Colby stepped forward.

Her palms were sweaty. She wasn't used to being on the opposite side of the law. She took a deep breath and let it out slowly to control her nerves. "Here you go, ma'am."

"This ID doesn't look like you."

"That was taken before I had my head shaved. Lice."

The woman stepped back quickly, filled the prescription, and shoved it across the counter.

"Have a nice day, ma'am." Job done.

As they walked back toward the van, Wolf nudged her in the side. "That was a fucking stroke of brilliance. Lice. Good one, Eagle."

"Got the pills with no questions, didn't I?" She puffed up, feeling her esteem in the eyes of her contemporaries bolstered a little. "Now what?"

"You'll see."

On the drive back downtown, Wolf collected everybody's pills and separated them. One clear Ziploc had Roxycodone, or blues, as they were called on the street, and the other had oxycodone, distinguishable by its round shape and light-green color. Some of the guys kept a few pills, while others turned them all over. After he'd separated the pills, Wolf handed the bags to Sheriff in exchange for a wad of cash. Wolf doled out one hundred dollars to each person.

The mood in the van improved as the guys discussed how they'd spend their money. Bug seemed particularly excited about his evening prospects. He popped a couple of the pills he'd kept out and washed them down with a beer from the cooler Sheriff had stocked for them.

She almost laughed aloud as she stuffed her share of the cash into her jeans pocket. The homeless men probably didn't know the difference, but the pills Wolf had just handed Sheriff would bring close to nine thousand dollars on the street. Pretty good haul for one day. Her next challenge was to find out how the pills were distributed and who ran the operation. On the way to top up her mobile, she phoned Frankie and left a message about today's progress.

❖

Adena bypassed the DRC and went straight to her law office, hoping Chris would be late. She needed time to process her feelings about Colby's touch last night. And why had she seemed shocked when she learned her family name? She couldn't have known her father because she was from New York, unless she was lying about that. What else was she hiding?

And why had she become so defensive at Colby's questions? Her advice about letting the police handle the case must have irritated her because she expected Colby to understand a need so deep she'd face danger to fill it.

Her heavy messenger bag slipped off her shoulder and she fumbled with the long strap, grabbing it just before all her files dumped out on the ground. "Graceful, Weber, really graceful."

Maybe having Colby challenge her this morning had upset her because it felt personal, though not quite as personal as their conversation the night before when she'd *admitted* she was attracted to Colby.

She'd barely had the strength to pull away, craving Colby. Her insides had roiled with the new sensation and churned up a palpable dose of excitement and fear.

She was still reeling from her last memory when she spotted Chris's yellow VW bug parked in its usual space. When she opened the door, her office smelled of coffee.

"Well, good morning, boss lady. This is the first time you've been in before ten...ever. What's the matter? Did..." She stared at Adena. "Coffee?"

"Yes, please, Chris." She dropped into the swivel chair beside her assistant's desk and waited, staring blankly out the front door.

"You should anyway," Chris said.

She accepted the steaming cup of coffee and inhaled the strong aroma. "Should what?"

"Talk about it. I just left out the preliminaries because you always say no. What happened?"

Did she really need a fourth voice in her head telling her how wrong any kind of relationship with Colby would be? "It's complicated."

"Then you have to tell me because your life's never complicated. Now spill. You know I won't repeat one single word."

In the five years they'd worked together, she'd never had cause to question Chris's integrity or discretion. She and Lois were her only confidantes. Should she tell her about the attack last night or get straight to the crux of the matter? Colby was the issue.

"Stop filtering and tell me what's really bothering you."

Sometimes working with a person day in and day out had definite drawbacks. Chris was just too good at cutting through her bullshit. "I met a woman—"

"Now that's what I'm talking about!" Chris jumped from her desk and did a happy dance around her chair. "It's about damn time. Is she good in bed?" *Straight to the nitty-gritty.* "What does she look like? Who is she? What does she do? Where does she live? How did you meet her? Details. Now."

Answering the questions in her head as Chris asked them, Adena was having serious second thoughts about this conversation. "I...we...oh, God. I met her at the DRC."

Chris stamped her feet on the floor, the dance over, and perched one hand on her hip. "Really? Is *this* what you've come to? I know you're not into bars anymore, but seriously, the DRC? Isn't there a better place for lesbians to meet? I'll sign you up on a dating website, compose a sexy profile, and you'll be beating them off with your favorite dildo in no time."

"Why did I bother? I should've known better. You're just like Lois."

"You've told the judge? I'm surprised she hasn't had you committed." Chris finally sat down and rolled her chair closer. "Okay, I'm over the shock. Tell me what's going on."

"You won't like my answers. We haven't had sex and probably won't. She's tall, slim, with the most dazzling green eyes, a shaved head, and way too much courage for her own good. Her name is Colby, and she's currently unemployed and homeless. There's just something about this woman that gets under my skin. I know I shouldn't be attracted to her, but I can't help it." She waited for Chris's inevitable disapproval, aware of how pathetic and desperate she sounded.

"What do you like about her?"

Not the response she expected. "Well, the few times we've had serious conversations, she sounded genuinely fond of her parents and appreciative of her upbringing. You don't hear that often. She's compassionate and caring because she always asks about other people. She's a veteran and has a strong sense of responsibility. Did I mention that she just makes me...hot."

"Oh my, Counselor. I don't think I've ever heard you say that before."

"Because I've never felt it before, but it can't go anywhere. I have a rule against socializing with guests from the DRC or clients here."

Chris placed her hand over Adena's. "Honey, the heart wants what it wants. I'll never judge you for that. Now don't worry. We'll figure it out."

For just a second, Adena believed that maybe it was possible to care about Colby, to get to know her better, and maybe even— no, it wasn't. "Thanks for listening, but hearing it aloud, I realize how crazy it all sounds. Please don't share this with anyone. In the meantime, I have work to do." She refilled her coffee and started toward her office. "Is Ollie coming in this morning?"

"Should be here shortly."

"Would you tell him I'd like to see him?"

"Sure, but you're going to want to take care of this first." Chris handed her a note with exclamation points all over it—Chris's indication the message took priority. When Adena hesitated, she said, "The mayor wants a meeting."

"Shit. You should've given this to me first."

"I know, but your news was way more interesting." Chris blew her an air kiss.

Adena closed the door to her office and dialed the number to the municipal building. Her nerves jangled like she'd had an overdose of caffeine. She got a sick feeling in her stomach because she had nothing new to tell the mayor. "This is Adena Weber. I'd like—"

"Oh yes. The mayor has been waiting to speak with *you*."

She didn't have time for nearly enough deep breaths before the mayor came on the line.

"Adena, I'm afraid we've run out of time on this DRC situation. Some council members and a few donors want to meet with you right away. When can we make that happen?"

"I'm not sure, Freda. I have court cases."

"Everybody's time is valuable, but we at least need a progress report. The city budget is coming up for approval soon, and we have to decide on our position. You understand."

Adena understood the tiny pittance the city allocated to the DRC annually wouldn't make or break their operation, but the publicity associated with its withdrawal could have a devastating effect on other donors. "Of course, Mayor. What suits your calendar?"

"Tomorrow afternoon at four?"

She scrolled through her schedule on her cell. "Fine. I'll see you then." She hung up, wishing she had a murder trial or anything to stall the vipers seeking answers she didn't have.

While she waited for Ollie, Adena reviewed the accounts for the past two years' activity at the firm and the DRC. Her father had been adamant the DRC never be closed no matter what she had to do. Did that include giving up the practice and working for the non-profit fulltime?

A light tap sounded at her door before Ollie stuck his head around the corner. "You wanted to see me?"

"How are you today?"

"Good, but you look worried." He walked around the desk and hugged her before taking a seat next to her. "Is this about my offer to take over the DRC?"

"I love that you don't mince words, Ollie. You're so much like Dad it hurts sometimes. And yes, I want to talk about your offer. I think you're right. We need an infusion of cash in a hurry, and you're the only man for the job."

"I'll turn it around. The cold weather has hit us hard. Flo's doing her best, but money only stretches so far. I'll reach out to some of our donors and see if we can fill the gap."

"Wait until after my meeting with the mayor tomorrow. It might end badly, and I don't want your efforts to be wasted."

"Do you want me to handle the meeting?"

"No, I need to do it, for myself and for Dad. You understand."

"Of course. In the meantime, do you want to take on some more cases to keep you busy?"

"If you need help while you work on this, I will, but I'm not anxious for a full caseload again." Once she'd said the words, she felt lighter, as if she'd been carrying a burden and was now free of it. She couldn't possibly be considering leaving her father's law practice. She felt guilty enough about handing over the DRC operations even temporarily.

"No, no. I'm good with my intern and the Elon law student I'm mentoring. He's been a godsend. Are you sure you're all right, Adena?"

"Of course."

He rolled his chair closer. "Your father worked all his life so you'd be taken care of and be happy. He wasn't a warm-and-fuzzy father, but he did his best. The law practice and the DRC were his dreams. If they're not yours, find your own path. There's no shame in that. I'll see they both endure. You have my word."

CHAPTER ELEVEN

Colby was careful not to arrive at the DRC the next morning until Adena had gone. She showed up feeling conflicted about the case and Adena's possible connection to it. Without evidence to exonerate Adena, she couldn't even consider a personal or sexual relationship. God, how she wanted to touch her again, slowly, until Adena moaned and completely surrendered. *Damn it to hell! Get your head back in the game, Vincent.*

When she walked into the dayroom, Cowboy and his gang were huddled in a corner whispering. Not a good sign.

"Eagle," Cowboy called, and motioned for her to join them.

"What's up, guys? It's too early for serious talk. I haven't had my second cup of coffee."

"Bug got arrested," Wolf said.

"For what?"

"Probably running his mouth and showing off his wad of cash," Coyote added. "He gets stoned and can't keep quiet."

"What was he charged with?"

Cowboy moved closer. "Possession of controlled substance with intent to sell."

She'd promised Adena she wouldn't bring drugs or violence to the DRC, and while this group had already done that, she would at least try to insulate the center and Adena as much as possible. "That sucks, but can't we talk about this later? I'd really like a shower."

"No, it can't wait," Cowboy said. "We need your help. Now." His eyes were hard and the set of his jaw tight.

"Okay, sure. What can I do?"

He motioned for her to sit but spoke to the others. "You guys go shower or whatever while Eagle and I talk. We'll get this figured out." When the other men walked away, Cowboy turned back to her. "You're a computer person, right?"

She nodded.

"Bug was our go-to guy for that stuff, but now we're fucked. We've got another drugstore run this afternoon, and we need new IDs."

Maybe it was too early, maybe her single cup of coffee hadn't done its trick, but it took a few seconds for Colby to understand what he was asking. "You need me to make fake IDs?"

"Quiet down." He looked around for anyone within hearing distance. "Can you do it?"

"That takes supplies I don't have. A scanner, computer with photo and editing programs, heavy stock paper, or a laminator. And if we're adding holograms, it gets even more complicated."

"I've got everything you need." He patted a duffle bag at his feet. "At least the little fucker didn't have that with him when he got popped."

She was afraid she already knew the answer to her next question but had to hear him say it. "And where do we do this?"

"Right here, of course. The computers are good, and the guys watch out for you in case anybody tries to get too close, namely Flo or Adena. We don't want them involved."

"That's nice." She tried not to sound sarcastic, but Cowboy's stare told her she'd failed.

"We're just trying to stay alive out here. Nobody else has to get hurt."

Colby flinched and a deep chill settled in her chest. "Nobody *else*? What the fuck, Cowboy? I'm not playing that game. I saw enough death and dying in Iraq to last a lifetime. A drug scam is one thing, but killing is something else. Count me out." She used her military experience as a cover for the shock of realizing Cowboy and his crew might be mixed up in more than drugs—maybe even murder.

"Keep your damn voice down. I meant in general people don't get hurt from our business, except maybe an occasional drug addict, and that's on them. Miss Adena's dad was killed, but none of us did that. We're running a simple supply-and-demand operation." While he spoke he never made eye contact, and she didn't trust one word he said.

Her display of moral indignation had given her time to regain her composure and had put him on the defensive, making him less prone to see the cracks in her story. "If you swear nothing's going on but selling some prescription drugs, I'll do the IDs."

"I swear it." He placed his hand over his heart, but she knew in her gut he was lying.

"Can I ask you something?"

He nodded.

"Is life on the streets so bad that vets have to get mixed up in something like drug dealing? I know desperate times and all that, but we're supposed to be honorable, fight for what's right, and follow the rules—at least that's the dream."

"Homelessness changes a man. You look at right and wrong different. We risked our lives and what do we get? VA clinics with six-month waiting lists and, oh, by the way, you need a car to get there because they're an hour or more away."

She'd seen it many times on the streets of New York as well.

"It's hard for proud soldiers to beg for food and shelter. We lose dignity and self-respect because we don't have a home and can't provide for ourselves. We're not doing this because we want to. We're doing it because we don't have a choice."

She studied Cowboy's face, the tight lines around his mouth and the hardened look in his eyes, realizing she was seeing only part of the man he used to be. She'd learned firsthand that having a home was closely tied to self-respect and social status, and trust meant something entirely different when you weren't in control.

"So, are you going to help us?"

"I have a couple of conditions."

"Such as?"

"Nobody gets hurt, and I want a bigger cut." Any self-respecting criminal would seize an opportunity for more cash. He'd expect it.

"What makes you think I have that kind of control?"

"I've seen the way the guys defer to you. If you don't sanction it, they don't do it. Am I right?" She was fishing, but the time had come to take a few chances.

Cowboy pushed back his wide-brimmed hat and sized her up for a few seconds. "I always knew you were sharper than these guys, but you got one thing wrong. I'm not in charge of the operation, just the street side of things. I tell the guys when to make a run, where to go, when to change IDs, and who gets paid what. If a guy balks or gives me crap, his cut gets smaller. If he threatens to go to the cops, he loses his income and maybe gets thumped. Anything else is decided way above my head."

And she'd thought Sheriff doled out the cash. If she had a cell phone with a record feature right now, Cowboy would be so screwed. Instead she tried to remember his exact words for her report later. "But you have the authority to up my cut for computer expertise, right?"

"Consider it done." They shook on the deal. She had a job to do, but making the veterans who were bound to Cowboy suffer bothered her more than a little. And using the DRC equipment for illegal purposes was directly violating her promise to Adena. "Just out of curiosity, how much *do* I get out of this extra work?"

"Twenty-five dollars for each new ID."

"Fifty and not a penny less. I do excellent work. And I still get a cut when I make runs with the guys." Fake IDs were worth five times more if they sold them on the street, so she knew Cowboy wouldn't balk.

He nodded. "You drive a hard bargain, Eagle, but I think we'll have a long and prosperous relationship."

"What names do I use on the new cards?"

"Make shit up. That part isn't important. Just keep the date of birth as close to the last one as possible, same height, weight, and modify the addresses slightly. Nothing too complicated and don't worry about holograms. Our IDs don't have to be fancy. Nobody expects it. Now get to work. We need to be ready to roll by two this afternoon."

Fake IDs did matter because doctors and pharmacists paid very close attention to them, especially when filling prescriptions of highly addictive medications. However, Cowboy might not be concerned if the ring already had a doctor and pharmacist working for them. In the real world, homeless folks who showed up with oxy prescriptions on a regular basis would raise a red flag. Colby vowed to pay closer attention at the pharmacies to see if any particular persons waited on their group.

Cowboy gave the other guys orders to scatter throughout the dayroom, alert her if anyone got too close, and run interference if necessary. The men would rotate being with her at the computer under the guise of preparing work resumes. She looked into the duffle bag and pulled out an envelope containing nine identification cards, all the guys who'd been with her on her first drugstore run. When the new cards were finished, she planned to keep these as evidence and find a way to get them to Frankie, but she needed one more thing.

"Cowboy, could you send one of the guys to that Office Depot on Church Street? I need more supplies."

"Like what?"

"Teslin paper, butterfly laminate pouches, and a thirty-two gig memory card."

"What for?"

"Because like I said, I do excellent work. If I save the cards on a flash drive, it'll be quicker to change them next time. Besides, I can't very well save them on this computer, can I? Someone might find them."

"Makes sense. How much does something like that cost?"

"Give them a couple of hundred."

She started scanning the old IDs as soon as Cowboy walked away, preferring to do one part of the process at a time before moving to the next step. After scanning all the cards, she could edit on the computer without anyone noticing. Since she was using the same photos, she wouldn't have to physically insert a new one. As she edited each card, she asked the guy working with her to separate the card from the rest of the teslin paper.

She downloaded a North Carolina hologram and a barcode to make the cards look more authentic and applied them before slipping each into a laminating sleeve. Bug's work had been adequate, but hers would be excellent. Editing all nine cards took a couple of hours, and the final step was laminating them in plastic. This was the part that couldn't be disguised as resume preparation. She'd have to find a more private place to finish the process.

JR was taking his turn with her at the computer. "Do you know where Bug did the laminating? It takes awhile, and I'm afraid someone will notice out here in the open."

"I think he did it in the men's bathroom because of Flo and Adena. There's an outlet for hairdryers and razors. Not sure if you can do it in the women's room. Too open."

She collected the supplies she needed along with her own things and headed toward Adena's office. The first day she'd been at the center, she'd seen a small private bathroom tucked in the corner. She knocked and then checked the dayroom for Flo or Adena. When she didn't see them or get a response, she slipped inside and locked the office door behind her. After the hand-sized laminator heated up, she tucked each new card inside a plastic pouch and ran it through the machine. The process was over in less than fifteen minutes, but the slightly chemical smell of burning plastic lingered. She weighed her options: leave and risk someone discovering what she'd done or try to mask the odor and possibly get caught in a private space.

She turned on the adjoining shower, stripped, and relaxed against the fiberglass surround, enjoying the hot spray across her shoulders. Bug's arrest had been a stroke of luck, almost assuring her a step up from runner in the drug operation. Her skills were essential, at least until Bug got out on bail. She'd call Frankie and see if his stay could be extended. Lathering her hands with a squirt of body wash, she scrubbed her head, noting her hair was finally beginning to feel like hair instead of bristles. She rinsed, toweled dry, and dressed quickly, hoping for a quick snoop around the office before slipping out.

The desk was unlocked and she rifled through the drawers, but nothing struck her as unusual. If Adena were involved in drugs, she wouldn't be stupid enough to keep evidence here, but she probably wouldn't keep anything at her law office either. Colby had a hard time imagining Adena doing anything illegal, but she had to be thorough. She flipped through the papers on top of the desk and came up empty. As she returned the desk to its original condition, someone rattled the door handle and then knocked, loudly.

"You in there, Adena?"

Flo. So not good. Colby crammed the laminator back in her bag. The plastic odor still hung in the air so she sprayed Axe deodorant under her arms and spritzed a whiff into the air before opening the door.

"What the hell are you doing? Did anyone give you permission to be in here?"

"Not exactly."

Flo's eyes were pinpoints as she glared at her and then glanced around the room. "What do you mean not exactly? This is a private office."

"The other showers were full and I'm doing a job interview." She worded her response carefully so she wouldn't be totally lying. Her work for Cowboy had been an interview of sorts. "I'm really sorry, but I thought you'd understand just this once."

"Even if what you're saying is true, which I seriously doubt, you should've asked before invading someone's private space."

"You're right. I apologize. It won't happen again." She respected Flo and her position but refused to be intimidated. They locked stares until Flo stepped aside and let her leave.

"See that it doesn't. And get some new deodorant. It smells like a dozen teenage boys jacked off in here."

On her way out of the DRC, she handed the small envelope with the new IDs to Cowboy. "Any need to keep the old ones?"

He shook his head.

"Do you need me for the run today?"

"Yeah, same place as before at two o'clock."

"I'll take care of the old cards and see you later."

"Sounds good, and thanks for today. You got us out of a tight spot. The boss will be happy."

She headed toward the library but diverted through the small green space beside the Historical Museum and pulled out her phone. Expecting a message, she was surprised when Frankie answered. "It's me. I've been promoted. I made nine new IDs for the runners today, and I've got the old ones. How do I get them to you for evidence?"

"You're doing great, sport. I've set up a post-office box for us to exchange information. Tell the clerk your name and she'll give you a key. Leave the stuff there."

"Will do."

Colby shifted her backpack and walked casually to the street, suppressing an urge to pump her fists in victory like she'd done the first time she'd successfully juggled three items at once. Cowboy had mentioned a boss, and maybe she'd eventually get an introduction. As un-DEA as it seemed, maybe she could catch the bosses without further damaging the street people who were forced to help them.

❖

Adena walked into her family home praying for a dose of strength before facing the mayor and DRC donors. The living room still smelled musky from years of her father's Cuban cigars. She inhaled deeply, and the faint scent of clove mixed with cherry summoned another surge of emotion. She turned in a circle on the hardwood floor, staring at the popcorn ceilings, waiting for her father to pick her up and swing her around until she was dizzy. Those days were gone. She was an orphan, and it hurt more than she'd imagined it could. Her eyes filled with tears. This might not have been such a good idea.

A portrait of her parents commissioned early in their marriage hung over the huge fireplace, and a leather recliner stood empty nearby, legal journals stacked precariously beside it. A pair of her father's old-fashioned wire-rimmed glasses rested on top of the magazines. When she'd kidded him about upgrading, his standard response was always, "What am I, a fashion plate for optometry?" She picked up the readers and hefted the weight in her palm, the legs sprawling sideways at odd angles. A tear splashed onto one of the thick lenses.

When had she last visited him? Had they shared a meal, a glass of wine, or a meaningful conversation? When had they spoken of anything except work? Memories were details wrapped in painful feelings. Where were her happy memories? Were they simply buried deeper? Even now could she release the reins of control and responsibility enough to enjoy life? Was Oliver right? Could she walk away from the law practice and the DRC without betraying everything her father worked for? So many questions without answers.

She replaced the glasses by his chair and went into his study. Cigar-smoke residue tinged the glass covering his legal diplomas with a yellowish haze. He'd been an accomplished man, and she was proud to call him father, but she'd missed the gentility and nurturing of a mother. Had the lack of emotional guidance steered her in her father's responsibility-laden footsteps, away from the desire for love, home, and family?

Colby's stories of her parents' concern about her air-force career, her mother lovingly crafting biscuits, her father's struggles with PTSD, and their closeness as a family had touched Adena in places that ached for love and intimacy. She believed in the concept of family and the commitment and longevity required to maintain it, but she'd never found the person who spoke to her heart and asked her to try.

Had Colby experienced such a relationship? Did she know how it felt to commit totally to another person? Had that commitment shattered her family and home and left her destitute on the streets? Adena knew beyond any doubt that love could wound and obliterate as easily as it healed and restored. Was it too late for her to try love?

She wandered through the other rooms of their ranch-style home, recalling memories in each one, saying good-bye: her father's fumbled explanation of sex while they ate Rice Krispies in the kitchen; discussing high-school prom dresses over pizza in the dining room; their all-night cram session in his study before college finals; her coming-out speech in the living room; and her decision to join his law firm while seated on the foot of his bed. Their talks had shaped her life and guided her to a career. In hindsight they had also touched her intimately and connected them emotionally.

Settling in her father's chair behind the large oak desk, Adena looked at the papers strewn across the surface, just as he'd left them, organized chaos. Why hadn't she closed the DRC that night? If she had, maybe her father would still be alive. Her chest tightened as guilt mingled with grief. She struggled to draw a full breath and her vision clouded. Why was her father killed? Was he targeted, and if so, why? She clutched the arms of his chair and sobbed.

When she finally looked up, shredded bits of tissue littered the top of the desk. She had no idea how long she'd been crying, but she could barely breathe. She blew her nose, wiped her eyes, and let out a few short puffs of air as the sadness passed.

After a few moments, she started clearing the used tissues from the desktop. The pocket-sized calendar her father kept for appointments was open to the last day of his life. Something written in red ink in the margin caught her eye, the letters *DE* followed by an equal sign and the number five. Her pulse pounded as she flipped through the calendar and found similar notations dating back three months before his death. What did it mean? Was it a clue? She didn't know anyone with those initials, and the numbers were too small to be fees unless they were a code.

She turned back to the beginning of the odd notations, excitement building with each entry, but she couldn't afford to jump to conclusions. What if these notes meant nothing to anyone except her father? And what if they were the key to solving his murder? Her heart raced as she scanned the desktop one last time. A copy of the DRC financials for the past year rested atop a stack of client files, and she wondered why he'd brought it home. She slid the calendar and printout into her coat pocket as she rose to leave.

"Thank you, Dad. Whatever this means, I'll figure it out." *This feels like a turning point. Finally something I can do.*

As she walked back through the house, she wondered what she'd do with the place. She had the house in Fisher Park and this one, but neither really felt like home, not the kind she wanted. She'd come here to rejuvenate before facing a situation that could jeopardize her father's legacy. Being around his belongings had done that and given her a possible clue to his murder.

❖

When Adena reached the municipal building, her father's friend, Matthew, owner of a local transportation company, waited outside the mayor's conference room. He struck an imposing figure, with his graying hair, Italian suit and shoes, and always with a Cuban cigar close at hand. Winston and her father had spent hours in her father's study concocting how to acquire the illegal and expensive indulgences and more hours stinking up the place with their ghastly scent.

"Adena, are you all right? Your eyes are puffy."

Shit. He could tell she'd been crying. Should she admit it? His question sounded sincere, but if she told him the truth—that she'd been at her father's home blubbering for an hour—he wouldn't know what to say. She'd feel embarrassed and stupid, and then he'd assume she wasn't stable enough to handle her responsibilities.

Why did she always deflect or gloss over anything emotional? She was still hurting over her father's death, vulnerable about this challenge to his legacy, conflicted about her career, and totally out of her element with Colby. "I'm fine, Matthew. Thanks for asking." Really, what else could she say?

"I'm so sorry about this. I tried to talk the mayor out of it."

"They have a right to be concerned about how their money is spent, and so do you." She wasn't sure where Matthew's allegiance to the center came from unless he and her father shared a past she didn't know about. He'd always supported the DRC financially and in the press, and that was good enough for her.

He placed his hand on her shoulder. "I don't want you to worry. If it comes down to it, I'll bankroll the entire center myself."

"What?"

She must've looked as surprised as she felt because Matthew squeezed her shoulder and added, "Surely you know how strongly I feel about the work you do there and how fond I was of your father."

"You're very generous. Thank you. I hope it won't come to that." On the way in, she updated him on some of the men he'd given jobs in the DRC's work program. The mayor's small conference table was populated by a who's who of Greensboro movers and shakers. She and Matthew took seats to the right of Mayor Tremble.

"Mayor. Ladies and gentlemen." Adena nodded but resisted the urge to address them by their given names. She wanted to win this battle on her own merits, not on any longstanding allegiance to her father. Most of these people had been guests in her family's home, and all had sought her father's legal advice at some point during his life.

The mayor said, "I'm sure this is uncomfortable for all of us, but in light of the recent newspaper article, we needed to have this meeting for the sake of transparency."

She almost chuckled at Freda's political speak for covering their asses. "By all means."

"Adena, have you discovered anything that might ease our minds going forward? We'll have to make a public statement soon," the city attorney said.

"The issue of leadership raised in this article was about our former director and has been addressed, as Oliver Worthington stated in his interview. As for Mr. Tabor's claim of refused service, we're still trying to locate him and determine when the incident occurred and how or if we failed him. I believe the article was strategically released on the anniversary of my father's death and the issues raised were meant to create controversy."

"To what end?" the mayor asked.

"Possibly to bolster sales. Technology is swiftly making printed news obsolete, and it's no secret the *Daily Record* is struggling."

"And you can't find this Tabor man?" Matthew asked.

"Not yet. We have no verification of him being a guest of the DRC, no computer record, no entry in the sign-in books, and no one else has ever heard of him. That's very unusual in a community this small."

One of the other donors shook his head. "That could just be an indication of the center's poor recordkeeping."

Councilman Harbinger loudly cleared his throat, and Adena held her breath. "And another reason we need a review committee to look into the situation. I'm not comfortable pouring money into an organization that can't even keep proper records."

Anger coursed through Adena, but she tamped it down before responding. She didn't want to appear defensive. "That's a logical assumption, but my instincts tell me there's more to the story literally, and I need a little more time to get to the bottom of it. I assure you the DRC is in good management hands and we're being fiscally responsible with every dollar of funding we receive. If you're not ultimately satisfied with my answers, I'll accept your decision to withhold support."

"How much time?" the mayor asked.

"Two weeks should do it."

"That's cutting it awfully close to the budget-review deadline," Matthew said. "Are you sure you can resolve this issue by then?"

"Absolutely." She hated to lie, but so much depended on her being totally convincing.

Harbinger leaned forward in his chair. "I'd like to go on record as saying I'm not comfortable with this. I vote no to any delay in withdrawing funds."

"This isn't a council meeting, Mr. Harbinger, but your objection is noted," the mayor said. She stood, the meeting clearly over. "I'm inclined to give you the time, Ms. Weber, but I expect answers. Any other objections?" She looked around the table but no one else spoke. "Very well. Two weeks. Not a day more."

Chapter Twelve

Colby, Stretch, and Runt played quarters under the Center City Park pavilion to stay out of the cold rain while Sing Song petted Parker, the park's orange tabby cat. The object of the game was to throw your quarter closest to the wall without hitting it. Colby had won several of the tosses, and the guys were getting annoyed. Maybe it had something to do with the bottle they kept drinking from though she was completely sober. She'd considered a couple of shots as the night cold deepened but decided against it.

"Eagle took your quarters away," Sing Song warbled. "You can't play worth shit today."

"Shut the fuck up," Stretch yelled. "Don't need your damn stupid mouth."

"Leave her alone," Runt said. "She's retarded."

"Guys, you going to play again or just talk?" Colby was anxious to divert their attention from Sing Song before their agitation led to violence. She'd been on two more drug runs with these guys, and they'd gotten into fights on both of them. The more they drank, the more unpredictable their tempers became. She'd much rather spend time with the veterans, but they'd vanished early in the evening.

"Let's play," Stretch said, taking a pull from the liquor bottle secreted inside his coat. He threw his quarter and it slid very close to the wall. "That's what I'm talking about. Let's up the ante."

"Not in the middle of a game." Runt swung his arm at his side like he was preparing to roll a bowling ball and tossed his coin. It slapped against the wooden wall and bounced back well away from Stretch's. "Shit. That sucks."

Colby took aim and purposely pulled up short. "Damn. Stretch took that one."

"You met the big boss yet?" Runt asked Colby as he waited for Stretch to throw.

Stretch shoved him hard out into the rain. "Shut the fuck up."

Rain soaked through Runt's light hoodie and ran down his face. "Just asking. She's been helping us a lot lately. Thought she'd have met him by now."

"I said shut the fuck up and I mean it," Stretch said. "If he wants to meet her, that's his business, not yours. Learn to keep your trap shut. Now get your ass over here and throw."

Runt swept the wet hoodie off his head and tossed his quarter too hard, well out of play. Colby threw hers lightly over the brick pavers, and it nudged just in front of Stretch's.

"Fuck me. She won." He dug into his pocket for another coin. "Again. I got to get my money back."

They played three more games before hearing the announcement that the park would close in fifteen minutes. Her last throw was limp and fell far from the wall. Runt landed his first win of the night and held out his hand for payment. She handed over her quarter and took a seat beside Sing Song. "I'm out, guys. Just got enough money left for breakfast in the morning." She was lying, but they didn't need to know.

"Chicken shit." Stretch handed his quarter to the winner, pulled his hoodie over his head, and crossed the park toward Elm Street with Runt following him.

As they rounded the corner, she saw a figure near the edge of the park in a long raincoat with an umbrella. The person had been standing there through several games. When the men left, the stranger walked toward her and Sing Song. As he got closer, Colby stood and moved between him and her friend, remembering the attack on Adena on the bridge.

"If anything happens, go for help," she said.

"Nothing's going to happen." The figure tipped her umbrella back and pushed the rain hood off her head. "Good evening, Colby, Sing Song."

"Adena? What're you doing here? It's almost eleven o'clock." Colby had avoided her for four days when Adena cut through the park on her way to or from her office and the DRC. But the distance had done little to quell the feelings Adena had sparked. Her warm eyes cut through the chill the rain had caused and reminded Colby of their attraction, of their admissions, and of those precious few touches. Even standing in a downpour wrapped in an all-concealing trench coat, Adena was the sexiest woman she'd ever seen.

"Not happy to see me?"

"Of course I am, always." She took Adena's hands and pulled her out of the rain.

"Now that your friends have gone, could I talk with you for a moment?" She glanced at Sing Song, who rose and pointed toward the parking deck. Colby nodded. "You're very protective of her."

"We sort of look after each other, though she's not much of a conversationalist. What's up, Adena?"

"Do you know anything about those men?"

How could she answer Adena's question without evading, lying, or giving away her true purpose? "What do you mean?"

"I've seen them around and trouble usually follows. I'm afraid they might be into drugs or something else illegal. They always have money, don't seem to work, and don't have need of the DRC. I shouldn't judge. I'm just concerned you'll get into something dangerous...again." Adena blew into her gloves and rubbed her hands together.

"They're all right most of the time, until they drink, but that could be said about a lot of people." She wanted to steer Adena away from the topic of her drug-running associates. "What are you doing out so late?"

"I helped Flo close the DRC and had some bills to pay. It's a never-ending process."

"What you need is some fun. Get out your money, Counselor."

"What?" Adena stared at her like she'd lost her mind.

"Quarters. I'm going to rob you of all your quarters. If you don't have quarters, I'll take nickels and dimes. Now pony up." She liked the way Adena's face scrunched around her eyes as she tried to figure out if she was kidding. "I'm serious. You need to laugh."

Adena pushed aside her raincoat and dug into the side of her messenger bag. "So this is what passes for entertainment with the homeless?" As she counted out her coins, she stopped. "I'm sorry, Colby. That sounded condescending."

"Stop being so politically correct and prepare to lose your money." She explained the rules of the game and waved to Adena. "After you, my lady."

"Okay. I'd say we're about six feet from the wall, the wind won't really be a problem, but my hand is cold, so the shaky factor might—"

"Wait." Colby stepped in front of her and waved her arms. "Stop right there. You're taking all the fun out of the game. We don't plan, calculate, and apply the laws of physics to quarters. We just play. That's the whole idea behind a *game*."

Adena looked at the coin in her hand and then at Colby. "Sorry, foreign concept."

"Totally, but there's hope for you yet. Just toss it."

Without taking her eyes off Colby, Adena threw the quarter and it plopped like a dead weight right in front of the wall. "How's that? I'm afraid to look."

"You nailed it. Now step aside and watch how a pro does it." She placed her quarter lightly on the tips of her fingers and gave it a flip. The coin bounced off the wall and landed straight up in a crack between two bricks well behind Adena's. "No way."

"I won!" Adena raised her arms in the air and did a variation of a happy dance while pointing at the wall. "Oh my God, I won."

"So you *can* do this?"

"Quarters? No, seriously, this is my first time."

"No, I mean have fun, laugh."

Adena stopped dancing and stared at her for a few seconds as if considering what she'd said. "I hadn't thought so recently, but apparently I can. Thank you for reminding me. Now, what do I get?"

Colby considered the double entendre briefly before picking up the two coins and placing them lightly in Adena's hand. "Double your money. That was impressive." The most impressive part was seeing Adena laugh and have a good time. Colby could've watched for hours.

"Okay, ladies, park's closed. I have to ask you to leave." The young attendant seemed almost reluctant to break up the joviality.

Adena said, "I can't remember the last time I laughed at something so simple and enjoyable, but I can't take your money." She offered Colby the quarter.

"It's against the rules of play to give back winnings. I can afford twenty-five cents."

As they walked toward the exit, Adena said, "Does that mean you've found work?"

"Nothing steady." At least that wasn't a lie, if being a runner was considered real work.

"Would you be interested in helping with the renovations at my house?"

Colby leaned forward, unsure she'd heard correctly over the rain pounding around them again. "I beg your pardon." She hoped she had misunderstood because the prospect alternately thrilled and terrified her.

"Renovations. My house. You said you were a woodworker. Whether I decide to live there, in my parents' home, or sell both, the place has to be livable." She rubbed her hands together again but didn't meet Colby's gaze, as if asking for anything came hard for her. "I'd appreciate whatever you can do...and I'll pay you, of course."

How could she say no to an opportunity to spend more time with Adena? But how could she say yes to a woman who might be involved in her drug investigation? It would be so much easier if she could just ask her. Before she finished mentally arguing the pros and cons, she heard herself say, "I could do that, but not every day. I have this other thing that comes up sometimes."

"The not-so-steady job?"

"Yeah, and I'm already committed."

"And you honor your commitments?" Adena's tone held a hint of surprise.

"Absolutely. It's not always easy, but you're only as good as your word."

"Yet I remember you saying you'd probably disappoint me."

"That depends on your expectations and whether or not I made a commitment."

Adena stared at her for several seconds, and her look of surprise changed to a reserved smile. "That's excellent news. Just please tell me you haven't gotten into anything illegal with this part-time job." Her dark eyes searched Colby's face with so much concern she almost confessed, but she stopped just in time.

"I'll be fine." She hated evading Adena's question. It made her seem shady and untrustworthy, and Adena had admitted honesty was important to her. "I'll do a good job for you."

Adena opened her umbrella, and suddenly the covered space felt private and intimate. "Why don't you come by sometime and we'll discuss what I want."

"How about in the morning before work? I can be there anytime."

"Seven thirty?"

"I'll see you then...and thank you, Adena." She watched Adena walk north on Elm Street until she disappeared from sight. Her heart raced and her body grew warmer at the possibility of spending more time with Adena, but was she fooling herself? She already spent entirely too much time thinking about her. Would she be complicating the situation or would it be the perfect way to eliminate Adena as a suspect? How could she be around Adena and not jeopardize the investigation by falling totally in love with her?

The park attendant was putting the chains up across the entrances, so she dashed to the restroom and brushed her teeth. She and Sing Song had altered their accommodations frequently to keep from developing a pattern the police might notice, but she was growing tired of sleeping on the hard ground, often wet and cold. As she walked toward the parking garage, she pulled out her phone, tucked it under the hood of her sweatshirt, and called her parents.

"Hi, Dad. How's it going?"

"Colby, good to hear from you. Your mother will be upset she missed your call. She's at the beach with her college friends for a few days. Are you all right?"

What she'd give for a few days at the beach—warm, relaxed, snuggled close to Adena.

"Honey, you all right?"

"Sorry, Dad. I drifted off thinking about how much I'd love to be at the beach instead of soaked to the bone. This is just a slow job, but I've had lots of time to think."

"Is that a good thing?" Her father didn't pry, but always left the door open if she wanted to say more. She loved that about him.

"I'm thinking about getting a place of my own when I get back, maybe even trying a relationship for longer than a few months. I want someone who makes me as happy as you and mom make each other, someone to share things with, to...really love."

Her father was quiet for a few seconds. "Well...you know your mother and I never want you to move out, but that's unrealistic. The important thing is that you're happy, always." His voice cracked at the end, and she felt a bit guilty for bringing up the subject when she was so far away, but maybe it was best so they could think about it until she returned.

"Speaking of relationships, have you heard from Kali?"

"She came by and talked with your mother after you'd spoken to her. Your mom helped her see the futility of trying to make you do something you didn't want to." He laughed, and Colby wanted to hug him and relax in the strength of his unconditional support.

"Thanks, Dad. It was for the best. Are you and Mom okay?"

"We're fine. Just missing our girl."

"Hey, I might finally be putting some of those carpentry skills you taught me to work. I've offered to help someone with some renovations. Think I can handle it?"

"Of course you can." His voice was tinged with pride, and she imagined him puffing his chest out. "You learned from the best. Just remember, always measure—"

"Twice and cut once. I'll do you proud, Dad."

"You always have. Any idea when you'll wrap this investigation up?"

"Not yet, but I'll stay in touch. Give Mom my love."

"Will do."

She hung up and ducked under the exit ramp to the ivy-covered ground that she and Sing Song would call home for the night. Her companion was already asleep, her snores soft enough for the rainfall to mask them. Colby snuggled into her sleeping bag and thought about her day tomorrow. She'd have to be totally professional with Adena and keep her eyes and ears open for anything that might connect her to the drug operation. As she drifted to sleep, she prayed she wouldn't find anything.

❖

Adena had watched from the sidewalk near the park tonight for several minutes as Colby, Sing Song, and two rough-looking men played some kind of game under the pavilion shelter. The men weren't guests at the DRC, but she'd seen them on the streets with others she recognized as drug users and dealers. How had Colby met them, and what was their connection?

Their interaction looked congenial with only occasional flare-ups, and they seemed to share a fragile respect for each other. She wasn't close enough to hear what was being said, but the tension in their bodies, the shrugging of shoulders, waving of hands, and laughter spoke as clearly as words. She was concerned Colby seemed so at ease with these volatile men.

But she'd actually had fun playing that stupid game of quarters too. For a few minutes, she'd forgotten about the murder investigation, the story about the DRC, and the mayor's ultimatum. For a single snapshot, she and Colby were the only two people in the world, doing something mindless and laughing, with no boundaries between them. Just hearing the foreign sound of laughter coming from her mouth had been comical. And Colby's chuckling had sounded so heartfelt Adena never wanted it to end. But when she'd asked Colby if she was involved in anything illegal, she'd skirted the question. So why had she asked Colby to help with renovations to her house? She *never* invited people to her place for any reason, but she'd done so with Colby twice recently.

"Why am I trying so hard to save *this* one?" Her body warmed at the thought, but she refused to accept her physical attraction as the answer. Even if she *saved* Colby, whatever that meant, she still couldn't get involved with her. They could never be equals or have a lasting relationship when she wielded all the power. It wouldn't be fair to Colby, and it wouldn't satisfy Adena's desire for a true partnership.

What about sex? "Jesus, you've lost it, Weber. Are you really that desperate?" The woman is homeless and that carries all kinds of possibilities you don't want to deal with. "Okay, I get it." She carried on the argumentative dialogue with herself until she arrived home. Maybe having Colby work for her was a bad idea. In the morning, she'd tell her she'd changed her mind. Her principles and DRC guidelines were clear: *Volunteers and staff are expected to behave in egalitarian ways that do not privilege one guest over another.*

CHAPTER THIRTEEN

Adena's alarm clock blared a Taylor Swift jingle at six o'clock the next morning. She slapped the off button and rolled over before remembering that Colby was coming to look at the kitchen. She spent much longer than usual in the shower, changed clothes twice, and even put on mascara for the first time in months. Her nerves were a mess, and she refused to admit why.

She stood looking over the small backyard, drinking her first cup of coffee and trying to settle her queasiness, when she heard a light tap at the front door. As she walked through the living room, she placed her hand over her abdomen and reached for the doorknob.

"Good morning, Colby. I've decided—" She stopped as the sun cast Colby as a silhouette and she was unable to read her face. She couldn't deliver this news without seeing the effect it had on her. For some reason, it mattered. "Come in, please." Once Colby crossed the threshold, Adena tried to gauge her emotions, but she'd moved quickly toward the kitchen.

"Why don't you show me what you have in mind before you make any hasty decisions. I might not be able to do what you want after all."

Adena retrieved the kitchen plans from beside her recliner and spread them out on one of the cabinet boxes. "The refrigerator goes there." She pointed to an open space closest to the living area. "The stove and sink will be set in the countertop here." As she leaned in just enough to indicate the locations on the plans, her shoulder brushed Colby's. Adena inhaled the scent of mint toothpaste, body soap, and a sporty deodorant, scents that shouldn't smell so sexy on any woman. She followed the line of Colby's neck from her ear to the collar of her sweatshirt. She reached out to touch Colby's face, but stopped in time and instead swept her hand toward the expanse of vacant space on the back wall. "The cabinets are going along here. I've chosen cherrywood, which will look great with the medium-toned flooring."

"Do you have the appliance measurements on the plans?" Colby was totally focused on the project, and it annoyed Adena that she appeared so unaffected by their closeness while she struggled to keep her hands to herself.

"In the spaces they're supposed to go and in the corner here." She pointed to a small graph on the top of the drawings.

"You're very thorough," Colby said, her voice huskier than Adena remembered. *Maybe not so unaffected after all.*

"I try to be. So, do you think you can do this?" Why was she even asking? She'd already decided not to let Colby do the work, hadn't she? She pulled her bottom lip between her teeth. She couldn't think with this woman so close. She moved farther away and waited for her answer.

"I can do most of what you want." Colby's eyes swept up and down Adena's body for several seconds, each glance a physical caress, each second ticking off in slow motion.

"Is something wrong? Colby?"

"I tried not to say anything when I came in."

"What?" Silence lingered between them as Colby's breathing quickened and her nostrils flared. "What *is* it?"

"You look absolutely stunning. The suit fits you perfectly, and the gold in that blouse brings out the tiny amber flecks in your eyes. I don't think I've ever seen you wear mascara. And you just smell... delicious."

Oh. God. Not unaffected at all. She wasn't sure if she should be elated or terrified. She'd never heard anything so sincere, so heartfelt, and she struggled between reaching out and running. She'd planned to end their tentative agreement at the threshold, and now her body seemed to be responding independently of her mind. Her skin tingled and warmed. Her insides felt liquid and achy. Her lips moved, but the dryness of her mouth absorbed the words. She stared at Colby's reddish-blond halo of hair, the swell of her ass beneath baggy jeans, and the tall length of her that she wanted to explore.

"Adena? Are you all right?"

She nodded.

"You're doing that staring thing again."

Adena swallowed hard. "Sorry. You said there's something you can't do?" *Diversion. Good plan.*

Colby stepped closer and forced Adena to look at her. "I can't stay away from you. I know we agreed not to pursue our attraction, and I've really tried to avoid you, but..."

Adena grabbed the edge of the cabinet box, uncertain if her legs would hold her. "What?" It really would be so easy to just let this happen, but she'd be violating her own rules, the organizational code, and her sense of decency. Her face burned and she couldn't make eye contact. Colby had to see the effect she was having on her.

"I've embarrassed you, haven't I? Too honest?"

"Too unexpected." Colby took another step toward her, and Adena lost her train of thought completely. "I can't...I mean..."

"You don't trust me? Or maybe you don't trust yourself?"

The air between them thickened with heat, and Adena struggled not to grab what she craved. "Yes. I mean no. I don't know which."

"Are you afraid of me, Adena?"

In so many ways. She nodded, unable to speak as Colby concentrated on her lips.

"I won't hurt you." Colby slid her arms around Adena's waist and slowly teased their bodies together. "I'm going to kiss you now unless you tell me to stop." When Adena licked her lips, Colby said, "Thank you for this."

Colby held Adena's stare as her tongue rimmed and moistened her lips. Her breath was hot and welcoming as it blended with hers. Colby kissed the edges of her mouth slowly, as if worshipping her in tiny morsels, and Adena's throaty moan echoed through the empty kitchen.

"I knew your lips would be this soft." Colby licked again and lightly sucked her bottom lip. "Open for me. I want to taste you."

Colby's arms tightened, and Adena melted into them, opening her mouth as she surrendered, feasting on Colby's tongue as it gently explored and then thrust deeper. She slid her hands under Colby's jacket and sweatshirt, feeling her flesh, burying her nails in her skin and marking her. When she scraped her fingernails down Colby's back, she thrust her pelvis against her and moaned. What she was doing was wrong, but it felt so very right.

Adena spun them around and pinned Colby against the wall, her leg wedged between Colby's, savoring the pressure of her thigh. Colby was as firm as she'd imagined, and their kiss deepened for a moment before she felt Colby pulling away. She rubbed against Colby, pressed her breasts into her chest, trying to get what she needed, praying it wouldn't be her last chance, and sure it should be. Now that the fire had been stoked, she couldn't stop.

Colby kissed the side of her face and down her neck, slowly easing Adena's head onto her shoulder, and then just held her. "It's okay. Take it easy."

"You want to stop?" She couldn't believe she said those words.

"Never," Colby said, "but as much as we both want this, you'll be sorry as soon as it's over. I can't do that to you. I apologize for being so forward."

As Colby's words registered, Adena felt ashamed of her behavior. "You're right. I'm sorry. This is wrong on so many levels."

Colby still held Adena against her. "I've wanted to kiss you since the day we met, but if and when we go further, I want it to be at the right time and for the right reasons." Adena couldn't look into her eyes. "And I want you to know about me, things like I'm not sick or a criminal or liar, or whatever you're afraid of."

She tried to turn away, but Colby persisted. "And we might as well start now. I've never used hard drugs or been charged with a crime, aside from the time you bailed me out, and I don't remember doing anything illegal then. As far as it goes, I'm as mentally sane as the next person. I shower and brush my teeth at least twice every day—never thought I'd use that as a reference, but things change.

I'm disease free, tested a week before we met. I know you're concerned about a lot of other things as well—money, job, social status—but sometimes you have to dig below the surface, Adena. Look at the person beyond their circumstances."

As Colby rationally addressed each of her concerns, Adena's desire strengthened. Colby could've taken advantage of the moment, pressed for what they both wanted, but she'd chosen the high ground. That spoke to a strength of character Adena admired.

"I don't mean to be judgmental, but I have to be practical because of work. One of my steadfast rules has been not to get personally involved with legal clients or DRC guests. It was never an issue, until you. And if we're being honest, it's a violation of DRC policy to show favoritism to any of our community. I shouldn't have you working here."

"I won't tell anyone, if that's what you're worried about."

"I'll know that I violated a trust, and I won't respect myself." She'd never wanted anyone as much as she did Colby at this moment, but more than wanting her, she cared about her. Her reaffirmed decision to maintain her boundaries was one of the hardest she'd ever made. Was her precious integrity worth the sacrifice of losing Colby?

Colby held her a few more minutes, and Adena absorbed the strength and warmth of her. When she finally stepped away, a sliver of vulnerability she hadn't shown anyone remained with Colby. Had she exposed her need to Colby because she was so unthreatening? Was she really that shallow? Or was she open because Colby touched something deeper in her? Whatever the reason, she'd never regret their kiss. *Ever.*

She finally turned away and reached for her messenger bag. "I really should go, and you probably should as well. I'm sorry this can't work." Was she referring to the job or their kiss? Both left her with a sense of loss and sadness. She walked slowly toward the door, praying Colby wouldn't stop her, not sure she had the strength to release her again. As she walked toward her office, she pressed her fingers against her lips and felt the lingering heat of Colby's mouth. If she had hundreds of kisses after today, Colby's was the one she'd always remember.

When she arrived at the office, Chris was lying in wait. The look of newsworthy gossip always made her face brighter and her smile wider. "What's up?"

Chris leaned over the counter in front of her desk and whispered, "Judge Lois is in your office and doesn't look happy. If I had to guess, I'd say woman trouble. Shall I bring coffee?"

"Not right now and no eavesdropping at the door." Chris's loud sigh was mostly for effect, but Adena knew she was genuinely disappointed. "And if you have time, could you pick up my dry cleaning around the corner on your lunch hour and drop it off at the house? I don't normally ask things like this, but I'm almost out of clean suits. Please and thank you."

"Huh?"

Chris's confused expression made her pause. "If you're too busy or don't want to, I understand."

"It's not that. You've just never asked me to go to your place, not in five years."

"That's…" She started to say not true, but Chris was right. "Sorry."

"No problem. If I do your domestic bidding, can I eavesdrop just a little?"

Adena shook her head and opened her office door.

"Good morning, honey. How…" When she saw Lois's face, the rest of her question was unnecessary. Her friend's eyes were bloodshot and puffy, her shoulders sagged, and her workout sweats were the most unattractive attire she'd ever seen her friend wear. She opened her arms, and Lois collapsed into them as they moved to the sofa. "Oh, honey, what happened?"

"She's seeing someone else. I thought we…had an… understanding." Her tears soaked through Adena's silk blouse. "She claims it was never…exclusive. It…was for me."

Adena held her and waited until Lois's sobs quieted. "Did she break up with you for this other woman?"

"I broke up with her. I want more than a casual, fucking relationship. She says she's not ready for anything serious."

"Was she ever or did she purposely mislead you?"

"I don't know, Adena. I thought we were on the same page. How could I have been so naive?" She sat up and reached for a tissue, wiped her eyes and blew her nose.

"You weren't, Lois. You cared for her."

"I did, but I think I knew she wasn't that into me. Little things, you know? She didn't return messages or calls, made excuses not to have sex. She had unexplained weekends out of town. Hints that I missed. Why are women so complicated?"

Adena thought about her earlier conversation with Colby and all the differences keeping them apart. "Why is life so complicated? I'm really sorry you're hurting. How can I help?"

"You already have. I just needed to vent, but I should let you get to work. I'll be fine."

"You aren't keeping me from anything urgent. Stay and we'll talk more, or if it makes you feel better, I'll let you work some cases."

Lois rose from the sofa and started toward the door. "Nice try, but I was on my way to the gym to relieve some tension. How about dinner tonight, if you're free? It's been a long time since we just ate and chatted over drinks. I promise not to be too morose."

"I'd love that, and you can be as morose as you want. Eating in or out?"

"How about I meet you here after work, and we pick up takeout on the way to my place. That way if I fall apart over the appetizers, I won't embarrass you too much."

Adena hugged her and kissed her forehead before letting go. "You could never embarrass me. I love you. If you need me before tonight, just text and I'll be there."

"Thanks, Adena. But get ready because you have some explaining to do as well."

"What are you talking about?"

"You were definitely preoccupied when you came in. I wasn't that distraught. I want to hear all about it, or should I say her."

Adena's skin grew warmer. "There's nothing to—"

"Don't even try. You're blushing just thinking about it. You have all day to get your story together, and I bet it's a good one. See you here at five thirty."

As Lois closed the door behind her, Adena slumped into her chair. It would take more than a few hours to figure out her feelings for Colby Vincent, and considerably longer to explain them to Lois.

❖

Colby stood back and looked at the placement of the large kitchen cabinet that would serve as an island. After Adena went to work this morning, she'd chosen to be useful. It had been too long since she'd done anything really productive. She probably should've left but couldn't abandon the place where she and Adena had shared their first and maybe only kiss.

The memory of it coursed through her, and she felt totally alive again. Adena's lips had been so soft and her hands demanding. When Adena had pressed against her and rubbed between her legs, Colby had been forced to withdraw or be embarrassed. She'd never wanted a woman more but had sensed Adena's inner conflict.

As they'd separated, she'd wondered if Adena had regretted the kiss or just the circumstances surrounding it. Would they have gone further if they'd met under different conditions? Adena's body had said yes, but her expression had said no as she'd excused herself.

Colby had decided to take a chance on her feelings. The heart wants it wants, and she refused to reject a chance for love no matter how many problems came with it.

Now she returned to the manual tasks that kept her mind from wandering to topics she couldn't resolve. The carpentry tools she'd found along with the other building supplies fit her hands perfectly, and she was grateful for the hours her father had spent teaching her to manipulate them to create beauty.

The plumbers had already done their preliminary work for the cabinets, so placing them according to the plans was relatively easy. She secured the base cabinets that would house the sink along the wall facing the backyard. The cherrywood looked fantastic against the pale-yellow wall color Adena had chosen, and Colby could hardly wait to add the wide-plank flooring to the palette.

But that would have to wait for another day, if Adena let her return. It was almost five, and she wanted to clean up and make it to Grace Community Church for the six o'clock meal. She broke down the cabinet boxes, stuffed them into the industrial-sized dumpster, and headed for the shower. As she washed the thin layer of sawdust from her body and the sticky glue from her fingers, she revisited her day's work, pleased with her efforts. She hoped Adena would like what she'd done.

She dressed quickly, tidied the bathroom, and had just stepped out on the front porch when she heard someone walking up behind her.

"Who are you and what are you doing here?" The woman had spiky hair, a couple of piercings, and a look that said she wasn't afraid of a fight even with a bag of fresh dry-cleaning dangling from one hand.

"I'm..." Who was this woman and how much should she share about her friendship with Adena? "I'm working on Ms. Weber's kitchen renovation."

"She didn't mention anything about that to me."

Was she Adena's partner, girlfriend, legal assistant? She hadn't seen her at the DRC. "I just started today. Want to have a look?"

"No, I don't want to have a look."

The woman tried to get around Colby, but she blocked her path. "I don't think I should let you in. I don't know who you are either." Colby bluffed, hoping to get more information.

"I'm Christine Mitchell, Adena's administrative assistant at her law office, if it's any of your business. I think you should go before I call the cops."

Great. Not a girlfriend. "That's not necessary. You could just call Ms. Weber. She'll verify who I am." *Maybe.*

"I'll do that after you're gone."

"Fine. Good-bye." Colby closed the door and started toward Elm Street. If Christine were Adena's assistant, she'd have her own key. She was pleased Adena had a pit bull like Christine watching over her at work. She doubted anyone could get past her without being properly vetted, and with the type of people who needed criminal defense, that was definitely an advantage. In spite of their run-in, she liked Christine.

Colby was halfway to the church when she saw Adena coming out of her law office on Elm Street. She ducked into a doorway and watched as another woman approached. She was an attractive blonde with a tight figure wearing a rich Merino wool suit and sparkling jewelry. When she reached Adena, they hugged and held for several seconds. The embrace was close, and Colby's skin tingled with the intimacy of it. Adena caressed the side of the blonde's face and then they kissed.

Colby turned away. She didn't want to know if it was a friendly peck or an arousing joining like the one she and Adena had enjoyed earlier. This was the kind of woman Adena deserved, not someone who had only lies and a life on the street to offer. Although the street wasn't her real life, it was what Adena knew and, by necessity, rejected. Adena couldn't possibly date someone like her, much less love her. Colby reversed course, no longer hungry, and just walked.

❖

Adena bussed the cardboard food containers from the coffee table to Lois's kitchen while Lois mixed another batch of martinis. Lois's mood was surprisingly good considering she'd broken up with her girlfriend, or maybe the alcohol had something to do with her spirits.

"You seem calmer," Adena observed. "Has something happened? Did you talk with Beverly?"

"No, but I had time to think while I worked out. We weren't right for each other. I see that now, but it was fun while it lasted."

"That's a pretty quick adjustment. It usually takes longer to process the shock, grief, and disappointment, and accept that it's over," Adena said, not sure where her expert advice was coming from. She'd never really been in love and had no idea how it should end.

"Don't get me wrong. I'm still pissed she wasn't honest with me, but I'll survive." Lois added a splash of extra dry vermouth to the mixture and poured it into a shaker with ice.

"Do you really think we need another drink?"

"I can only speak for myself when I say definitely." Lois leaned against her at the kitchen counter. "If I'm drunk, you won't hold it against me when I make a pass."

"And you won't remember if I refuse?"

Lois placed the jar of olives she held back on the counter. "Would you? Refuse?"

Colby's kiss flashed through Adena's mind, and she licked her lips. *That* had been a kiss, the kind she'd waited years for, the kind that reduced her to a bundle of urgent, fiery hormones. Her clit stiffened and she felt moisture gathering. She rested against the counter and crossed her legs, staring at her friend, considering the question. If she couldn't have Colby, and she *couldn't*, what was wrong with having some fun with Lois? They'd dated before, the sex had been good, and they'd parted friends. "That depends," she said.

Lois straddled her legs and leaned into her. "On what?"

"You've just broken up with Beverly. Do you really think it's a good idea?"

"You know what they say. The best way to get over one woman is to get under another."

Adena tried to move away. "That's not very romantic."

"Since when do you care about romance? It's always been just sex between us." She lowered her head, slid her arms around Adena, and whispered, "Come on, Adena. It might help us both forget. Let's play."

Lois's lips tasted of vodka and olives, but they were hot and receptive. An initial blast of arousal shot through Adena, and she returned the kiss. The passion she'd suppressed for Colby surged. She hadn't touched anyone intimately in too long. She needed to feel alive, desired, and satisfied, and maybe she could forget.

When Lois cupped her breast and tentatively massaged her taut nipple, she thought of Colby and the way she'd claimed her, tenderly but with no reservations, no hesitation. Her body cooled. "Stop, Lois. I can't do this. Not now."

"Come on, Adena. It's just us."

"Is it? We're not the same as we were before, and Beverly is as tangible a presence as if she were standing right here."

Lois backed away and stared at her. "And who else? Are you thinking about someone else too?"

She felt her eyebrow arch in spite of her efforts to remain neutral. "No."

"Not true, but it's obvious you don't want to talk about her. If I had to guess, I'd say it's that homeless woman."

"Lois, please don't." Her feelings for Colby and the desires of her body were too new and tender to have Lois's hurt feelings and negativity trample on them.

"Fine. Let's call a truce. Maybe I was out of line. You've always been more the forever type than me anyway."

"I've never had a long-term relationship. How can you say that?"

"Just because you haven't had one doesn't mean you don't want it."

Was that true? Had she been holding out all these years for something she didn't even realize she wanted—true love, commitment, home, and family? What a cliché. But the image conjured by her words made her feel hopeful. She wanted what she'd dreamed love should be but hadn't seen, not between her parents or with past lovers. She'd always thought happiness came from hard work, but another possibility emerged. "Maybe you're right. Maybe I've been kidding myself."

Lois took her hand and guided her toward the door. "Haven't we all? But the good thing is, as long as we're still breathing, we can keep trying." She hugged her and held her at arm's length. "Sorry I got carried away. I'd hate to lose your friendship over sex."

"You're entitled to a moment of crazy, and it will never destroy our friendship. I enjoyed our evening. Thank you, and call anytime if you need to talk."

"Sure you'll be okay walking home alone?"

"Of course, this is my town." She hugged Lois again and took the lighted path along Elm and Hendrix streets.

When she opened her front door and turned on a light, she saw the kitchen transformation immediately. Visible from the front of the house, the cherry base cabinets stood boldly against her yellow walls, a foundation for the rest of the kitchen. The huge cardboard boxes were gone, the subfloor swept clean, and the locations of the top shelves marked with bold lines and measurements. She stroked the sleek front of the large island that anchored the space and imagined the heavily veined granite slab on which she'd prepare meals and parties.

Colby's craftsmanship was outstanding, the cabinets aligned perfectly, shimmed for proper balance, and the doors fit snugly. She pulled one of the drawers out, and it slid back into place noiselessly. The strong, capable hands that had held her so gently this morning had completed all this manual labor in one day. As she looked around the room, her tears fell onto the raw wood of the island. The space was beginning to feel like a real kitchen with potential to be the heart of her home, and Colby had made it happen.

She wanted to see this through, to give Colby a chance to finish the work and to possibly keep her out of trouble. But she also wanted to get to know Colby better, to spend more time with her and explore these new feelings. How could she do that without violating her principles? Which was more important, her values or her potential happiness?

CHAPTER FOURTEEN

Colby got up early and rushed to the depot, waiting just inside the doors, sipping her first cup of coffee. She didn't want to see Adena until she'd thought about their kiss and the one she'd seen between her and the blonde. Her feelings for Adena were complicated, and they were complicating this case. When Cowboy and the other guys walked by, she ditched her empty cup and rushed toward them. "Hey, how's it going?"

Cowboy motioned for her to join them. "Where you been? I looked for you yesterday." She'd apparently earned her place in the group, since no one took notice of his invitation.

"Around, walking, nothing special."

"I need more IDs. You got time to help me out this morning?"

She'd have to risk running into Adena, and, in spite of her promise, the only connection to drugs so far led back to the DRC. "Sure. You got all the supplies with you?" He nodded toward Coyote, who carried the familiar backpack. "Any news about Bug?"

Wolf grunted. "The little shit is going away for a while. At least he won't have to worry about where he eats and sleeps, but he won't have any fun either."

When it was her turn to sign in at the DRC desk, Flo pulled Colby out of line. "What's going on?"

"What are you talking about?"

"I told you from the start not to mess with Adena. She's already bailed you out of jail once, and that's one time too many. What the hell are you into with this crowd?" She nodded toward Cowboy's band of misfits.

They stood toe-to-toe but she refused to back down. "They're veterans. I'm a vet. Seemed like a natural fit. We're hanging out. Is there a law against that?"

Flo put her hands on her hips. "Don't get smart with me. I can smell trouble, and the scent's all over you. If you cause any more problems for Adena or this center, you'll answer to me."

"What's going on?" Adena leaned against the doorframe of the dayroom. "Flo?"

"Just having a friendly word with the new girl." She stared Colby down, daring her to contradict her.

"It didn't look very friendly to me. Colby?"

"We're fine here, ma'am."

"Good. Then everybody can get back to business." Adena glared at Flo as she passed on the way back to her office. "Can I see you for a minute, Colby?"

"I'm in a hurry this morning. I need a shower, to brush my teeth, and get to—"

"I'll only take a minute of your time. Please."

Damn, she hated when Adena said please. She sounded so sexy, and it made her weak and pliable. "Okay." She followed like a trained puppy back into her office.

Adena closed the door behind them, then moved to the center of the small room. Colby stepped to the other side. Their chemistry was volatile and made close-quarters communication difficult. "How can I help?"

"You've already done enough," Adena said. "My kitchen looks like a professional spent days in there. It's beautiful. Thank you."

"No problem. I enjoyed working with my hands again, but I've gone as far as I can without help. The bottom cabinets were easy to install, but the top ones require at least two people. Sorry if I overstepped when you asked me to leave, but I just wanted to do something useful. You've done so much for me—taking me in here, bailing me out of jail, breakfast, patching up my side. You even let me sleep under your roof. It was the least I could do. It'll be beautiful when it's finished. Just tell whomever you get to do the work that the ceiling slopes slightly toward the east. That's why I wrote the measurements on the wall where the cabinets go." Adena never looked away as Colby spoke, and she wondered if she'd said something wrong. "What?"

"I know this is completely opposite of what I said this morning, but could you possibly finish the work?" She reached toward her, but Colby stepped back. "What's wrong?"

"I just...we shouldn't..." She struggled for the right words and settled on the truth. "I'd need your help with the remaining cabinets, and we shouldn't be alone. I'm too attracted to you, and you've made it clear you don't want anything else to happen. Besides, I don't imagine your girlfriend would approve. I don't do cheating."

Adena moved so close Colby felt her body heat and smelled the light, flowery fragrance of her soap. "What girlfriend? I don't cheat either."

"The blonde I saw you kissing on Elm Street yesterday." She sounded petty and jealous, but the sight had been like a punch to the gut occurring so soon after their kiss.

"She's not my girlfriend, but what about Kali?"

Colby was surprised at the mention of her ex's name, and it probably showed on her face. "How do you know about Kali?"

Adena looked at her feet and her eyebrow arched. She was obviously uncomfortable with the question. "I might've overheard you talking to her one night."

Colby placed her finger under Adena's chin and gently lifted until they were looking at each other again. "So, if you did overhear that conversation, you know I was breaking up with her. And before you ask, it had nothing to do with you. I should've done it months ago."

A tentative smile tweaked the corners of Adena's mouth before she turned serious. "The fact that we're both single only complicates things further. We shouldn't spend time together, but that doesn't mean I don't want to." Adena waved her hands like she wasn't sure where to put them, her eyes focused on Colby's lips. "Why do I always want to break the rules with you, Colby Vincent?"

"You do?"

"So much." She licked her lips, and Colby felt instantly weak.

"Then what are you so afraid of?"

"Do I seem afraid right now?" Adena placed her hand on Colby's forearm and squeezed.

"You're pretty bold considering where we are, but I still see uncertainty in your eyes. Has someone hurt you in the past?" Colby had seen that look of deep sadness in her mother's eyes so many times while her father was dealing with his PTSD. She sensed that Adena's grief went beyond the loss of her parents to a chronic skepticism about love.

"So many questions. I'm taking the day off tomorrow. Come by and we'll work on those upper cabinets. I'll *try* to act like a professional."

Adena caressed the side of her face, and jolts of pleasure shot through her. "O...kay."

Slowly stepping her back against the wall, Adena said, "And if I fail miserably, will you forgive me?" The twinkle in her eye mesmerized Colby as Adena skimmed her lower lip with her thumb.

"Adena, can we—" Flo poked her head inside the office. The look in her eyes reminded Colby of the enemy in Iraq.

To her credit, Adena didn't flinch. She slowly removed her hand from Colby's face and whispered, "I'll see you tomorrow."

At that moment, Colby admired Adena more than ever. She hadn't pretended or blamed Colby for their situation. Adena's words were strong, certain, maybe to her own detriment, and Colby felt validated. She wanted to stay and defend Adena but knew it wouldn't be necessary. After what she'd just seen, Adena was more than capable of taking care of herself. As she squeezed past Flo in the doorway, Colby imagined the sermon Adena would get about fraternizing with guests.

She found Cowboy and the others in the computer lab and started working on the new fake IDs. Raven was posted outside the lab to make sure she wasn't disturbed. This time, her old driver's license was in the discard pile. The case was growing stronger against the vets, but still no progress on finding out who was really behind the operation. As she laminated the new cards, this time in the computer room, she tried to gauge each man's potential as a state's witness. Could she save them from serious time if they agreed to flip on the bosses? These men were trying to survive, and no one else was offering a legitimate option.

When she finished, she stuffed the supplies back in the pack, handed it to Raven, and met Cowboy outside the DRC. "These are good to go."

"Thanks, and you'll take care of the old ones?"

She nodded.

"You free tomorrow night, say eight?" Cowboy's grin was wider than usual.

"I guess. Why?"

"Someone wants to meet you. Be in front of the DRC at eight. Sheriff will pick you up. Be nice and don't say anything stupid when you meet him."

"Meet who? I don't like surprises. I've had PTSD, remember?" She wanted to get more information but couldn't push too hard.

"You'll like this guy."

"Are you going with me? Sheriff is sort of weird. He keeps saying he knows me, and I get the feeling he'd like to disembowel me with his huge hunting knife."

"He won't touch you, especially now. I'm not riding with you, but I'll be there."

"Okay, I guess. See you tomorrow."

Colby walked farther east down Washington Street over the bridge and dialed Frankie. "I've got a meeting tomorrow night at eight. This could be the break we've been waiting for. I'll check in afterward with details. I've also got more fake IDs. I'll leave them in the PO box like last time."

As she walked back toward downtown, Colby had a feeling her luck was about to change. Tomorrow she'd spend more one-on-one time with Adena, and tomorrow night she'd hopefully meet the man at the top of the drug-operation chain. Things were definitely looking up.

❖

Adena watched Colby until she was completely out of sight before turning her attention to Flo, who hadn't spoken since she entered the office. "Well, Florence, I assume you have something to say."

Flo dropped into a chair in front of the desk, and Adena sat down next to her. "Would it do any good? You can't take your eyes off her. I can't believe what I just saw. You had her backed against the wall, with your *hands on her.*"

As Flo recounted her version of the story like a lurid porn movie, Adena's body heated and the initial excitement returned. "Yes, I did."

"Have you lost it completely? That girl can sue the center and you for everything you have just because you touched her. Is that what you want?" She held up her hand. "Wait. That obviously isn't what you want, but it could be the end result. What's going on, Adena?"

"It's complicated."

"It seems pretty simple to me," Flo said. "You touched her inappropriately. You violated our rules and regulations. You took advantage of your position with the center. You've put us all in jeopardy. If she files a complaint, we're finished."

For some reason, Adena wasn't as panicked as she probably should've been. Everything Flo said was true, and her conduct could lead to exactly the result she was trying to avoid, but she couldn't deny her attraction to Colby any longer. She'd tried to reason it away, ignore it, assuage it with another woman, but nothing worked. She felt something for Colby she hadn't experienced before, and she wasn't willing to walk away yet.

"You're right, Flo, but I'm not prepared to discuss this. If you feel the need to report me, I'll understand. Of course I hope you don't, at least until I figure a few things out."

"This is so unlike you, Adena."

"And that's exactly why I have to see it through, whatever *it* is."

Flo took her hand. "You're the most logical, unflappable person I've ever met, so if this woman has you twisted in knots, I'm doubly concerned. I strongly advise against any further interaction with her that isn't strictly professional." She paused for a second, her eyes drilling into Adena's. "I'm wasting my breath. Please be careful. You're not the only one with something to lose." She gave her hand a final pat and started toward the door.

"I know, Flo, and thank you for worrying about me and the center. That's why you're so very good at your job. Now, would you please get me the last two years' contribution records and a list of our guests?"

Flo gave her a final you've-completely-lost-it expression and closed the door behind her.

What am I doing? The question circled in Adena's mind, but the answer invariably came from the ache in her body. *I want her.* And what if the connection was only physical, only temporary? She'd never be the center of Colby's life—a life dependent on survival at any cost. Could she risk the disappointment of being just an option but never a priority, or would the pain be too much?

She tried to forget Colby and the effect she'd had on her, again, as she returned phone calls and completed other DRC paperwork. After a couple of hours, she collected the contributor and guest lists Flo had compiled and headed for her law office. She stopped by Dolce Aroma and picked up a latte and a baklava for Chris. Food bribery went a long way toward squelching Chris's complaints when she needed extra work done.

When she opened the front door, Chris was whistling to a particularly upbeat song on the radio. "Good morning. You sound like you swallowed a handful of canaries."

Chris stood behind her desk and almost danced from one foot to the other. "Oh. My. God. You are not going to believe what happened to me last night."

"First, are we alone, because I'm afraid this could be X-rated."

"All alone and definitely X-rated, maybe even triple-X. I met this guy at that new club, Chemistry."

She placed the coffee and pastry on Chris's desk and backed away. "Enough. You lost me at guy."

"No, you're going to like this. Trust me. He had a smoking-baby-Jesus-hot girlfriend with him, and after a few drinks, they asked if I'd be into a threesome."

Adena waved her hands to erase the image forming in her mind. "I really don't need to hear this. It's too early for porn, and I think a few professional boundaries, at least about sex, are good. Please stop."

Chris poked a pouty face. "You're no fun."

"True, but I've gotten used to it. Could I get a list of all our clients with the initials DE?"

"Sure, but I just have to say it was *mind-blowing*. I might be bisexual." Chris plopped back into her chair with an exaggerated sigh, grabbed the baklava, and said, "Thanks for the coffee and yummy. Speaking of yummy, I saw a strange woman at your house yesterday when I dropped off your dry cleaning. Almost called the cops."

Adena froze halfway through her office door. "Really?"

"Yep, and I'd bet you money it was the homeless girl you mentioned, Colby something. She was hot. Am I right?"

Without turning around, she said, "She's doing some carpentry work for me."

"Sure she's not doing some plumbing work on your rusty pipes?" Chris chuckled.

Heat flushed Adena's face. "Very funny. My list, please."

While she waited for the client list, she checked messages and prepped her cases for next week. Then she scanned the contributor and guest names from the DRC. The notes in the margin of her father's calendar might not even refer to a client, but she'd been searching his personal files for the past five days with no luck. She felt in her gut the information was significant, if she could just figure out what it meant.

She found only three DRC guests with the initials DE: Della Ellis, Donald Enfield, and Dorothy Euliss. The contributors' list produced two more names: Dwight Ernest and Delmar Errington.

She knew the contributors relatively well, and they weren't legal clients. They'd both been long-time supporters of the DRC and attended all their charity functions. She'd recognize the DRC guests on sight and had represented Enfield in a pandering case once.

A few minutes later, Chris tapped on her door and dropped the firm's client list on her desk. "Sure you don't want to hear about my *awesome* night? It might get your creative juices flowing, if you get my drift." Her fiftyish, tattooed assistant couldn't pass up an opportunity to mention Adena's nonexistent love life.

"Thanks for your concern, but no. If you're so anxious to share your sex life, maybe you should write a book. I'm sure it would rival *Fifty Shades.*"

"You have *no* idea." She fanned herself as she exited.

Adena flipped through the client database and confirmed her earlier assumption that neither Ernest nor Errington was on it. She found Enfield's name and only two additional possibilities, Denton East and Derrick Evans. What did these seven people have in common, if anything? Which one had her father been referring to when he scribbled the initials on his calendar, and what did the numbers following the initials mean?

She punched the intercom to Chris's desk. "Do you use any kind of code with the letters DE for billing, type of service, scheduling, insurance, payroll, anything?"

"Nope. Tell me what you're looking for, and I might be able to help."

"That's the problem. I don't know." She disconnected and went back to the lists. The only obvious connection was the DRC guest, Donald Enfield, whom she'd represented in court. His name appeared on two lists. None of the names were on all three. *What does it mean, Dad?*

She gathered all the pages and stuffed them into her bag along with her father's calendar and the picture of the suspect she'd gotten from Detective Carrick. She'd spent hours poring over the names, trying to find a connection that simply wasn't there. She reached for the phone when Chris buzzed her.

"Detective Carrick on the line for you."

"Hello, David. I was just about to call you. What's new?"

"I haven't been in contact because I haven't had anything new to tell you."

"And now?"

"It might be nothing, but we arrested a guy for drug possession with intent to sell and carrying a concealed weapon. He's a veteran, goes by the nickname of Bug. He gave us two names, Shaun Rossi and John Tabor, but we've confirmed through fingerprints that he's Rossi. I think he's probably a regular at the DRC."

"He is." She drummed her fingers on the desktop. "Wait. Did you say John Tabor?"

"Yeah, why?"

John Tabor was the man supposedly interviewed by Martin Linen who'd complained about being turned away from the DRC on a freezing night. Carrick would have no need for that information. She let it pass. "Nothing. Go on."

"He was out of his mind when he was picked up and had a large hunting knife on him. The patrol officer said he mumbled something about the man who died at the DRC. They tried to get more out of him, but he passed out. They notified me, but when I got to the jail, he was still so inebriated I couldn't question him. I'll make another pass when he's dried out."

Adena's heart raced. "Do you think it's him?" Could this finally be over?

"I'm not confident he's the killer. I've sent the knife to the lab for testing, but that'll take a while. Even if the knife is similar to the murder weapon, it's a popular make and there are hundreds like it out there."

She sank back in her chair. "So we're back where we started, again?" Except she now suspected the man Linen had talked with was using a false name.

"Not necessarily. We could get very lucky and find blood evidence on the knife. That would be huge. We'll just have to wait and see."

She started to vent her frustration, but the detective had experienced enough of her wrath over the past year. "Okay. Thank you for calling. Please keep me informed."

He hung up, and she stared at the ceiling. "When will it end? I'm not sure how much longer I can hold it all together." She buzzed Chris again. "Would you please pull Shaun Rossi's file, if we have one, and also check for John Tabor." She should've checked their names before, but she'd been too focused on the other lists. If these men had been clients of the firm, she wanted to know more about them. If they hadn't, she'd ask at the DRC until she found something, anything about the man who'd possibly killed her father and the one who'd helped tarnish his legacy.

CHAPTER FIFTEEN

Colby stuffed her bedroll into a locker at the DRC after her shower the next morning, grabbed a shirt and jacket from the interview rack, and headed to Adena's with her backpack thrown over her shoulder. She'd seriously thought about not showing up to work on the kitchen, keeping her distance to remain professional or at least more objective. But the thought of not going caused more unhappiness than she was prepared to endure. She'd started to question her desirability after being on the street. Adena's interest was a total rush. If only a little ego boost were enough, but she hoped for so much more.

She knocked on the thick oak door and waited, as the tapping of Adena's footsteps grew louder. Her heart raced and her palms grew sticky. What was wrong with her? She wasn't here to get laid; she was here to do a job—two jobs actually—and it was time she acted like a DEA agent, not a love-struck teenager.

Adena opened the door and Colby stifled a moan. She wore a pair of clingy jogging shorts and a snug tank top with no bra. "That's what you're working in?"

As she waved her in, Adena said, "I thought we'd get hot and sweaty. Is there a problem?"

"Only if you want me to work." She was staring but couldn't stop. She'd never seen the alabaster skin beneath Adena's business trousers, the bare flesh of her shoulders, or the perkiness of her breasts without support. And her ass in those shorts was criminal.

"Now *you're* staring."

"Give me a minute. I was taught to enjoy the beauty in life, and you definitely qualify."

Adena's skin flushed and she pulled at the tail of her tank top. "Thank you. Are you wearing that?" She motioned to the sweat pants and shirt that covered Colby from neck to ankles.

"It's all I had clean. Couldn't get a space in the laundry line this week."

"I've probably got something that will sort of fit." She nodded toward the back of the house, and Colby followed.

Adena's bedroom looked like an abandoned motel room with an old side table, dented coffee pot, and an air mattress on the floor.

"Sorry about the mess." She rifled through a box of clothes and pulled out a pair of shorts and another tank. "Try these."

Colby held the clothes to her chest and looked around for a place to change. She grabbed the hem of her sweatshirt, and Adena headed for the door.

"I'll see you in the kitchen." When she came out of the bedroom, Adena was the one staring. "Wow. I forgot how much taller you are than me. Makes those shorts *really* short. And the tank is very tight across your...shoulders."

Colby started to suggest she put her sweats back on, but seeing Adena's eyes light up as she looked at her was worth her slight discomfort from the ill-fitting clothes. "Let's get started."

"I have coffee and bagels with cream cheese from Dolce. I can't expect you to work on an empty stomach." Adena motioned for her to sit in the recliner and pulled up an ottoman nearby. "I got you two." She handed the bagels to her and Colby dug in.

"Oh my God, I'd forgotten how good fresh ones taste. I'm used to the ones they throw out. Sorry, guess you don't need to hear that."

"Don't you have the Chicken Lady's Little Green Book of places where free meals are served around town?"

"I'm not always early enough. Sometimes they run out, and sometimes I..."

"Give your food to someone else?"

"Some folks need it more. What can I say? I'm a sucker," Colby said.

"You're a considerate person."

Heat crept up her neck. "Maybe we should get started. This was great. Thanks." She stood and offered to help Adena up. When their fingers entwined, a slow crawl of arousal claimed her. Adena's hands were soft and warm, her skin smelled of soap and flowery perfume. Adena's breath hitched, and her eyes widened as Colby pulled her closer.

They stood only inches apart for several seconds. Adena focused on her mouth, and Colby stared into her brown eyes, watching the flecks of gold deepen as her breathing increased. When her lips parted, Colby dipped her head for a kiss.

"We really should get to work."

Adena released her hands and the separation was startling. The air grew thinner and colder, and her nipples puckered beneath the light cotton fabric. "Right." As she tried to cover her chest, Adena glanced down.

"Oh, God. You're absolute torture, and you're not even trying." She turned away quickly and pulled a cabinet box into the center of the floor.

Colby didn't move as she slowly adapted from the heat of their touch to the cool loss of it. She eventually grabbed the box cutter and ripped through the tape to open the box, anything to take her mind off Adena's firm, tempting ass as she dragged boxes into the room.

"This one is first." Adena pointed to one of the cabinet containers, trying to focus on anything except the hungry look in Colby's eyes and the burn in her own body. "It goes in the upper right corner. I'll get the stepladder while you cut the rest of these open. Be careful. That box cutter's really sharp."

"Okay, Boss."

Adena retrieved the ladder and then stood in the center of the kitchen, wiping her sweaty palms on her shorts and staring at Colby as she ripped one box after another. "You've obviously done that before."

"A few times."

Everything about Colby tempted her. The confidence with which she moved, her concern for others, the loving way she spoke about her parents, the subtle red of her hair, her green eyes, full lips, and powerfully sensuous body—all made it so damn hard to keep her distance. She'd dated and slept with desirable women, but her attraction to Colby transcended normal yearning and went straight to craving.

"If you don't stop looking at me like that, we'll never get any work done."

"I'm sorry?"

"You're practically drooling, Counselor."

"If you had photographic evidence, I'd probably cop a plea. I'm sure my intent would be obvious." She started to peel a box open but stopped when Colby pressed against her back.

"Are you interested in progressing from intent and opportunity to the act?" Colby kissed her neck and chill bumps ran down her spine. "The sexual energy in this room is interfering with my ability to do good carpentry."

"Please," Adena said.

Colby nipped her ear and tried to turn her around. "Please what?"

She wiggled out of Colby's grasp and leaned against one of the boxes. "Please don't."

"We've been flirting since I got here. Can you honestly say you don't want this?"

"No, I can't."

"Then why? Aside from the professional considerations, the fact that I'm homeless, don't have a job, and you'd be embarrassed to introduce me to your friends?"

Even standing in the middle of her disaster of a kitchen, wearing clothes two sizes too small and enumerating all the reasons they shouldn't be together, Colby still appealed to her so much she ached.

"It's not about you, Colby. We've discussed this before. It's an ethical issue for me. Yes, I'm attracted to you, but I can't go there, as much as I'd like to."

"Everything about you begs for this—your mouth opens slightly when I'm close, your nostrils flare, your eyebrow arches, you breathe erratically and fiddle with your hair, and when you lick your lips, it's like an invitation. And I definitely want to accept it."

She cupped Colby's face and stared into those dangerous pools of green. "I want you. Desperately. You stopped last time because you understood my dilemma. Our circumstances haven't changed."

Colby was asking to give her exactly what she wanted. With the slightest encouragement, or at least no objection, she could be satisfied in minutes. *And then what?* Her mind hijacked the moment. If sex was all she wanted, why hadn't she accepted Lois's advances the other night? And once she'd had her, what would Colby do? There could never be a place for her in Colby's life or vice versa. Colby was a transient, and no one ever stayed in Adena's life very long. If she was going to be alone, it was best not to be hurting as well.

"Hypothetically, if we had sex, what would happen next?"

Colby backed away, her face a palette of confusion. "Next? What do you mean? I thought you just wanted sex."

"Is that all you want?" Why was she even asking the question?

"Absolutely not, but it's all I can offer right now. You can't possibly imagine a future with me?" Colby's tone sounded matter-of-fact, but her eyes projected hope and pain.

Adena *had* started to consider the possibility, but Colby's statement brought her back to reality. "You're right, so I think it's best if we don't complicate things."

Colby's eyes lost some of their sparkle as her words registered. She kissed the side of Adena's face and picked the box cutter up again. "Of course. I'm sorry for putting you in this situation again. You've made your position clear." Colby's shoulders rolled forward and she worked open the boxes more slowly.

Adena couldn't bear to see her so dejected. If she ever hoped for real intimacy between them, it was time for honesty. "Colby, would you stop for a minute, please?"

Colby turned toward her but didn't meet her gaze.

"Even if our circumstances changed, I'm not sure I could be in a relationship with you...or anyone else." Her voice was barely above a whisper.

Moving toward her slowly, Colby came close enough to reach out but stopped far enough away not to crowd her.

"I'm afraid..." She choked her truth out like a bitter pill. "Of loving and being hurt. Of never being a priority." She immediately wanted to take the words back. She felt vulnerable and exposed, unable to draw a full breath.

Colby pulled her into a gentle hug. "It's all right. Everybody's afraid of something."

"Not you." Adena chuckled. "You'd fight the devil himself."

"With a good-enough reason, maybe, but that doesn't mean I wouldn't be afraid."

Adena had no right, but the question that gouged at her insides demanded a voice. "What *are* you afraid of, Colby?"

Colby guided them gently to the floor atop a flattened box. She stared at Adena's hands for several seconds before finally answering. "I'm afraid of never finding the kind of love my parents have. They've been through rough times, but they're still kind to each other, still support each other's dreams, and still love each other as much as ever. I want to feel that kind of chemistry, passion, and heart connection once in my life."

Adena recognized the same words Colby had used when she broke up with her girlfriend on the phone—chemistry, passion, and heart connection. That's what Adena wanted too, but was it realistic? She'd convinced herself that hard work and commitment to a worthy cause were enough for happiness and a fulfilling life.

Her rationalizations unraveled in the face of Colby's sincerity and her own desire to finally be truly heard. "Everyone I've cared about left me, either through illness, violence, or personal choice, but the result was still the same—pain so deep it left scars. I'm protecting myself, not from being alone, but from caring enough to hurt when it ends. I sound pathetic." She looked down at the floor so Colby couldn't see the weakness in her eyes.

"I'm sorry. I didn't know."

"So, you see, even if our circumstances changed, could you honestly say you wouldn't leave, that I'd be important enough to hold you?" Colby's silence was the only answer she needed. At least she had the decency not to lie.

"If given a choice, I'll never lie to you, but I can't promise I won't leave. I can tell you I've waited for someone like you all my life—a woman who values family and commitment as much as I do, a woman who gives back to the community and feels the same passion for me that I feel for her. But can you see yourself with someone like me? Be honest. If right now, exactly as I am, is all I'd ever have to offer?"

Adena took a deep breath and turned away. She would definitely spend more time with Colby and get to know her better if only their circumstances were different, but saying so wouldn't make it so. "I'm sorry, Colby. This situation is difficult for both of us. I really appreciate your honesty. Now, it's up to you if you want to continue working or not. I'll understand if you decide to go."

Colby stared at her for several long seconds, the green of her eyes dark with emotion. "Let's get to work. I need to burn off some frustration."

"Are you sure?"

"Absolutely," Colby said as she rose and pulled Adena with her, "but it might cost you dinner." She positioned the ladder for their first installation.

"Deal."

Colby picked up the leather tool belt Adena had never worn and strapped it around her waist. Adena felt a rush of heat as a vision of Colby in nothing but the belt filled with sex toys flashed through her mind.

"Hand me that..." Colby placed her hands on her hips. "If we're really *just* going to work, you need to stop looking at me like that, or at least control your facial expressions better."

"Sorry?" It was hard to apologize for something she really wasn't sorry for. Damn it. Why did her mind always win in the war between logic and emotion?

"As I was saying, hand me that small corner cabinet. If you'll support it from underneath, I can level and install it from up here."

Colby climbed the ladder, and Adena tried to focus on anything except her long naked legs. The tool belt covered more territory than the short shorts that barely concealed the swell of Colby's ass. The temptation to touch her was strong.

"I'm ready whenever you are." Colby gave her a look that said she knew exactly what she was thinking. It wouldn't do any good to deny it.

"Right." She lifted the small cabinet and steadied it while Colby secured it in place. Her arms weakened from the proximity of their bodies.

"Hey, try to hold it steady or I might drop it on your head."

"Sorry. I was distracted."

Thank God, Colby didn't respond with one of her usual evocative comments. She was having a hard-enough time concentrating with Colby's crotch in her face and imagining what she'd like to do to it. She forced herself to think about work, the responsibilities she'd turned over to Oliver, and the mystery of her father's cryptic notes. When his murder was solved, she'd have to concentrate on something else, maybe decide about her future career path. Did she want to continue as a criminal-defense attorney, become a full-time nonprofit administrator, or pursue something entirely different?

Without a break in her work routine, Colby asked, "How is it working at the DRC?"

The question sounded a bit awkward. "Fine. Why?"

"I meant through the years. Have you ever had any problems with folks? Homeless people bring a lot of complications. You know drugs, alcohol, mental illness, and disease? Some have criminal histories that are hard to leave behind."

Adena remembered her conversation with Detective Carrick yesterday afternoon and forgot Colby was waiting for an answer.

"Adena, are you okay? You look really far away right now."

"I was thinking about a call from the detective working my father's case. They arrested a guy who was under the influence of drugs, and he mumbled something about my dad's murder. He had a hunting knife in his possession."

"Does the detective think he's the suspect?"

"He's not sure at this point. More lab tests, you know. But to answer your question, yes, some of our guests do have a lot of challenges."

"What was the arrested guy's name?"

"Shaun Rossi, but he gave the name of John Tabor too. He went by Bug on the street."

Colby dropped the hammer, and it almost smacked Adena on the foot.

"Hey, watch it."

"Sorry. It slipped."

The next hours passed quickly as she and Colby established a silent rhythm. The simple hold-this-pass-that tasks allowed her to watch Colby work uninterrupted. Gliding her strong hands over the wood grain with reverence, she applied each nail with precision. She paid attention to the tiniest detail, measuring several times before trimming and securing each unit. It was like watching an artist practice her craft. As a trickle of sweat rolled down Colby's side, Adena wondered if she'd be as attentive to a lover. *Stop it.*

"Okay. You can let go now. That's the last one."

Colby had been going like a workhorse since they began, but Adena's arms were starting to ache from holding the cabinets up so long. She stepped back and surveyed the finished product. "They look fantastic. You're very talented with your hands. I meant with cabinetry. Really. Thank you so much."

Colby admired their work. "They do look amazing. So, what's next?" Colby looked at her wrist and then around the kitchen. "What time is it? I was relieved of my watch and haven't gotten another."

"Seven thirty. I didn't realize we'd been at it so long. We worked right through lunch. Why don't you have a shower while I arrange that dinner I promised?" Adena said.

"I've got to go. Yes to the shower, but dinner will have to wait." She gave her handiwork one final glance and dashed from the room.

When she returned, Colby was wearing tight-fitting jeans, a dress button-down shirt only slightly wrinkled, and a coat that resembled a suit jacket. Adena's mouth felt parched as she scanned her from head to toe. "You look very…nice. Job interview or date?" Why did she ask about a date? She'd made it clear she couldn't get involved with Colby, so she needed to leave the personal comments off. "Sorry. It's none of my business."

"Do I really need to be here for this conversation?" Her grin was warm and her green eyes sparked. "I do have a job interview of sorts, so I borrowed a couple of things from the center. Wish me luck. And thanks for letting me help with the kitchen. I needed something productive to do."

"I'll have the plumbers hook up the sink and appliances next week and also have the countertops installed. After that, I'll be ready for the bathroom work. Interested?"

"Sure. I can do tiling and the woodwork. I can lay the kitchen floor too, if you want. Just let me know."

"Sold." She pulled a house key on a stretchy pink cord from her messenger bag and handed it to Colby. "I'll let you know when the bathroom is prepped. I'm usually out of the house by seven or seven thirty and home by six, unless I'm helping Flo at the center. Work at your own pace." As Colby walked toward the door, Adena tried to ignore the fact that she'd just given her a key to her house, a job renovating her bathroom, and, against her own advice, another opportunity to spend time together.

CHAPTER SIXTEEN

Colby hurried down Church Street to the depot and arrived just a few minutes before Sheriff pulled up. She'd hoped someone else would be going along for the ride, but he was alone. She scooted into the front seat of his mobile ashtray and strapped on her seatbelt. "What's up?"

"Same old, same old. You?"

She grunted and let his disinterested question pass. Master of conversation he was not, and that suited her. She didn't want to risk pissing him off because this guy gave her the creeps. His dyed black hair was almost as shiny as his leather jacket, his teeth could've used a dentist years ago, and his jeans were so tight that his package was too obvious. He puffed a cigarette like a lifeline, and even with the window down, the smoke permeated her clothes and choked her.

She'd never sat in the front seat on their drug runs, so she looked around as he drove in silence. He had an open can of beer in the cup holder between them and the hilt of a large hunting knife stuck up beside his seat. Why did everyone in this group carry a knife? She remembered Adena telling her earlier about Bug's arrest, his knife, and drugged comments about her father's death. Geeky Bug didn't strike her as a killer, but the man next to her could fit the bill. Any of the guys she hung out with could've had the means and opportunity to kill Franklin Weber, but what would a homeless vet or drug runner have to gain by killing the man who helped provide shelter and other services for them? He hadn't been robbed, so money wasn't the obvious motive.

"Do you know who I'm meeting tonight?" She had nothing to lose by trying to get more information.

"Yeah, I know."

"Well?"

"Well what? I voted to keep you out of the operation altogether. Women cause problems, sooner or later, and something about you ain't right."

He might be uglier and scarier than most, but his instincts were pretty good. "Why don't you like me, Sheriff?"

"Told you. Something's off with you. I've seen you before but can't place where."

"Not likely. I'm from New York. Ever been there? Or maybe we served together in the military at one of those dust bowls in Iraq."

"Nah, that ain't it, but it'll come to me."

She hoped she remembered before he did. If they'd run into each other in New York, chances were he'd been involved in one of the investigations she'd managed. But she was pretty certain she'd have remembered his ugly mug. No sense stressing yet.

Sheriff pulled in front of a two-story Federal-style brick home nestled beside a golf course. Dentil cornices above the elliptical windows highlighted the plain front and gave the house a regal feel. Before her father began woodworking and building, she wouldn't have known one style home from another. Now she enjoyed the differences and the stories they told about the past. "Nice place. This guy must rake in the dough."

"You have no idea."

"How will I get back downtown?"

"Not my problem." He sped off, her open door slamming shut as he peeled away from the curb.

She looked down at her clothes and suddenly felt very underdressed, but it was the best she could find on the DRC rack. Before she could ring the bell, Cowboy opened the door. "Right on time. Come in."

She checked the entrance alcove for anyone else before confiding. "I'm sure glad to see a familiar face."

"Relax. You're in charge of this meeting. Just listen first and wait for the question."

Strange advice, but she could follow simple instructions. She trailed Cowboy down a hallway through the center of the renovated home toward the back into a paneled den. She took a second to adjust from the bright chandelier lights to the dim lamplight of the office space. An older man with graying hair wearing an expensive Italian suit sat behind an ornate desk. He rose as she entered, flanked by two muscular men who looked like linebackers.

"Ah, our guest of honor has arrived. Welcome, Ms. Vincent." She shook his hand before sitting in a leather wingback chair in front of the desk. "I'm so glad you could join me. Would you care for a drink?"

"Vodka rocks, please." She needed a shot to settle her emotions from the day with Adena but not enough to impair her senses. This meeting had the potential to further her drug case or maybe blow it wide open. The smaller of the two men handed her the drink with a cordial smile. She air-toasted her host and took a small sip.

"I guess you're wondering why I invited you here?" He rolled a cigar between his thumb and first two fingers and then sniffed it. "You like Cubans?"

She shook her head. She'd learned to be patient in adversarial situations, to watch and listen, but she needed some answers. "Actually, I'm wondering who you are."

"Forgive me. I'm Matthew Winston, owner of Winston Transportation, international transport conglomerate, and these two impressive gentlemen are my associates, Ty and Grif."

"Nice to meet you." Bingo. The final W of the triad identified. Winston was definitely the boss, based on the way Ty and Grif moved when he did and Cowboy mimicked his stance.

"Cowboy tells me you're new in town, a homeless vet, and interested in a money-making venture. He also said you've been a stand-up guy when he tested you."

She nodded and took another sip of her drink to squelch an angry comeback as she remembered the beat-down she'd gotten when she first arrived and her recent arrest.

"The things I value most in business are loyalty and discretion. You've exhibited both, and I believe in giving people opportunities."

Opportunities to go to jail? Winston struck her as the type of man who liked the sound of his own voice, so she remained silent.

"I need a person with particular technical skills, skills Cowboy assures me you possess."

"I know something about computers. It was my SC in the air force."

"You've done some IDs for us?"

She nodded.

"I need our business computerized, and our regular computer person has gotten into a bit of a jam. Dear Bug will be in jail for quite a while, not a bad idea really since he was getting too attached to the product. I assume you know what I'm talking about?"

"Prescription drugs," Colby said. She wanted to be able to testify in court that Winston confirmed the nature of his illegal dealings in her presence.

"Nearly as profitable as cocaine and heroin without half the law-enforcement scrutiny. The business has gotten too large for the old-school ledger method of bookkeeping, so I'd like you to computerize everything."

For such a successful businessman, Winston was putting a lot of faith in someone he knew very little about. It didn't make sense. There had to be a catch.

"But we've just met."

"True, but I'll have certain *safeguards* in place, just in case."

"Such as?"

He grinned, and Ty and Grif chuckled. "They wouldn't really be safeguards if I told you what they were. Let's just say if you cross me, no one will ever see you again, and they'll never find your body."

"I don't plan to cross you, but you're taking a chance. If I were in your place, I'm not sure I'd be so trusting."

Winston rose and stood in front of her. "I appreciate your concern, but I respect Cowboy's ability to read people and evaluate talent and my own skills at risk management. Are you interested in the job or not? You'll earn a lot more than making weekly drug runs, and you'd be off the street. We'll set you up in an apartment, for access, you understand."

"An apartment?" She should be ecstatic about having a roof over her head, but what about her connections with Sing Song and Adena? How would she explain her sudden disappearance to Adena? She already expected her to leave, but Colby wasn't ready just yet. "Shouldn't I be on the street?"

"Not for this job. You'll be taking in money weekly, logging it into a program, keeping records, and forwarding the proceeds to me. You can use any computer program you want, but code the entries so it's not obvious what we're doing in case it falls into the wrong hands. Can you handle that?"

"I've designed hardware, software, and supercomputers for the air force. I think I can manage a simple accounting program. What info do you want me to track?"

"The runners and the pharmacies Cowboy uses will be listed on a hard copy that Sheriff drops off each week with the money. That and the totals should be enough. When Cowboy needs new IDs, he'll meet you somewhere to do those exchanges."

This sounded too good to be true. Why was he willing to give her such unfettered access to his illegal activities and let her handle the money? He was either a very crafty businessman or a very high-risk one. And if he had *safeguards* in place to spy on her, why hadn't he utilized the person who put those in place instead of bringing in someone new? But she wasn't about to ask that question when this was like the golden ring in her investigation. "Where will I keep this money for a month?"

"A safe, of course. Let me worry about that. You don't have to make deliveries. Someone will make drop-offs and pickups at the designated times. You'll give them the take and a computer printout of the month's activities."

"I assume you know I don't have a computer."

"Everything will be provided—furniture for the apartment, utilities, whatever type of computer you prefer, spending money, and a car if you need it."

"I don't need a car, but I'd like to be as close to downtown as possible. I've grown fond of the area and some of the people. Will that be a problem?"

"I think we have a place in South Side that will work. And we'll get you a smartphone so we can contact you. Agreed?" He nodded to Grif, who left the room.

Colby hesitated. She wanted Winston to think she was seriously considering the offer but wasn't too eager. "Agreed."

Winston shot Cowboy a quick grin. "Don't you want to know how much the job pays?"

"It's got to be more than I'm making now, and if we're going to trust each other, I have to assume you'll treat me right."

This time Winston laughed aloud. "You picked a good one, Cowboy. You've earned your bonus this time for sure." He opened his desk drawer and pulled out a stack of hundred-dollar bills. He peeled off two thousand dollars and handed it to Cowboy before twisting a rubber band around the remainder and tossing it to her. "This should get you started. Buy some decent clothes and shoes, but nothing too fancy. I don't want you drawing attention. Tell Grif what kind of computer you want."

"There is one thing I need to mention." In her excitement about access to the drug operation, she'd almost forgotten her job renovating Adena's house.

"Go on," Winston said.

"I've got a part-time carpentry job, and I'd like to finish. Will that be a problem?"

"As long as you're available when I need you, the rest of your time is your own. Either Grif or Ty will contact you with drop and pickup times. Cowboy will coordinate the street operation, and Sheriff will do the actual deliveries to and from your place."

Ty and Grif she could stomach much better than Sheriff. Ty looked like the college-football type who dated cheerleaders and used brawn more than brains. Grif reminded her of one of her best gay friends back home. He was probably in love with Ty and would follow him to hell if he asked. She took the last swallow of her vodka and placed the empty glass on a coaster. "Sounds like a perfect job. Thank you for the opportunity."

"One last thing," Winston said. "You'll communicate only with Ty or Grif about the business from now on. Sheriff has his job. Cowboy has his. So if you have questions, you go to Ty or Grif. We won't talk again, unless you screw up. Understood?"

"Yes sir." She rose, shook his hand again, and followed Cowboy out the back door.

She doubled over, hands on her knees, unsure if the rush she was feeling came from the vodka she'd chugged or the incredible position she'd been handed in the middle of her drug case. "Holy crap, Cowboy, you could've given me a heads-up. That was intense."

He slapped her on the back. "Breathe. You did fine. This guy is the man."

She never imagined she'd meet the brains of the operation so soon, but she was both excited and suspicious. She pulled a couple of long breaths and schooled her grin before standing. "Thank you for putting in a word for me. It means a lot. Just out of curiosity, why haven't you moved up in this operation?"

"I'm happy recruiting new vets and being the street boss. I get compensated plenty, don't you worry. Besides, somebody's got to make the tough decisions so the boss can keep his hands clean." He winked at her, and Colby had the same cold feeling she'd felt when he mentioned no one else had to die.

Cowboy was definitely not an example of the principled soldier Colby had expected when she took the DEA assignment. He wasn't just trying to survive after the government had left him destitute like the other guys. He enjoyed bossing the others around and wasn't afraid to utilize violence to keep them in line. "How we getting back downtown?"

"That would be me." Grif bounced down the steps, handed her a smartphone, and pointed toward a black SUV. On their way back Grif asked, "What kind of computer do you want?"

"Mac laptop, moderate speed and memory. Accounting software doesn't need a lot of horsepower. That good?"

"Sure. I'll have it set up when the apartment's ready."

Colby couldn't wait to be free of these two so she could call Frankie with a report. Her handler wasn't going to believe it.

Grif stopped at the corner of Elm and Market, and Cowboy lumbered off toward the park. She'd started to get out when Grif said, "Hey, I'll get the apartment details to you soon. The place should be furnished and ready to roll in a few days."

"Thanks. See you around." She walked up Elm Street toward Hendrix. Maybe she'd sleep in the small park at the dead end near Adena's place. Without her bedroll, she'd be at the mercy of the elements. When she was certain no one was around, she pulled out her mobile.

"Frankie, it's Colby."

"How's it going, sport? Sounds like you have news?"

She relayed every detail of her conversation with Matthew Winston and her belief that he was at least the top local man in the drug organization. She finally took a breath and said, "Can you believe it? Has anything like this *ever* happened before?" Frankie was so quiet Colby thought she'd lost the connection. "Hello?"

"No, it hasn't, and that worries me. This could be a setup. Is there any possibility you've been made?"

"I don't see how."

"This guy wouldn't have gotten so far in business being stupid or careless. Stay on your toes. Any guesses where the prescriptions are coming from?" Frankie asked.

"Not yet."

"My bet would be the DRC doctor, Everett Raymond."

Cowboy's crew had already involved the DRC in illegal activity, and Colby would have to follow the evidence, regardless of her promise to Adena. And what if Adena was involved? "Possibly, but I don't want to jump to conclusions yet. Can you check the drugstores in the area without arousing suspicion to see how often his name pops up?"

"No problem. Routine inventories of pharmacy records are pretty normal business. But we also have to establish the nexus between Worthington, Weber, and Winston in the conspiracy to close this case," Frankie said.

"If there is a connection. We don't know that for sure. Agent Curtis only said he suspected a link, not that he had any evidence to prove one. And even if there is a relationship, maybe it's not criminal." And maybe she was just hoping, for Adena's sake, to preserve her family's name and reputation...and so they might have a chance when the investigation was over. If they ever had a chance, it would be when she could devote more time to convincing Adena she cared about her and wouldn't hurt her. The time was definitely not now.

"Frankie, can you also get me a list of DRC donors?"

"Sure, that's easy enough. Be careful, Vincent, and remember, technology isn't foolproof. Anything can be blocked, tracked, interrupted, or hacked. I hope you know what you're doing."

"I've got this part covered. Don't worry." As she ended the call, she hoped she was really as certain as she sounded.

CHAPTER SEVENTEEN

As Adena prepared for work, she again admired Colby's handiwork in her newly remodeled space. The wide-plank flooring in the kitchen was beautiful and the cherry cabinets an attractive contrast. Her center island was the perfect prep space for meals and a gathering place for guests, if she ever had any. Her master bathroom, now swathed in luxuriously white subway tiles, would be complete when the plumber installed the vessel sink. She should be thrilled that her house was starting to look like a real home. So why was she here alone, sipping coffee, and feeling depressed?

Truthfully, she missed Colby. Since she'd admitted her fears and shut down any chance of a relationship, they hadn't spoken in four days. She'd rushed home in the evenings, hoping to find Colby still working on the house, intending to invite her to dinner, and had been disappointed each time. Colby hadn't even been back to the DRC to retrieve her personal items from the locker.

She couldn't blame Colby for avoiding her. She'd encouraged their conversations and enjoyed physical intimacy more than she cared to admit. But clinging to lofty principles that wouldn't keep her warm at night, she'd pushed Colby away, afraid of her own feelings. Alone in her renovated sanctuary, she missed the one person who could make it feel complete. The only thing preserving her sanity was a hectic workload.

She'd taken on more pro-bono work and had also covered some of Ollie's cases while he worked on fund-raising for the DRC.

She'd scanned the files she'd asked Chris to pull on the clients with DE initials every night after work, hoping to find a connection to her father's calendar notes and perhaps his death. She'd do the same tonight.

She refilled her coffee, took a seat in the banquette by the window, and spread the files across the table. Della Ellis and Dorothy Euliss were DRC guests whom she'd never represented in any criminal proceedings. She scratched through their names on her list again in different colored ink and turned to the remaining DRC guest, Donald Enfield. He'd been charged with trespassing downtown, and she'd gotten him off with time served. She flipped through the two-page file but didn't find anything unusual. Dwight Ernest and Delmar Errington were wealthy businessmen who contributed generously to the DRC. She discounted them as legal clients and marked through their names on the list, again.

The next two files were clients she'd represented for drug arrests, Denton East and Derrick Evans. They had been charged at different times with possession of medications without a prescription. She'd pled them to a lesser offense, paid their fines, and they'd been released from jail after a short incarceration. Both men worked part-time for Winston Transportation. She looked through their files again and found nothing unusual.

She picked up another file and opened the cover, staring at the picture of Shaun Rossi, the man who'd been arrested for drug possession and carrying a concealed weapon, and had used the alias John Tabor. Carrick had found no evidence to connect him with her father's death. She carefully reread his chart. Oliver had represented him in two previous cases of drug violations. She glanced at the employment information and found he also listed Winston Transportation.

She flipped to the notes she'd compiled during her initial reading. Donald Enfield had also worked part-time for Winston Transportation. Until her father's death, he and Winston had lunch once a month at Starmount Country Club. Winston had offered the services of his company to the new nonprofit from the day it started. He provided jobs to homeless men who needed work and had helped several find full-time positions and reestablish themselves. Every charitable organization needed a patron like Matthew. It wouldn't be unusual for his employees to run afoul of the law occasionally, like any other business that employed large numbers of high-risk people.

What a waste of time. She pulled out the final file at the bottom of the stack marked *John Tabor*. This was the only one she hadn't read before. When she looked at the first page, she dropped the folder in her lap. Stamped across the client information page in big red letters was the word DECEASED. A triple-line obituary, dated eighteen months earlier, stated only that he'd served his country in Desert Storm, died from lung cancer, and was survived by cousins. Her suspicions were finally confirmed. Martin Linen had interviewed Shaun Rossi, who'd used John Tabor's name. The next question was why. If Rossi had a beef, why not use his own name?

She closed the files and stuffed everything back into her bag. None of this information put her any closer to figuring out why her father had scribbled *DE* on his calendar or what the numbers after them meant. She had no concrete reason to believe his doodles had any significance at all. Just a feeling, nothing more. As if her personal life wasn't frustrating enough, she added this puzzle to the mix. She took a sip of her cold coffee and had started to the sink to dump it when she heard a noise at her front door.

"Colby?" She gripped the empty cup in her hands, unsure what to say.

"Sorry. I thought you'd be at work. I'll come back later." Colby started to leave.

"Don't."

"Don't come back later?"

"Don't leave. I'd like to talk to you, if you have time."

Colby slowly moved away from the door but didn't come farther into the house.

"Would you sit, please? Want a cup of coffee? I have an extra blueberry bagel and honey-walnut cream cheese, your favorite. Mine was delicious. You take two sugars and cream, right?" She was babbling, but she was desperate for Colby to stay long enough to have a conversation, the details of which were unclear.

"Just the coffee. Thanks."

"Have a seat." She pointed toward the window banquette, but Colby perched on one of the bar stools a discreet distance away. She hadn't looked directly at her since she arrived.

Adena poured fresh cups and handed one to her. "So, how have you been?" *So lame.*

"Fine."

"I hope to furnish the house before long. Just can't decide on my style." *Like I can't decide on my life.* She struggled for words but just kept staring at Colby. "You've got new clothes. Your jeans are hardly worn, that Polo is definitely your color, and the Vans suit you. Did you rob a bank or something?" Colby cringed at the question. "Sorry. I'm nervous...and trying to figure out what's changed about you."

"Maybe it's the hair. I'll be able to comb it again soon, not just fluff it. Got an advance on a new job too and decided I could use some fresh things."

"You look great." This new-and-improved Colby Vincent had her mouth watering even more than the old one. Style suited her and seemed to give her more confidence. Only the poor really understood how money affected a person's self-perception and presentation. As she watched Colby fiddle with her cup, she decided to just be honest. "Have you been avoiding me?"

Colby drummed her fingers on the handle of her coffee cup. "I've been busy. Do you like the work?"

Another diversion, but she hadn't denied avoiding her. "Oh yes! Please forgive me for not saying so immediately. Everything's beautiful, and I can't believe you've done it all in such a short time. Thank you so much, really."

"Just a few more touch-ups and I'll be finished. That's why I came by."

Adena's heart throbbed painfully. Finished. Colby wouldn't be returning to work in her home—or for any other reason. "I see." Her mouth was dry as she struggled with an overpowering feeling of sadness.

Colby shifted on the edge of the stool, one foot already on the floor. "That new job I mentioned is a pretty good one, and it comes with an apartment, so you won't have to worry about me being on the street anymore."

Colby would be off the street, no longer a DRC guest. Her mind filled with possibilities—a chance to get to know each other, an actual date, not having to pretend or hide. But how had this happened? Colby hadn't asked for employment information or even completed a resume that she was aware of. "Where? How?"

"An opportunity came up and I took it. A friend recommended me to another friend. You know how these things go." She looked toward the front door and sipped her coffee, still not meeting Adena's eyes.

Opportunities this good didn't just happen out of the blue and not without a lot of reciprocity. "Tell me about the work you'll be doing?" She had no right to pry, but she was concerned about Colby falling in with the wrong crowd.

"Computer stuff, what I did in the air force. Nothing dangerous."

"And an apartment? That's a nice bonus."

"Yeah, that's what I thought, but I'm not about to turn it down. This could be my way back. You understand, right?"

Something about this whole conversation felt off. "Where is your new place?"

"I'm not sure. It isn't ready yet."

How could she not be sure where her apartment was? Hadn't she looked at it before accepting the place? More alarm bells. "Will you let me come visit?" Where had *that* question come from?

Colby looked as surprised by the question as she was. "Probably not a good idea."

"I'd like us to be friends, if possible. There's no reason we can't now."

"You mean now that I'm not homeless?"

The question was a legitimate one, but it stung just the same. "Now that I won't be violating any rules or ethics."

Colby stood, placed her cup in the sink, and walked toward the door. "Yeah, there *is* a good reason. You're afraid of us, and I'm too attracted to you to lie about it. We won't see each other much anymore since I won't be hanging around the DRC, so it should be easy to forget a kiss and a few hugs. I'll come back another time and finish the work, and I'll leave your house key on the island."

"Colby, wait." But the door had already closed behind her. "Damn it. Damn it to hell." Would it be so easy to forget what had happened between them? Adena's heart told her it wouldn't.

❖

Colby kicked an empty beer can down Church Street toward the city center. She hadn't expected to see Adena this morning and wasn't prepared. When she'd walked in on Adena, she'd stood at the door unable to speak and fought every instinct to hold her and tell her how much she cared. But Adena had made her wishes clear—no sex and no relationship. Colby's only recourse was to get in and out quickly, finish the renovations and turn her attention to the drug case. Things were heating up, and the further Adena was from her the better. Now that they could finally see each other, it wasn't safe.

She'd just reached the intersection of Church and Friendly when her new mobile vibrated in her back pocket. She pulled it out and checked the caller ID. Ty. "Yeah, what's up?"

"Ready to see your new place, Eagle?"

When had he become a follower of the menagerie? "Sure, tell me when."

"Right now. Stay on Friendly over to Davie Street. Keep going south until you come to the railroad overpass, go under and up onto Martin Luther King, and head east. You'll see my SUV in front of the condos on the right."

How did he know where she was? GPS. Of course they would have her phone tracked so they'd know her location all the time, one of their safeguards no doubt.

In a few minutes, she found Ty leaning against the side of his black SUV talking on his mobile. He hung up as she approached and dangled a set of keys in front of her. "You're going to like this. Grif decorated it himself. He loves that shit. Guess it comes with the swish."

She whacked him on the arm. "Don't be such a homophobe. Let's see it." She was excited about her first solo place, even if drug money was paying for it. Maybe she'd be here long enough to test living on her own and straighten out her feelings for Adena. She hadn't been able to think about her future seriously when her main priority was surviving.

Ty led her to the ground floor unit and opened the door.

"Surprise!" Grif jumped at her and waved his arms like a model for *The Price is Right*. "Do you love it or what? Isn't it fab?"

She scanned the spacious lower level from the front door past the dining space to the kitchen. Windows on both ends flooded the area with light, and she loved the open concept. Grif had decorated with contemporary furnishings, a style she hadn't realized she liked. The traditional architectural features of the building blended nicely with the modern and gave the condo a cozy feel. He'd added pops of red and yellow throughout to accent the neutral walls and high ceilings.

"I really like it, a lot. Thanks, Grif. You've nailed my style, if I have one."

"I knew you'd love it. Do I know interior decorating or what, girl?"

Grif ran ahead of her in the space and pointed. "One flat-screen TV here and one in the master bedroom for your viewing pleasure. I put this lightweight bookcase in the dining area to serve double duty as a sideboard or for books, music, or whatever. For informal meals, you've got two barstools at the peninsula. The kitchen is equipped with dishes, pots and pans, glassware, utensils, and a fully stocked fridge. Wasn't sure what you like, so I covered it all, vegan to meat lover. And you're close to all the best restaurants downtown, so enjoy."

She wouldn't have thought of half these things if she'd been moving into a new place alone. "Wow, Grif. You're amazing."

"I know, right? Just call me Marty Stewart. You have two bedrooms upstairs, but I staged one as an office with a futon that's very comfortable for guests. Your Mac along with the name and password for your wireless network are on the desk. The bed is made with Egyptian cotton sheets, six-hundred thread count, and there are fresh linens in the bathrooms."

"You really thought of everything, didn't you?" She held out her hand, but Grif grabbed her and hugged her hard against his bulky chest. "Really, thanks so much." She pulled away and waved as he and Ty left.

Stretching out across the red sofa, she stared at the ceiling. She almost felt awkward in the comfort after crashing on granite benches and sleeping on the ground. But she'd only been visiting the homeless world so she could ease back into society without much difficulty, unlike Sing Song or the veterans. This place seemed like a dream, but if she wasn't careful it could turn into a nightmare. If Winston was tracking her movements by mobile, the condo was probably wired as well. She'd be cautious until she had an opportunity to check for bugs.

She looked through the other rooms upstairs, emptied the clothes she'd bought at the Thrift Shop onto the bed, tucked the new Mac into her backpack, and headed to Fincastle's on Elm Street. She wanted to check the computer for tracking and monitoring software before she did any work, and the best way to start was in a public place with free wifi.

Colby ordered the Magnolia burger with Muenster cheese, onion straws, lettuce, tomato, apple-smoked bacon, and comeback sauce on a buttermilk roll and a large side of fries. She'd only ordered two real meals since she'd been in Greensboro, and this was the first one she'd pay for herself. A Hardee burger didn't count as a real meal in her book. She wanted to eat one of everything on the menu just because she could. The specter of starvation had made her ravenous.

The waiter brought her food, and Colby sent up a silent prayer of thanks before cramming a fistful of fries into her mouth. She tried to chew slowly but couldn't believe how amazing it tasted. Everything else receded as she focused on the juicy burger and perfectly fried strips of potato. Too soon her plate was empty and she washed the last morsel down with soda.

"Wow, you were hungry. Can I get you anything else?" the waiter asked.

"It was great. Could I have more soda, please? And do you mind if I sit here and do some work? I'll leave if you get busy."

"Sure, no problem. It's a little early for most folks. Take your time."

Colby pulled the new computer out of her backpack, turned it on, and waited for the wifi connection. If Matthew wanted to know what she was doing, programs like I Spy logged everything—what she typed, files she downloaded, who she talked to and emailed, website searches, programs she ran, and so much more—all time-stamped by date. He probably already had that fail-safe in place, but the smartest guys in the intelligence community had trained her to disengage or bypass these programs without leaving a trace.

Since the unit was new to her, she first checked for remote-control software or virtual-network computing software that allowed someone to connect to the computer without her knowledge. She didn't find any, and none of the program icons looked suspicious. Then she looked for third-party apps connecting through an open port, but again nothing seemed out of place. But this particular step could be deceiving. If the spying software only recorded data and sent it to a server, it wouldn't show up in the firewall list. The excitement of the virtual chase slithered up her spine. She hadn't done any of this work since the air force and would've been disappointed if it was too easy.

She checked all the outboard connections from her computer to other servers, which usually required another program, but she wouldn't need one. A quick scan of sent bytes showed which program was sending the most data from her computer. Someone was definitely monitoring activity on the unit. She isolated the offending program and with a few keystrokes modified the code enough to block the program from being deleted or destroyed. When she closed this case, she'd simply seize the entire computer along with all its information. In the meantime, she didn't care if Winston monitored what she was doing.

She'd decided to use an Excel spreadsheet to track the drug business. The program was simple, quick to configure for Winston's specifications, and easy for him to understand. She opened a sheet and started inputting the information she knew needed to be included. She'd thought about the code names for each runner and the drugstores, and when she was happy with them, she'd email a copy to Ty, after she made a hard copy for Frankie. Sometimes old-school was simpler and better than technology.

When she looked up from her computer next, every table in Fincastle's was full and the waiter was eyeballing her. She nodded, packed her stuff, and headed back to the condo. No sense wasting a perfectly good bed with clean sheets. She'd have a nice, long, hot shower and then sack out until she wanted to wake up. A real mattress, fresh linens, soft pillow—heaven.

CHAPTER EIGHTEEN

A dena waited until Cowboy's crowd settled around a table in the DRC day room before she approached. She wanted to gauge their collective response to her question about Shaun Rossi and John Tabor and then divide and conquer if necessary. When Cowboy saw her heading toward them, he stood, removed his hat, and offered his chair.

"Good morning, Miss Adena."

"Good morning." She looked at the gathering and counted heads. "Who's missing?"

No one at the table looked at her for several seconds as they exchanged quizzical glances with Cowboy. He finally spoke. "Bug got arrested."

Bug, AKA Shaun Rossi. Adena folded her arms to hide the chill bumps and raised hairs. She didn't want to believe that anyone in this group of usually nice and polite men was involved in her father's murder, but she had to know. "For what?"

The group was silent again until Cowboy spoke. "Drugs maybe? That's what I heard."

"That's too bad. He seemed like such a quiet, nonconfrontational guy."

"Must've been the drugs," Wolf said.

Cowboy elbowed him hard. Was Wolf trying to say Bug wasn't any of the things she'd observed? And if so, what was Cowboy's interest in keeping it quiet? Then she remembered when she'd shown

Cowboy the picture of the suspect in her father's case, he'd glanced at it briefly, dropped his head, and denied he knew the person. Was he lying? Did he know more?

Wolf rose, and the rest of the guys followed his lead. "I'm out of here. Places to go. Things to do. People to see."

Adena caught Cowboy's arm as he started to leave. "Wait. Please?"

He nodded and said, "See you fellows outside," then rejoined her at the table.

Adena searched for a tactful way to approach the subject but decided on the most direct route. "Cowboy, do you know something about my father's death that you're not telling me?"

He was able to maintain eye contact only for a second before glancing at something behind her. "Why would you think that?"

"Just call it a feeling. If you do have any information, please tell me." He looked at the floor. "You met my father, didn't you?"

"Mr. Franklin was a very good man, Miss Adena."

As a young adult, she'd had difficulty reaching that conclusion. His concern for others didn't begin at home, and she'd resented him for that. "Yes, he was. I was in elementary school when he first started talking about a safe space for the homeless to learn skills and receive support. He'd work all day defending cases in court, come home for a quick dinner, and then meet Ollie to discuss how to make the DRC a reality. Now it's my turn to carry on his legacy, but I'm finding that more difficult than I imagined."

Cowboy finally looked at her. "Why?"

"The police think a homeless person killed my father. I don't want to believe that, but they seem convinced. The detective told me Bug said something about the killing—"

"No, ma'am! Bug would never do a thing like that. We gave him the nickname because he wouldn't hurt one. He's not like—"

"Like who, Cowboy?"

"Some of the other guys out here."

"Please tell me what you know. I'll do everything I can to keep you out of it."

"I can't help you."

She got a sick feeling, now certain he was hiding something. "Does that mean you're not willing to help?" He'd skirted her questions twice, and this time she was determined to get straight answers.

"It means I can't."

"Because you don't know anything or because you'd get into trouble somehow? With your friends? Is someone threatening you? What am I missing?" Her voice was louder than she'd intended, and several other guests were looking at them.

"I'm really sorry, Miss Adena."

"Did you know John Tabor? Why would Bug use his name?"

Cowboy rose and headed toward the door without answering. She started after him, but someone grabbed her arm.

"Come with me." Flo pulled her toward the private office. "What's up with you? You're interrogating a guest like you're a cop. Want to fill me in?"

"Not really."

"Let me put it another way. What the hell's going on, Adena? We don't treat guests like that. What's the deal?"

She slumped into a chair and covered her face with her hands. "My dad's case."

"And you think Cowboy had something to do with it?" The tone of her voice made it clear Flo didn't share her suspicion.

"Not really, but I do think he knows something. I can feel it."

Flo knelt in front of her and took her hands, forcing Adena to look at her. "Tell me."

She shared her concerns based on Cowboy's reaction to the suspect's photo and the group's response to her questions about Bug. "Am I just too close to see things clearly? Has a year of searching for answers skewed my perception?"

"I'm the last person to poo-poo a woman's intuition, but maybe just this once you should let the professionals handle this. If there is a connection between Bug and the case, Detective Carrick won't rest until he finds it. And if the other guys are involved, he'll ferret that out too."

She sagged in her chair as the fight drained from her. "You're right. I'm just tired of waiting and hoping. I can't move forward and there's no going back. The stress is finally catching up to me."

"That's entirely understandable. Give yourself a break and be patient a bit longer." Flo squeezed her shoulders before rising. "And try not to alienate all of our guests in the process."

"I'll try." Adena rolled her chair to the desk and shuffled through the growing stack of unpaid bills. "Have you seen Colby Vincent in the last few days?"

Flo threw her hands up in resignation. "Here we go. I'm not sure which is worse, your obsession with your father's case or with this woman."

"I'm not obsessed. I'm worried."

Flo grabbed an Excel spreadsheet from the corner of her desk and ran her finger down it. "She hasn't checked in for three days, which could be a good thing. Isn't our goal to help folks assimilate back into society?"

No matter how logical Flo's answers sounded, Adena couldn't shake the feeling something was off with Colby's sudden good fortune. "But we haven't done anything for her. She didn't utilize our services to look for work or housing or—"

"She did use the clinic on more than one occasion." Flo's grin held an I-told-you-so edge.

"All right. Give it a rest."

"Only if you do." Flo backed out of the room, grinning the whole way.

Colby had said she'd gotten an apartment and a new job, both major improvements from street life. So why was she still worried about her? Everything about Colby Vincent from the day they met had been strange—her behavior, what she said, how she spoke, her concern for others but total disregard for her own safety, the feelings she expressed for Adena and the ones she evoked, and an overpowering sense that she wasn't as she seemed.

Adena needed definitive answers and consistent behaviors in order to trust and feel safe, but she'd received the opposite from Colby. She'd learned long ago that people usually told you who they were, if you'd only look and listen. The person Colby was telling her she was clashed with the person Adena felt she truly was. She wanted to trust her heart, but she was afraid.

She finished the DRC paperwork, checked in with Chris at the office, and headed to Crafted for lunch. When she walked in, Lois waved at her from the bar.

"Hey, you. I was worried you were upset about the last time I saw you."

"Come here," Adena said, wrapping her arms around her. "I wasn't upset. Are you feeling better? Any more contact with Beverly?"

"Yes and no. Move on. You just missed your partner in crime."

Adena looked around. "Carrick was here? I need to talk to him."

"Not Carrick. Doc Everett. He said business was booming at the DRC and he had to rush back. Very dedicated man."

"Unfortunately business is always good, and we're very lucky to have him dedicate his time." She ordered pulled pork on greens and watched Lois plow into her fish taco. "So, what's going on? I hope your lunch choice indicates you're back in the dating pool."

Lois looked puzzled for a second. "Oh, fish in the sea. Taco. Got it. Ha ha. No, I'm not there yet, but soon. I hate to wallow."

"It's not a good look."

Before Adena had eaten two bites of her lunch, Lois balled her napkin up and dropped it on the plate. "That was delicious and badly needed. You heard about the stabbing in jail last night? The bailiffs were blathering like a bunch of breeders at a baby shower."

"Huh?" She waved for Lois to continue, while she tried not to spray sweet-potato chips all over the bar.

"Guy named Shaun Rossi, shiv to the heart. Bled out in seconds. No one knew a thing until they found him this morning. The sheriff's department is in a snit trying to figure out how it happened when the prisoners are locked down. Duh. Can you say rotten apple?"

Adena finally swallowed and took a sip of water. "Damn it to freaking hell." Anger swelled in her, and she dropped her fork onto her plate. How could something like that happen in a secure facility?

And why did every potential lead in her father's murder ultimately wind up at a dead end?

"Did you know this guy?"

"He was a regular at the center. Carrick thought he might've known something about Dad's case. He hoped to question him soon."

"I had no idea. I'm sorry, honey." Lois kissed her on the cheek. "And I'm sorry to drop a bomb and desert you, but I've got a jury trial resuming in fifteen minutes. Talk later?"

"Sure. Go do judge stuff."

Shaun Rossi was dead. Another setback.

❖

Colby woke up sideways across the queen-sized bed and shifted against the firm mattress, enjoying the comfort and decadence she'd missed for almost a month. She'd been here three days, and as long as she didn't think about the drug money paying for it, the place felt restful and homey. But she'd been tiptoeing around the unit until she had a chance to check for bugs. She slept in pajamas at night, showered and covered up quickly, and never used the bathroom with the door open. She never called Frankie or made personal calls from the condo. Maybe she was being paranoid or just cautious. She'd find out today when she cleaned.

She pulled on a pair of sweats and headed for the Keurig coffeemaker Grif had left as a housewarming gift. As she sipped a blessed shot of espresso, she wondered about Sing Song and the veterans. Now that her job involved only the bookkeeping aspect of the operation, she seldom saw them. She'd walked the central business district a couple of times but hadn't spotted any of the old crew. Maybe she'd try again tonight. And after a little time had passed, she planned to volunteer at the DRC to help out. *And to maybe see Adena again?*

After a couple of shots of caffeine, she pulled out the vacuum, mop, and dusters. She vacuumed the living-room rug and hardwoods before moving to the kitchen and half bath downstairs. She flipped the sofa over, surreptitiously checking for listening devices as she did the housework. Pros didn't usually hide bugs under chairs and sofas because they muffled the sound. The best bet was lamps, light fixtures, or decorative accessories.

When she finished mopping, she started dusting and immediately spotted small listening devices on both table lamps. She found the third underneath a vase on the bookshelf, a fourth in the smoke detector in the kitchen, and the fifth imbedded in the motion sensor for the security alarm near the front door. Only the two units near the exits had video capability.

As she dragged the cleaning supplies upstairs, she felt almost sick. Infiltrating a drug ring was part of her job, but having them spy on her was another matter. She didn't find any devices in the office, but Winston was monitoring her computer. She hoped he had the decency to allow her privacy in the bedroom and bath. No such luck. She located a video bug on the flat-screen television in front of her bed and another in the overhead smoke detector in the bathroom.

"Fuck you, Matthew Winston." She flipped each unit the bird and yanked them loose from their connections. Her body shook as she tried to remember if she'd been careful enough to preserve some sense of dignity over the past three days.

It took only fifteen minutes for Winston's response. When she answered her mobile, she was still seething. "What?"

"You took offense to your accommodation?" Winston's condescending tone came through the line like a splash of cold water, and she was instantly calm. _So much for his no-contact rule._

"You understood wrong. The accommodations are excellent. It's your perverted need to spy on me in the privacy of those accommodations that I take offense to. Are you so hard up that you have to spy on a woman taking a shower to get off? Pathetic."

"Maybe the installer got a little overzealous."

"Maybe? You can watch everything I do, listen to every conversation I have, but you _are not allowed_ to spy on me in the bedroom or bath. Is that clear? If that's what you need to prove my loyalty, I'm not the right person for the job. I can clear out today."

"Hold on, Colby. The guys were just trying to be thorough, but I understand why you're upset. Part of the setup was for your safety and ours. Now that you've removed the offending devices, are you okay with the others?"

She gave him a few minutes to stew while she considered her position. "I'm not sure I can work under such close scrutiny. You're giving me access to your entire operation, but you can't trust me in my own home?"

"Okay. I'll have them remove everything. Will that make you happy?"

It would indeed, but she wanted him to do more than just trust her. She wanted him to trust her completely. And maybe she could use the situation to her advantage. "That's all right. Just no spying in the bedroom or bath again. Agreed?"

"So it's settled? We're good?"

"Almost. Would you instruct the security company to authorize access on my mobile so I can monitor activity in the condo when I'm out? It might come in handy, and with all the money coming and going, I'd just feel safer."

"It'll be done within the hour. Anything else?"

"That's it from my end," Colby said.

"Good, because I'm going to need your services for quite a while. My former computer man got himself killed in jail last night. Someone drove a shiv in his heart." The way he nonchalantly delivered the news sent chills up her spine.

Shaun Rossi, AKA Bug, was dead. She knew his real name from the fake IDs she'd produced for him. He'd gotten a little out of control on a couple of their drug runs, but nothing that would necessitate killing him. Maybe Winston didn't like loose ends, especially those with drug-abuse problems. A junkie in jail was like a baby without food, noisy and desperate for attention. When Colby hung up, she went to her bathroom, turned on the shower, and called Frankie on her other phone.

"It's me. I'm going to turn off my new phone and drop it in the post-office drop box late tonight. Clone it ASAP and make sure it's back in the box by morning. It has a program installed that gives you visual access to my condo, if you need it. Better safe than sorry. Also, would you check on the death of a guy named Shaun Rossi in jail last night? Thanks." Was there more to Bug's murder than the drug business? In one way she was like Winston; she didn't like loose ends either.

She worked on the operational spreadsheet for a while but couldn't really concentrate. Grabbing her new used jean jacket, she walked to Adena's house, by way of the post office, to finish the detail work in her bathroom. Opening the door to a place she was probably no longer welcome felt strange, but she'd promised to complete the job.

As she installed the shoe molding and applied the touch-up paint, she remembered the last time she'd been here. The sexual tension between her and Adena had been palpable, but Adena's principles and fears ran too deep. She'd left wishing the case and her stay in Greensboro were already over.

She cleaned her paintbrush and organized the other tools, while imagining a life in this place with Adena. The house now felt almost ready for habitation, like it breathed new life. Any dwelling could be a home if the people who lived there cared for each other. She wanted nothing more than to stay and convince Adena they had a chance. But an old saying came to mind: when one won't, two can't. She placed the house key on the island and locked the door behind her.

She walked toward the center of town, her steps heavy with sadness and uncertainty. She'd spent her life waiting for someone who sparked her passion the way Adena did. But she'd never convince Adena she cared while having to lie about her identity. Would Adena reject her completely when she discovered Colby had lied from the day they met about who she was and what she was doing in Greensboro? And if the drug investigation tainted the DRC, would Adena discard her regardless of who she was or how honorable her intentions were?

"Poor little new girl ran away. Where she went no one could say." Sing Song fell in step beside her. The blond spiky hair, blue eyes, and delicate features were such a contrast that Colby did a double take every time she saw her. "Did some old pimp take you in and fill you up with lies and gin? Where you been the last few days? I looked for you till my eyes did haze."

"Not your best effort, Sing Song, but it's good to see you. Have you been okay?"

She nodded.

"I've got a condo. You should come by sometime, if you want." She'd really started to care about this curious woman who appeared and disappeared at will.

"I don't like to live inside. Makes my skin crawl and blisters my hide."

"Okay, but if you change your mind, I'm on MLK across from the train tracks."

Sing Song waved as she headed in the opposite direction, rhyming as she walked. "Take good care and don't get hurt. They'll squish you like Bug and make you squirt."

"Hey, wait." She ran to catch up. "You know Bug is dead?"

Sing Song nodded, her eyes fixed on the ground.

"Tell me what you've heard."

"Bug got high and talked too much. People don't like babbling and such. Thought he was safe behind bars, but someone sent him to the stars. Stuck a shiv deep in his heart. Bug bled out and then depart. Gotta go." She turned and ran, waving her hands and yelling nonsense.

"For a mental case, you certainly know what's going on around here, Miss Sing Song." If only she could say the same. Had Bug threatened Winston's operation, or was his death some sort of jailhouse justice? Whatever the reason, she needed to piece together this drug case soon because she now occupied the job he'd vacated, an inherently dangerous position.

CHAPTER NINETEEN

"Hey, boss lady," Chris said. "Uh-oh, you look like a steaming cow patty on a frosty morning."

"Lovely greeting." Adena wasn't in the mood for the usual banter with her assistant. She continued to her office, dropped her bag on the floor, and sat down, reaching for the phone.

"Stop. Coffee in two minutes, and then you'll tell me what's wrong. Don't move." When Chris returned with the hot cup of morning glory, she was uncharacteristically quiet.

How could Adena sum up all the things that seemed out of balance in her life? "Colby finished the renovations at my place, and they're amazing. I had my first consult with a decorator. Soon I'll have a fully functional home that's actually livable."

"Those are all good things, right?"

She nodded.

"So why do you look so morose?"

"I told Colby I didn't want to see her, but she did the work anyway, while I wasn't home. She left the key yesterday, no note and no good-bye. I'll probably never see her again."

"Which is what you *said* you wanted. I'm confused. The woman is a genius with her hands, gorgeous, apparently listens to what you say, and you like her, but you don't want to see her. What am I missing? Is it the homeless, jobless, rootless thing...which I totally get?"

Adena sipped her coffee. "Succinctly put, but no."

"Then what? I'm running out of guesses."

She turned the cup in her hands, staring blankly at the firm's logo.

Chris slapped the desk. "You're afraid."

"How did you know?" She was so transparent. Her heart ached, and she felt like such a failure. She was whining to her assistant about something she should've taken care of weeks ago.

"Everybody has baggage—fear of abandonment, not being enough, not trusting, never being a priority."

Adena flinched when Chris nailed her greatest fear. "I can't take the risk of—"

"Letting her in emotionally, being happy, caring too much, being left, getting hurt?"

Her throat tightened and she could barely breathe. "Any of that."

"Honey, we all fear those things. Love is a gamer's worst nightmare. You think you're making the right move until everything blows up in your face. But damn, it's worth the risks. If you don't take a chance, you'll never feel that love high or how much it hurts to lose it."

"I know exactly how much it hurts. I've lost everyone close to me."

"But you've never been *in love*. She makes your heartbeat rival a thunderstorm, your pulse feel like you're running a marathon, and your insides like a furnace. Am I right?"

She nodded. "You're so poetic. I never knew you had such a sensitive side."

Chris shrugged. "It's a gift."

Adena's eyes misted as she remembered the few times in Colby's arms, the comfort, warmth, and security, but those were physical responses. Regardless of how she felt, her fears wouldn't change even if their circumstances had.

"I'm not telling you how to live your life. I'm only suggesting you think about what you're *feeling* instead of what you're *doing*. The outcome is often quite different."

"How did you get so smart about love?"

"I've had my heart broken more times than I can count, and I keep going back for more. There's no better feeling in the world than loving and being loved. It's very healing...and *so* worth the heartache. Trust me." Chris reached for the phone when it started ringing.

Adena had barely survived the loss of her father. Was she ready to open herself to the potential for more pain so soon? What if Chris was right and caring for Colby could heal her and help her thrive? Could she take the chance?

"Detective Carrick for you." Chris handed her the phone.

She took a deep breath and shifted into work mode before answering. "Hello, Detective, any good news? I heard about Shaun Rossi's stabbing."

"Unfortunately, my follow-up interview with him was scheduled for this morning, but we might've caught a break."

Adena's heart stuttered. "Tell me."

"The lab finished the analysis on his knife and didn't find any traces of your father's blood or skin cells."

"Couldn't he have cleaned it after—"

"Could've, but not likely considering his circumstances. CSI removed the handle and found only minute traces of Rossi's own blood and skin. I'm confident he didn't kill your father."

"And how is this a good thing?"

"We've narrowed the field. That's always helpful."

Bug had seemed like a nonviolent nerd who wouldn't harm anyone purposely. She'd needed reassurance that her instincts had been right about something. But she was also deeply disappointed because their only viable lead now seemed lost. "Anything else?" A long pause was her answer. "Well, thank you for calling. I appreciate the update."

Chris stuck her head around the door and waved a pink message at her. "You don't really want to see this, do you?"

"What is it?"

"Duh, a message—from the leader of this great city."

Adena waved her away. "I'm going to pretend I never saw that. If she calls again, stall. I need more time, and she's not going to be inclined to give it to me."

The mayor wouldn't be put off for long. When Chris closed her door, Adena retrieved the client case files with the initials DE from her bag. She'd gone over and over her notes, and the only connections were that three of the people worked part-time for Winston Transportation and frequented the DRC. She dialed Matthew's mobile, hoping her father's old friend could help or maybe just listen. Today she felt a deep need to connect with someone who knew and appreciated her father.

"Hello, Matthew. It's Adena Weber."

"How are you, my dear? Any luck with that newspaper article yet?"

"I'm afraid not, but that's not why I'm calling. I know you're busy, but I was wondering if you have a few minutes for coffee."

"Of course. How about Green Bean on Elm in thirty?"

"Perfect." She hung up and started walking. She was grasping at straws to think Matthew could help her, but she had to try. As she cut across Elm Street beside the park, she looked for Colby, hoping but not really expecting to see her. She caught a glimpse of a sandy-haired woman darting behind the pavilion but didn't have time to investigate.

When she arrived at Green Bean, Matthew was sitting at a table by the front window with his bodyguards on either side. She'd seen the two men for years flanking Matthew at charity functions throughout the city, but never understood why he needed protection. She nodded and smiled as she approached their boss.

Matthew rose, dropped his signature Cuban cigar into an inside coat pocket, and gave her a hug. "So good to see you, Adena. You've lost more weight, but that's understandable." He held her chair and offered a perfunctory smile she'd seen at dinner parties and board meetings, the extent of his social niceties. Matthew was a man of business. "How can I help? I love seeing you, but I doubt this is a social call."

"Very astute as usual. Do the names Donald Enfield, Denton East, and Derrick Evans mean anything to you?"

He scratched his chin while stirring his coffee. "No."

"What about John Tabor?"

"I recognize the name from the newspaper. What's this about, Adena?"

"I believe Shaun Rossi was interviewed by Martin Linen as John Tabor. He made unsubstantiated claims about the DRC."

"How do you know Tabor was really Rossi?"

"Because John Tabor has been dead for eighteen months, and Shaun Rossi used Tabor's name when he was arrested recently. They had to run his fingerprints to confirm his identity."

"Why would Rossi lie to the papers?" Matthew took a slow sip of coffee, seeming to mull over her news.

"I'm not sure. Maybe he was paid to discredit the DRC. We'll never know because he was killed in his jail cell last night."

"How horrible." Winston placed his hand over hers. "I don't like you messing around in matters like this, Adena. Your father would want me to look after you."

Matthew's words sounded sincere, but the look in his eyes was distant, his touch mechanical. She'd been acquainted with this man for years but never considered them particularly close. His offer to fully fund the DRC at the mayor's meeting and now his overabundance of concern about her safety felt misplaced. Or was she just overly suspicious?

"And what about these other three men?" Matthew asked.

"They're DRC guests occasionally and employed by your company part-time."

"In our reestablishment program, I assume?"

She nodded.

"Why are you so interested in these men? Is this about Franklin's death?"

"Murder. Why does everyone have trouble calling it what it was?" Her anger caught her off guard and she tried to rein it back in. "Sorry. I'm very frustrated."

Matthew squeezed her hand. "I understand, my dear, really I do, but I can't provide information I don't have. My company employs over four thousand people in ten countries. Just because I live here doesn't mean I know everyone who works for us locally. I thought the police were convinced a transient killed Franklin."

"They might be, but I've never subscribed to that theory."

"I hate to say this, but maybe they should look in the obvious place, the center. I know how protective you are of everyone there, but some of those men have very shady backgrounds. And now with so many homeless veterans, they come already trained to kill. Sounds like someone did you a favor taking out that Rossi character."

"Exactly the opposite. I wanted definitive proof, which I'll never get now. But Carrick is convinced he's not the killer."

Matthew leaned forward in his chair. "Really? How can he be sure if the man's dead?"

She told him about the trace evidence found on the knife that didn't match her father's DNA. "I really can't let this go until I find the truth."

His eyes darkened and his voice lowered to a tone that felt almost threatening. "I wish you would, Adena. I'm afraid your persistence will only lead to more trouble."

"What do you mean?"

"Whoever killed your father won't be above doing so again to protect his identity. Maybe he already has with this Rossi. Please be careful." He tugged at the perfectly composed Windsor knot in his tie.

"Enough of this unpleasantness. Tell me about the center. I got a call from Ollie the other day. He was in soliciting mode for funds to cover the cost of night accommodations from the early winter weather. I told him I'd help, of course, but not officially until the mayor gives her go-ahead." He pulled a check from his inside suit pocket, filled it in, and handed it to her. "But what she doesn't know…I hope this keeps you going for a while." He rose. "And I'm sorry I couldn't help with those names. Take care."

She watched him leave before looking at the check. Five thousand dollars would indeed help the center get through the winter. She should be happier, and maybe she was just being selfish, but she'd gladly give up the money for just one viable lead in her father's case.

❖

Colby picked up a scarf and pretended to examine it in the small vintage design store while she really watched Adena and Matthew Winston in the Green Bean across the street. She'd spotted Adena on Elm Street and followed her, intending to ask if they could talk, but she'd seemed in a hurry. When Adena entered the coffee shop, Colby had almost slipped in behind her, until she'd spotted Winston and company.

Maybe Winston had been a long-time friend of her father's like Oliver Worthington had and Adena was just meeting him for coffee. Perhaps he was making another donation to the DRC and wanted to deliver it in person. Maybe he needed legal advice. But there was another possibility she didn't want to believe—the W-cubed connection in the drug-diversion operation. Adena could be meeting with Winston to discuss their illegal venture and how to continue without their resident geek. Would Winston tell her he'd hired Colby to fill in? Would it matter, or would Adena just be happy their moneymaking plan would continue uninterrupted?

She'd tried to ignore the possibility of Adena's connection to this operation, but too many things pointed toward her. The majority of the drug runners were DRC clients. She and Bug had made fake IDs using DRC computers, unchallenged. The doctor who volunteered at the center was most likely providing the prescriptions. She'd bet Matthew Winston, the man behind the drug business, was a major DRC donor. Adena's father had been murdered behind the center, which might not be connected to drugs, but she'd worked too long in law enforcement to believe in coincidences. She already had enough circumstantial evidence to consider Adena a suspect, but her gut didn't agree. When she saw Winston hand Adena a check, she felt a wave of disappointment. Drug proceeds or DRC donation? Was there a difference?

She waited until Winston's entourage and Adena left the area before she crossed over to Davie Street toward the Murrow Boulevard post office to collect the prescription and donor lists Frankie had compiled. She needed something to distract her from what she'd just seen. In the weeks she'd worked with Frankie, Colby had considered staking out the box they used to exchange information just to see what her handler looked like but always changed her mind. She liked the idea of having an unidentified guardian angel.

But today it would take more than an angel to improve her mood. She hadn't seen Adena and Winston together before and had almost convinced herself Adena wasn't involved in the drug case. Now she had to seriously consider the possibility. Could she really be so wrong about the woman she was attracted to, had kissed and desired since the day they met? She retrieved the items from the post-office box and walked back to her condo, not even remotely enthusiastic about continuing this investigation. But the sooner she found the truth, the sooner she could put an end to the agony of not knowing.

Now she intended to find out who was writing prescriptions for the drug runners. Frankie had suggested Doctor Raymond, but she wanted to be certain before she pointed a finger in the direction of the DRC. She and Adena might not have a future, but she didn't have to complicate Adena's life any further.

Settled in her second bedroom with a cup of coffee, she scanned each sheet of the drugstore list and highlighted the prescriptions that originated from Doctor Raymond, concentrating on the process without considering the outcome until she'd lined the last page. When she glanced at the papers covering the surface of her desk, the yellow markings told a story—Doctor Raymond's signature appeared on too many oxycodone prescriptions to be legal. Almost every client he saw left with a prescription for oxi or roxy. She had to prove that Raymond, and not someone else, had actually signed the prescriptions. It was too easy for someone to steal prescription pads. She made a note to have Frankie retrieve the actual documents and have an examiner check for forgeries.

The DRC donor list provided less useful information. She confirmed her suspicion that Matthew Winston was a regular, substantial contributor to the program, but nothing else. The men he used to make drugstore runs frequented the center, and she'd soon have the list of names to prove it. But she needed more, the final connection between Winston and his drug operation—proof of the origin of the prescriptions. As she gathered the pages together, Colby realized Adena was more directly connected to the drug ring than Winston, but she still refused to believe it.

In spite of her efforts to stay away from Adena, she'd fallen hard for her—the classy professional who represented indigent clients, worked after hours at a homeless center, and risked her life to find the answer to her father's death—a woman more dedicated to a memory than Colby had ever been to anyone except her parents. If Adena went to jail or was in any way adversely affected by this investigation because of Colby, she'd never forgive herself.

CHAPTER TWENTY

As she greeted morning guests at the DRC, Adena counted the days since she'd seen Colby—exactly ten. She'd mentioned a new job and apartment, but when Adena asked for details, Colby had skirted the issue, again. Why was it so important that Colby be honest with her? She didn't know what was important to Colby Vincent, but she felt pretty sure it wasn't her.

"What's wrong with you?" Flo asked.

"Nothing. Why?"

"You're unusually quiet, and you keep looking down the line like you're expecting someone special. Bald girl?"

"No."

"She hasn't been in for several days. I heard one of the guys say she's got a job and a place to live."

"And that's exactly what concerns me. What job? Where's she living?" As soon as the words registered with Flo, Adena knew she'd made a mistake.

"You already knew that. What does it matter as long as she's employed and has a roof over her head?"

"I'm just afraid she's gotten into something illegal. You know I always worry about our guests, even after they're gone."

Flo rolled her eyes. "But you've worried about this one since the day she showed up."

Adena distracted herself with the line snaking its way to the door. Sing Song was running toward her with a frantic look on her face.

"Is Doc Everett here today? Got a rash that won't go away."

Adena stared at her for several seconds without answering as disconnected pieces of information swirled through her head and finally snapped into place. "What did you say?"

"Doc Everett?" Sing Song swept past her toward the clinic.

"You're brilliant, Sing Song. Can you handle this?" She called to Flo as she rushed to the clinic. Doctor Raymond's nurse, Carolyn, was behind the desk checking folks in. "When you have a chance, I need a list of the days the doctor worked over the past three months."

Carolyn glanced at her. "Three months? Really?"

"Yes, please." When she reached her office, she grabbed the list of notes she'd taken while reviewing the case files and spread them out beside her father's calendar. If she was right, she was about to decipher part of the meaning of her father's cryptic notes. At lunch, Lois had referred to Doctor Raymond with the affectionate term used by everyone at the DRC, Doc Everett. She should've made the connection sooner.

When Carolyn brought the printout, she meticulously counted and compared the days Doctor Raymond had worked with the numbers listed in the margin of her father's calendar. Every week the numbers were different. A sinking feeling settled in her chest. Wrong again. The figures on the calendar were consistently higher than the number of days Raymond had worked. If her father suspected something was amiss with Raymond, what was it and why hadn't he mentioned it to her? She shoved the papers into her bag and headed back to the clinic. Everywhere she turned felt like a dead end.

Adena waited until Sing Song left the DRC and followed her. When they reached the street a respectable distance from prying eyes, she asked, "Do you know where Colby's new apartment is? You two are friends. Please help me."

Sing Song kicked loose asphalt with the toe of her holey sneakers for several seconds before waving for her to follow. They walked up Washington Street, south on Davie, and up to Martin Luther King Drive. When they reached the South Side neighborhood, Sing Song stopped and pointed to a two-story unit.

"That's Colby's place?"

Sing Song nodded and, as she walked away, said, "Think you better make a call. She don't like surprises at all."

"I don't have her number." Adena stood on the street arguing with herself about whether to violate another of her many rules and infringe on the privacy of a former DRC guest. If she wanted answers, she'd have to confront Colby directly and pray she wouldn't lie.

She held her breath and knocked on the front door. When Colby answered, she knew coming here was a bad decision. Colby's emerald eyes were cloudy, and the dark circles under them absorbed their normal sparkle. The corners of her mouth were tight and her cheeks sunken. The sick feeling in Adena's stomach threatened to crawl up her throat. If Colby had gotten hooked on drugs, she'd never forgive herself.

"You shouldn't be here." Colby scanned the street behind her as if searching for something or someone else.

"I just figured that out." She struggled to control the urge to run and take Colby with her. Colby had looked happier and healthier when she'd lived on the streets, though that observation defied logic. If they could just go somewhere and talk, maybe things would work out. The silence between them stretched until Adena felt something in her snap. "Sorry, I'll go."

"Wait. Since you're here." Colby grabbed her hand and led her up the stairs to a second-floor bathroom. "If we're going to talk, it has to be here. Don't ask why." She lowered the lid of the toilet and motioned for Adena to sit while she leaned back against the door. Colby's gaze constantly darted around the small space, and the energy vibrating off her was wild and electric. She seemed afraid.

"Are you all right, Colby?"

"This probably isn't a good idea."

"Are you in some sort of trouble?" Adena couldn't let it go.

"Why are you here, Adena?" Her voice was hard and direct, piercing her heart and making this visit seem even less of a good idea.

"I'm not really sure..." If she expected Colby to be honest, she had to be as well. "That's not really true. I need help, and that's not an easy thing for me to say. I feel like I'm entangled in some sort of

Machiavellian plot, but I don't know how or why. My feelings about my father's death, the DRC, and...you...are like being drawn and quartered."

"Do you see those things connected?" Colby settled on the edge of the bathtub facing her.

"I'm not certain they are. Maybe it just feels that way because I can't figure them out. You've been a mystery since the day you walked into the center, and I've been conflicted about my attraction to you. If we can have an honest conversation, maybe we can piece together the random bits of information about my father and the center...and eventually about us."

"What kind of information?"

"Arbitrary stuff like why my father was keeping track of something related to Doctor Raymond at the clinic. And—"

"Keeping track? How?" Colby's attention was suddenly focused only on her and not in the loving and attentive way she wanted, but laser focused in a desperate, this-is-important kind of way.

"He scribbled the initials DE, for Doc Everett, in the margin each week, followed by a number. I thought it was the number of days the doctor volunteered at the center, but it's not. The numbers are too high."

"Can I see your father's calendar?"

"Of course." Adena pulled the calendar out of her bag and handed it to her.

Colby scanned the pages for a few seconds.

"What is it?"

"Will you wait here while I check something?"

"What's going on, Colby? You're scaring me a little." Colby seemed to have skipped over the part about them having an honest conversation about their feelings and zeroed in on the information about her father and the center.

"Don't worry. Just stay here. Please." She didn't wait for Adena to answer before sprinting from the room.

What could possibly be wrong? Why was Colby so concerned? One bad scenario after another played through her mind while she sat there. When Colby finally returned, her lips were tightly drawn into a frown. "Are you going to tell me what this is all about?"

Colby closed the calendar and handed it back to her. "What do you want from me?" Her voice was hard and flat, her eyes cold. Was she trying to force Adena to leave?

"I want the truth about what's going on here, what's so important about the information I just gave you...and when you're leaving."

Colby sighed deeply and looked at the floor as if Adena had drained the fight from her. "Straight for the jugular."

"Are these difficult questions?"

"At the moment, yes. I can't tell you what you want to know."

"Why? Just tell me that," Adena said as she rose and went to her.

"If I told you that, you'd know everything."

"And that's a bad thing because..."

"Because I'm not—" Colby's cell phone chirped and she looked at the display. "I'm sorry, Adena, but you have to go. I'm expecting someone." She tapped a quick text into her phone and slid it back into her pocket.

Adena stepped so close Colby had to look at her. "I want to explore these feelings between us. I've never said those words to anyone, and I'm petrified. I don't know why it has to be you, but I can't find out alone." Just saying the words aloud gave her butterflies and a feeling of vulnerability so powerful she almost panicked.

"But a few days ago you were afraid of where this might lead."

"I'm still afraid, but now you're not a DRC guest. We're free to explore this...if you want to." Adena paused, considering another possibility. If Colby was leaving, she'd find a way to hide her feelings again, to deny, pretend, and carry on. "Have you changed your mind?" She wanted to know quickly.

"Never," Colby said, "but we can't talk about it now. Rain check, *please*?"

Adena couldn't bear the separation any longer. She ran her hands slowly down Colby's arms, reveling in the warmth and responsiveness of her skin. The electric joining ran the course of her body. She kissed Colby's lips, pressing harder, needing something tangible to take with her. Their kiss deepened. Their bodies surged together, and Colby's hands cupped the back of her head and held her in place. Adena slowly backed them against the bathroom door. She hugged her more tightly and had reached for the buttons on Colby's shirt when her phone beeped again and she pushed Adena clear, gasping for breath.

"I'm sorry, Adena. You *have* to go. We'll talk soon. I promise." Colby raised Adena's hand to her lips, kissed her knuckles one by one, opened the door, and led her downstairs to the front door. "I'll call you."

"Please don't do anything foolish. I couldn't bear it if you were hurt again." She stared into Colby's eyes, unable to leave, a feeling of foreboding weighing her down. Words she'd never imagined saying sprang forth. "Colby, I think I lo—"

Colby pressed her fingers to Adena's lips. "Not yet. I *will* call you, because I feel the same way. Soon, my love, very soon."

"I really hope so." Adena kissed her cheek and opened the door. When she did, a tall man who stank of cigarettes and carried a small duffel bag walked past her into the apartment. He stared at her hard before Colby closed the door, leaving her with a chilling feeling she'd seen him before and not under pleasant circumstances. Why would Colby be meeting with this man, and why had she led her directly to her bathroom when she entered? As she walked back to her office, she knew one of her fears had come true—Colby was involved in something either dangerous or illegal, possibly both.

Colby closed the door behind Sheriff, her nerves an angry tangle. She never wanted Adena to be in danger, and she felt Sheriff could be exactly that. He gave even her the willies, but hopefully Adena wouldn't return until the case was over and she could explain. But if she did return, Colby would protect her with her life, just as she'd done on the bridge that night.

She directed Sheriff to the kitchen counter. "Would you start counting? I have to send a quick email to Ty about our last deposit."

"No problem."

She took a beer from the fridge and placed it beside him. "Help yourself if you want more. I'll be right back."

She dashed upstairs to savor the few amazing seconds she and Adena had just spent together. Adena wanted to explore a relationship—at least until she found out who Colby was and that she'd broken her promise about keeping the DRC out of trouble. Maybe she could explain the drug situation had existed at the center before she arrived. She cared for Adena, more than cared. She was certain their connection was a once-in-a-lifetime chance. Even now she couldn't face the possibility Adena was involved in the drug business.

The other grenade Adena had dropped was her father's suspicion about Doctor Raymond. But what had Franklin Weber stumbled upon? Colby shuffled through the stacks of papers on the corner of her desk and pulled out the prescription list she'd highlighted. She flipped through the pages of the diary she'd made copies of and began to compare and count. When the information formed a pattern, she dropped into her chair. "Oh, no." Exactly what she didn't want to have happen. Had Mr. Weber suspected Everett Raymond of writing illegal prescriptions, and had it gotten him killed? She'd need more information before making that leap, but these documents were a start.

Would Adena be able to continue the work she did for the homeless community when it surfaced that drugs were being run from the center? Would the center even exist after the search warrant was executed and the investigation completed? Who was responsible for Franklin Weber's murder and how could she prove it? Adena would be devastated if someone who frequented the DRC had killed her father. Colby could hear Leon telling her to concentrate on the drug case and leave the homicide to the locals, but she couldn't. Adena deserved answers, and if she could provide them, she'd do it no matter what.

She hid the documents in the bottom of her desk and went back downstairs to join Sheriff. He had several stacks of bills laid out along the kitchen counter and was counting each one while intermittently sniffing a line of white powder.

"Been entertaining this morning, Eagle, or was it an all-nighter?" Sheriff asked, losing count and starting over.

She didn't answer. He'd dropped off money on several occasions without any problem. She had a feeling this wouldn't be one of those times. She needed him to get out of the condo ASAP so she could get back to her real job.

"Wasn't that the woman who runs the DRC? What's her name, Weber?"

She still didn't respond, hoping he'd let it drop.

He stepped back and studied her, walking around, squinting, and finally stopping in front of her. "Now I fucking remember you! I knew it would come back to me eventually. You and her, on the bridge by Hendrix Street."

Colby remembered immediately and anger flooded through her. She hadn't gotten a good look at the attacker because he wore a mask, but his size and the ever-present stench of stale cigarette smoke were the same. Sheriff bristled and became more irritated when she didn't respond. She didn't need a fight with him over something that had nothing to do with the drug operation she was on the verge of closing.

"So?" She decided to let him vent and take it from there.

"So you stuck your fucking nose in somewhere it didn't belong." He snorted another line and wiped his nose with the back of his hand.

"I had no idea that was you. I just saw someone being assaulted and tried to help. That's what soldiers do. What was that all about anyway?" Hairs bristled on the back of her neck, and she knew they were headed down a dangerous path.

"She can't keep out of other people's business, just like her fucking father."

His statement registered in the deepest part of Colby, and she shivered. She placed the cash in her hands on the kitchen counter and deliberately separated it into piles, willing her hands not to shake. Her nerves jangled like they had before an assault in Iraq. She clenched her teeth and forced a pseudo-smile. She had to stay calm if she hoped to keep him talking. "Did he know something about the operation?"

"He was getting too close and had to be dealt with."

She grabbed another handful of crumpled cash to keep from seizing his throat. She hadn't read the report about Franklin Weber's homicide, but she took a chance and baited him. "I heard somebody botched that job."

"Fucking liar!" Sheriff stepped back from the counter and reached into his waistband. "Who said that shit? That job was clean." He waved his large hunting knife at her. "See this? It went through him like a slab of melted butter. I don't fuck up my jobs. Cops don't have a clue and it's been almost a year. Clean, I tell you."

"Okay. I was just repeating what I heard." She raised her hands and moved to the opposite side of the counter. Another confession she wished could've been recorded.

"Why are you hanging with her anyway? The boss won't like it. He wants her out of the business entirely." He leaned over the counter toward her, waving the knife in her direction. "Something about you never set right with me. Not sure why the boss trusts you."

"As opposed to an upstanding, stable individual like you?" She couldn't help herself but realized immediately she'd pushed too far.

"Fuck you, bitch. I can slice you open with a flick of my wrist."

"Like you did Franklin Weber?"

"Naw. I took my time with him, practiced my stabbing craft. But you, I'd enjoy slicing." He moved around the counter toward her.

"You already stabbed me once." She tried to back away, but he followed. "Get off me, Sheriff. The boss won't like it if he loses another computer geek." His face twisted into an expression that was probably associated with thought. "Back off."

"Nobody tells me to back off, bitch. You and that Weber woman are a waste of good bodies. You need to know what a real man feels like." He pressed closer, and his foul cigarette- and beer-soaked breath assaulted her nostrils.

"Know where I can find one?" She kneed him in the groin and jumped across the bar toward the living room. Money flew into the air and scattered across the living room in slow motion.

"I'll fucking kill you." He lunged toward her, slashing the knife through the air.

She grabbed a ceramic vase from the bookshelf to block his strikes. He charged again, and she slammed the vase across his forearm, deflecting the blow.

"Bitch."

"Stop this, Sheriff. We're on the same team." She couldn't reason with him. Fire and hatred burned in his bloodshot eyes. She somersaulted over the coffee table and straightened just as he sliced at her neck, barely missing.

"Fuck that. I should've finished you on the bridge." He jabbed at her with the knife, going for vital organs.

Colby deflected blow after blow until she was cornered against the front door and held only the bottom of the shattered vase in her hand. If she were going to die, she wished she'd told Adena she loved her. She might never have another chance.

Sheriff's eyes were glassy and red as he charged her again. The veins in his neck and forehead bulged as he raised the knife and brought it down toward her chest.

She was suddenly propelled violently forward, felt a sharp stab in her side, and heard a gunshot. She grabbed her midsection—hot, sticky. Her vision blurred as she looked up one final time.

Sheriff's mouth dropped open. The bloody knife fell from his hand, and he slumped to the floor. She dropped to her knees and tried to brace against falling face-first. Just before she hit the hard tile, she thought she saw Sing Song rushing toward her.

CHAPTER TWENTY-ONE

A dena was almost at the law office the next morning when her cell phone chirped. The text was from Flo. She dropped her messenger bag just inside the door and said to Chris, "I got a 911 text from the DRC. I'll be back as soon as possible. Cancel my appointments, and have Ollie cover my cases."

She fast-walked for five blocks to Washington Street and broke into a run when she saw the parking lot filled with black government and local police vehicles. The few DRC guests who'd stuck around were trying to get a look inside and verbally taunting the intruders who wore DEA jackets and vests. What was the Drug Enforcement Agency doing at the resource center?

As she approached, Flo waved her off. "You can't come in."

She recognized Officer Reynolds guarding the door. "You know me. Let me in, Officer."

He shook his head. "Sorry, Ms. Weber. The building is sealed until the search has been conducted. I'm sure the special agent in charge will want to talk with you."

"Search? For what? Do you have a warrant?"

Flo waved a piece of paper over the threshold, and she snatched it. She skimmed the document, rereading certain portions that didn't make sense. "Drugs? Are you insane?"

Reynolds shrugged as if he had no idea what she was talking about.

"Looks like I was right about your little bald girl," Flo said. "I knew something was off with her from the moment I met her."

"What does she have to do with this?"

"Her name is right there in black and white."

Adena's vision grew hazy as she inspected the warrant more carefully. The officer's signature said, Frankie Strong, DEA. Then she read the affidavit of supporting information provided by an undercover operative—*Agent Colby Vincent*. Her body suddenly felt heavy and she slumped against the brick wall of the DRC. So the woman she'd developed feelings for was not homeless, not a criminal, but a federal agent.

That's why Colby had seemed so different, unlike the normal homeless folks she dealt with. Colby was investigating criminal activity, not participating in it. She hadn't brought the problems to the center; she'd solved an existing illegal situation. *How could I not have known? Why didn't it occur to me that she was an undercover law-enforcement officer?*

A series of past interactions with Colby flashed through Adena's mind as she reevaluated each one in this new light. Colby had lied or evaded in almost every conversation, but she'd done it for the sake of her job—a job that would ultimately clear the center and her father's name. The DRC would eventually be vindicated in the press, regain public trust and funding, and the homeless community would continue to enjoy their only ally. With Colby's help, Adena could keep her promise to protect her father's legacy.

As this new information registered, Adena felt a sinking feeling. Even if Colby had a legitimate reason for hiding the truth from her, it still stung. And these new developments only reinforced the fact that Colby Vincent would leave Greensboro and return to her real home. Adena pressed her hand to her stomach. Colby would leave her too.

Doubt crept back in. Colby had been investigating the resource center and maybe her since she arrived. Was every minute they'd spent together carefully calculated to get closer to her and obtain information? No wonder she'd infiltrated the DRC and offered to work at her home. But drugs? Wouldn't she have known if drugs were being run out of her facility? *You couldn't even tell Colby was playing you for information.*

She choked down a wave of nausea as she remembered their kisses and how right they had felt. But Colby Vincent was paid to pretend and garner trust. Adena had disregarded her internal warnings about getting involved with Colby—so much for taking a chance on love. She was too embarrassed and ashamed to even look at Flo. Instead, she waited on the cold concrete steps for the search results that would determine the rest of her life.

❖

After what seemed like a few minutes, Colby flinched from the severe pain in her left side and opened her eyes to a shock of spiky blond hair too close to her face. "Where am I?"

"Cone Hospital. You all right, sport?" The voice sounded familiar, but the look didn't fit the person associated with it.

"Sing Song?"

"Sometimes. Agent Francesca Olivia Strong, DEA," she said, offering a mock salute. "I prefer Olivia, but you can call me Frankie. It was a better street name."

She had to be suffering from a concussion because this picture didn't make sense.

"You're Sing Song *and* Frankie Strong?"

The woman nodded.

Colby was having trouble mentally transitioning from Sing Song the deranged to Frankie her ghost handler. Her voice, the look in her eyes, and even her bearing were completely different in the two personas. "Pretty awesome undercover transformation. The case?"

"You got enough information for us to obtain warrants in the drug case, solved a year-old murder investigation, oh yeah, and got yourself stabbed in the process."

"How did you know I needed help?"

"You gave me access to the cameras in your apartment, remember? Thank goodness I was at the PD getting one of the guys to show me how the app worked. I hate technology. When we saw Sheriff getting nasty, we headed your way. Good thing too."

"My apartment. The evidence." She tried to sit, but a wave of dizziness knocked her back.

"Take it easy. You've been in and out of consciousness for almost two days." Frankie tucked the sheet back over her and fluffed her pillow. "We secured the apartment and collected everything. With Sheriff…dead and you unavailable, we totally locked it down."

"You killed Sheriff?"

She nodded. Frankie's eyes shifted to the floor and she swallowed hard.

"First time?"

"Guess we both popped a cherry on this case. Not what I expected."

"You'll be fine, and I really appreciate your intervention," Colby said.

"We'll see. You did a great job on this case, Vincent. And for your service, we've booked you a return flight to New York tomorrow afternoon, first class, compliments of DEA, if you're up to it."

"Tomorrow? But I have things to wrap up."

"It's not like you have to pack or anything." Frankie laughed.

"That's exactly what Agent Curtis said when I took the assignment."

"How about that? My boss was right about something for once."

Colby looked out the window. A yellowish streetlight flickered tiredly in the evening sky. "What about Matthew Winston?"

"Gone, along with one of his thugs, Ty. He probably saw the footage of your fight with Sheriff and bolted. We have warrants out, and in the meantime, we'll review the evidence, tie up all the loose ends, and make sure the case sticks when he comes to trial. Winston's other man, Grif, was apprehended at the airport with a suitcase full of cash. The runners were picked up, and Doctor Everett Raymond was questioned at the Greensboro Police Department."

"And the pharmacists?"

"We're still trying to sort out who was involved. Agents executed a search warrant at the DRC for several hours."

She struggled to sit up again but slumped against the pain in her side. "Damn. If that was going to happen, I wanted to be there."

"I know, and you worked for it, but the warrant had to be served ASAP. Besides there's nothing you could've done to soften the blow for Adena. It's probably best you weren't involved. She was pretty upset."

Colby's chest ached for the pain she'd caused. The image of Adena's stunned, incredulous, and then horrified expressions played through her mind. *Her* name was on that search warrant. By now Adena knew she'd withheld the truth about her identity and information that would affect the DRC and possibly her law firm. "Any chance she's involved in the operation?"

"Too early to say, but I doubt it. She seems like a pretty straight shooter," Frankie said.

"And Oliver Worthington?"

"He's probably clueless about the drugs as well."

"What happens now?" Colby asked.

"Now you go back to New York and pick up where you left off."

"As if." Was that even possible? Her former life seemed so far away from…from what? Adena and the possibility of a relationship? If there had ever been a chance, it vanished when federal agents swarmed the DRC. "What about the veterans? Will you offer them a deal in exchange for their testimony?"

"You liked those guys, didn't you?"

"Some of them. Cowboy was hard-core though. The rest were just looking to make enough to get off the streets. Will you put in a good word for them? Give them a chance. I'd be willing to come back and testify if you needed me to."

"Let's hold off promising anything until we get all the facts. I'm still waiting for the handwriting analysis on the prescriptions. The guy interviewing Raymond says he denies writing them all, but that could be an act. We'll see."

"As far as acting goes, you could win an Oscar for your Sing Song role. You had me from the moment we met. Why did you need me if you were already inside?"

"I was on the perimeter, and we needed someone who could infiltrate and work within the organization. You did it in record time. Might lead to a promotion or at least the station of your choice, if you play your cards right."

Right now her next professional move was the least of Colby's concerns. She needed to talk to Adena as soon as possible and try to explain. But what could she say? She'd lied to her from day one. If Adena listened at all, it would be more than she deserved.

"I need a favor."

"Okay." Frankie smiled down at her. "I bet I can guess."

"Get a message to Adena."

"That's not a good idea, sport. She could be involved in this case. We don't know for sure yet. Can't you wait a bit?"

"I don't believe she's involved in anything illegal, and apparently I'm leaving tomorrow. Tell her I'll be at the Biltmore Hotel on Washington Street tonight."

"She was here," Frankie said.

"Adena came to the hospital? To see me?"

"Right after your surgery, but you were heavily sedated."

"What did she say? How was she? Did she leave a message? Tell me everything."

Frankie held up her hand to stop the barrage of questions. "There's nothing to tell. She was obviously upset about the search warrant. She hung around until you got out of surgery and then left. No message."

"Frankie, will you please ask her to come by? I have to talk with her before I go back to New York."

"I'll try. No promises." Frankie handed her what looked like a gift bag.

"What's this?"

"Your boss, Leon Scott, was here too. He left this. It's your badge, gun, and cell phone. Call or text Adena and ask her to meet you if you feel that strongly about it."

"I will, but please, deliver the message in person, just in case she won't answer me. It's important."

Frankie nodded.

"And thanks for being there for me on my first case, even though I didn't know you were."

"My pleasure. And just for the record, Vincent, you're a good person. Not everyone treats homeless people with the respect you did. I know they appreciated it because I certainly did. I'll come by later and help you check out and into the Biltmore. And by the way, Detective Carrick with GPD wants to talk with you about the Weber murder. Feel up to it?"

"Sure."

"He's in the hospital on another case. I'll have him come up when he's finished."

When Frankie left, she slid back against the pillows, feeling unsettled. She was proud of her first undercover operation but upset she didn't get to see it through completely. The experience would bolster her resume for future assignments. She'd gotten a taste of living on her own and felt confident it was time to do so permanently. The compassion she'd developed for the homeless community would be with her always, and she'd never look at her privilege in quite the same way again.

Her feelings for Adena caused the most turmoil. She'd fallen for her, no doubt, but had buried her emotions under the cover of the job. Every lie she'd told, every misleading comment or skirted conversation tied another knot in her tangled web of feelings. How could she ever sort them out without Adena's help?

She retrieved her mobile and dialed. "Adena, it's Colby. Please call me. We need to talk." She left her number and hung up, praying she'd get a reply. Hours passed and nothing.

Frankie returned that evening and helped her check out of the hospital and drove her to the Biltmore. "Did you give Adena my message?"

"I delivered it personally. She didn't say anything. I tried to tell her you needed to talk, but she just walked away shaking her head. Did you talk to Carrick?"

She nodded, still processing Adena's reaction to her request. Of course she was upset, disappointed, maybe even angry, but why wouldn't she at least let her explain?

After she settled into her hotel room, Colby waited, but still no call from Adena. At midnight, she scheduled train passage to New York leaving at eight the next morning. DEA could keep their first-class ticket. If Adena wouldn't talk with her, she had no reason to stay.

CHAPTER TWENTY-TWO

W hat *are* we doing here?" Lois whined as she pulled into the parking lot. "And what is that horrible monstrosity?" She pointed to the eighty-foot-tall chest of drawers in front of the Furnitureland South building.

"I think that's self-explanatory." Adena teased her, aware that she'd tricked her into furniture shopping.

"You said we were going to eat oysters and drink martinis."

Adena brought her hand to her chest and sucked in a quick breath. "You mean I didn't tell you about the furniture stop on the way?"

"You most certainly did not, or I would have declined." Lois shoved the gear stick of her Mercedes convertible into park and released a long, exaggerated sigh. "Really, Adena? You know I hate shopping if I can't try anything on and take it home immediately. What's the point?"

Adena got out of the car and went to the driver's side, opened the door, and held out her hand. "The point is, you told me to take control of my life. This is part of the process, furnishing my house so people can actually visit."

Lois followed Adena past the huge piece of faux furniture, swiping her hand across a leg as they approached the steps. "You mean practically giving away your law practice and becoming a full-time nonprofit administrator wasn't enough of a change?"

Adena felt a second of panic. She'd sold the practice to Oliver. She took a few deep breaths to calm the anxiety. Obviously her changes would take some getting used to. "Ollie's offer was very generous. I won't have to worry about survival, and I'm staying on as an associate to keep my license active. Besides, I'll be doing what I love. Who could ask for anything more?"

"Maybe *someone* to love? Speaking of which, have you heard from Agent Vincent?"

Pausing in front of a showroom of leather furniture, Adena thought about ignoring Lois's question, but she'd been practicing her intimacy skills. "Colby has called several times and left messages, but I'm not quite ready to see her yet."

Lois pulled her into a shop out of the path of shoppers. "You haven't talked to her *yet*?"

"I went to see her in the hospital the day she was hurt." And she'd had to force herself to leave. She'd wanted to wait by Colby's side until she woke up, look her in the eyes, and tell her she loved her. But too much had happened and was happening that needed Adena's attention. She'd thought about leaving a message with Agent Strong, but Colby deserved more than just a quick note of thanks. She'd been stabbed once protecting Adena from Sheriff on the bridge and again uncovering the truth about her father's murder. She deserved more, much more, but Adena needed time. "I was there," she repeated, as if saying it again gave the act more weight.

"And left before the poor woman woke up."

"I had to think, Lois."

"It's about the lies, isn't it? The ones she had to tell you? And don't forget you lied to her about your feelings, ducking behind your high principles."

"That wasn't a lie." Adena tried to sound indignant, but even she wasn't convinced. "Not totally. I tried to tell her how I felt, once."

"But you *didn't* tell her, did you? She still doesn't know."

"The situation is totally different now, but that doesn't change the fact that everything I thought I knew about her was wrong."

Lois shook her head, and her blond hair brushed across the top of her shoulders, catching the appreciative glance of a woman passing by. "So, let me get this straight. You're judging lies based on motivation? If so, hers were way nobler. She was risking her life to make a difference. And let's not forget, she cleared the center and solved your father's murder. After the DRC issue was settled, you were basically a coward, afraid of your feelings and of getting hurt. Think about that until I get back."

"Where're you going?"

Lois sprinted after the woman who'd eyeballed her, chatted with her briefly, then pulled out her cell phone. The two exchanged numbers before Lois rejoined her in the second showroom.

"You're absolutely unbelievable."

Lois grinned. "Yeah. Ain't it grand? We're having dinner Friday night. When opportunity knocks, you have to answer. Remember that next time Colby gets in touch. She won't keep trying forever." Lois looped her arm through Adena's as they walked the hallway between showrooms. "You've come a long way, my friend. Don't stop short of the prize. Never thought I'd say that about someone who was once homeless. You deserve to love someone and be really happy. Find out if she's the one."

Adena's heart ached and she pressed the heel of her hand against her chest. She missed Colby, but they had so many things to talk about, problems to resolve. In the past three weeks, Adena had reexamined her life and reached some conclusions. She loved the law, but not as much as she loved philanthropic service. And she didn't love either as much as she loved Colby Vincent. Time to start living her life.

"You're exactly right, Lois. Now let's buy some furniture so I'll have a suitable place to nest."

❖

"Hey, sport, how've you been?"

Colby gave Frankie a hug as she picked up her suitcase from the Piedmont Triad International Airport baggage claim and followed her to the car. Her blond hair had grown a little and was styled close to her head. She looked as pleasing as her welcoming voice sounded.

"Not bad. How's your PTSD? Still struggling?"

"A bit. I'm on administrative leave for a while."

Colby resisted the urge to ask the question that had been on her mind the entire five weeks she'd been home in New York. She'd called Adena several times, left voice messages and texts, with no response. The request to return to Greensboro for an evidence briefing with the Assistant U.S. Attorney was a blessing and a curse.

"And before you ask, I don't know how Adena is. I haven't seen her or had any contact."

"Was she charged in the case?"

"We couldn't find anything that connected her or Oliver Worthington to the drug operation. The DRC didn't take too much of a hit reputation-wise, and they're still in business. Martin Linen admitted to accepting a bribe from Winston to run the story, but not to knowing John Tabor was really Shaun Rossi. Winston probably paid Rossi to say that stuff. The newspaper fired Linen and published a retraction, which cleared the way for city funding and a huge outpouring of public support and money."

"That's great news. What about the veterans?"

"Most have agreed to testify in return for immunity, except Cowboy, real name Thomas Garner. Did you know he's not even a vet, just played a good game? Winston hired him to keep the other guys in line."

"Interesting. He fooled me. Not a very good recommendation." As they approached downtown, Colby felt the pull of familiarity as they passed the areas where she'd found shelter, slept, and been fed during her stay. When she reentered the homed world, she'd eaten and drunk too much, slept too long, and purchased too many things she didn't need, just because she could. And then she'd stopped, realizing she was overcompensating after being deprived and afraid. Now she lived on far less and volunteered more often with the homeless in her area. Her immersion had taught her more about the world than her parents' retelling of their experiences ever could have.

"Do you have a place to stay tonight?" Frankie asked.

"Back at the Biltmore. I like the history of the place. Did you know it started out as the office for a textile company and was later used as a post office, apartment building, and an interior-decorating business before becoming the Greenwich Inn and finally the Biltmore?"

"No idea, but I'm not much of a history buff." Frankie pulled into a parking space near the U.S. Attorney's office and they proceeded to the fourth floor.

"What, no history facts about this building?"

"This place is too new to have history."

For several hours, she, Frankie, and the AUSA pored over the details of the case page by page. She interjected commentary as necessary but mostly listened for any information she didn't already know. "What about the handwriting analysis of the scripts?"

"Doctor Raymond didn't issue all of them. His nurse, Carolyn, helped out, and they were both charged. She and Dennis Lowell, AKA Sheriff, were an item, and she's the one who warned him that Franklin Weber was getting suspicious about the number of prescriptions they were writing." Frankie slid a clear evidence bag toward her. "These signatures were forged."

"Did Sheriff take matters into his own hands, or did Winston tell him to kill Weber?"

"Unfortunately that's a bit of the puzzle we may never put together. Sheriff can't tell us, and nobody else knows for sure except Winston."

"But Winston has been arrested, right? We have the computer, cash transactions, and my testimony."

Frankie looked out the window. "About that. He and Ty are in the wind. Winston has properties all over the world, and with his transport business, we'll have a hard time finding him."

"Great," Colby said. "I'm sure he cleaned out his bank accounts before we froze his assets, and you know how long it takes to lock down funds in a foreign country. He probably has enough money to hide for years."

The US Attorney shifted in his seat and tried to sound reassuring. "Don't worry, Vincent. We've put in a request for the US Marshals Violent Fugitive Task Force to take the case. He won't be able to hide forever."

"I'd sure like to be on that manhunt," Frankie said.

Colby had meticulously covered Winston's part in the drug conspiracy in her DEA statements, along with Sheriff's confession about Franklin Weber's murder, when Detective Carrick interviewed her. Why didn't Adena want to hear the truth from her? She'd chosen to uphold her oath and preserve the integrity of the case, which had cost her Adena. But having a choice wasn't the same as having control.

When the case meeting was over, Colby walked to the Biltmore, rolling her small suitcase behind her. She felt like she had that first night on the streets—alone and totally without direction. The AUSA wanted one final review of the evidence, and then she'd be free to go back to New York until the trials, which could be months away for some, years for others. Would she ever see Adena again?

She checked into the hotel, took a long hot shower, and wrapped a towel around herself before sprawling across the queen-sized bed. She considered taking a nap but was too restless. Maybe she'd wander down to Natty's and have dinner and a few drinks. Maybe she'd stroll by Hendrix Street…no. Adena had made her position clear, and stalking her wouldn't change that. She got up, pulled on a fresh pair of jeans and a top, and walked Elm Street. The next time she looked up, she was standing in front of Adena's house.

Colby argued whether to stay or leave as she paced back and forth on the sidewalk. She took two steps toward the door and three back to the street. If she returned to New York without having this conversation, Adena would never know who she really was, what mattered to her, how much she regretted lying to her, and most importantly, how much she loved her. She took several deep, slow breaths to calm her nerves, marched up onto the porch, and knocked, louder than she intended.

As she opened the door, Adena spoke without looking up. "Where's the fire? I'm almost ready. Come in while I—" Adena dropped a scarf she'd been pulling around her shoulders and stared. "You're here."

Adena was gorgeous in a short, form-fitting black dress with cutouts over the shoulders, a plunging neckline, and three-quarter sleeves. Her lips were darker with a hint of red gloss, and her deep-brown eyes were magnified by eyeliner and mascara. Colby's feeble attempts over the past weeks to convince herself she wasn't really in love with Adena vanished. She'd never be able to walk away from her again. "You look amazing," she said. "May I come in?"

Adena retrieved the scarf and crossed her arms, her face devoid of emotion. "I'm on my way out."

"I have a lot to say. Please, Adena, would you just listen?"

Adena stood in the doorway, giving no indication of allowing her inside. "You're supposed to be living your life in New York. I never thought I'd see you again."

"I told you some things are worth fighting for. If I have to fight for you, for us, I will gladly." Colby's insides were in shreds. "My life is here now, or at least I'd like it to be."

Adena looked into her eyes for the first time, and Colby saw a momentary flash of something bright, hopeful. Then Adena shook her head and Colby saw the doubt and pain.

"I couldn't tell you I was a DEA agent, but I won't make excuses. You deserved the truth—about the drug investigation, your father's murder, and my feelings for you. I'm so sorry I didn't give you any of that when you needed it most. It was my fault. How can I make this right?"

A long silence hung between them before Adena responded. "I'm very grateful you found my father's killer. Detective Carrick let me watch the video of Sheriff's confession and read your statement." Her words were flat. "You were stabbed. Are you...all right now?"

Colby nodded, unable to take her eyes off Adena. She'd hurt her, and somehow she had to let her know it would never happen again.

"I'm glad." She just stood in the doorway, blocking the entrance.

"I heard you came to see me."

"Just wanted to make sure you didn't die in Greensboro on your third attempt." A flash of pain streaked across her face before she schooled her expression.

"Adena, *please*, let me in."

"Tried that. It didn't work out so well."

Colby stepped toward her as a couple on the sidewalk stopped and stared. "Will you let me in before your neighbors call the police? The DEA takes a dim view of their agents being incarcerated."

"It's happened before," Adena said, her lips curving slightly at the corners.

"Only in the line of duty. If you don't let me in, I'll just camp out on your porch until you finally give up." She touched Adena's arm lightly and felt their connection immediately. She prayed Adena did as well. "Please?"

Adena stepped back from the door and waved her in. "Fine. I'll listen. You'll have to be brief. I have dinner plans."

Colby's momentary euphoria instantly turned to conflict. She didn't want Adena going anywhere dressed like that with anyone but her, but she had no claim on her. "Have you seen Sing Song? Sorry, Agent Strong?" She stalled for time to present the important bits in the best possible way.

"You came here to ask about Sing Song?" Adena's expression turned cold again.

"No. I...Can we..." She fumbled for words to bypass the case and go straight to her feelings, but Adena's words came more quickly.

"Were you investigating me, Colby?"

The anguish in Adena's voice made her cringe. She moved closer, wanting desperately to hold and reassure her. She understood that Adena needed answers, and she'd give her whatever she needed as long as those answers finally led back to their love. "Never."

"Did you think I was capable of dealing drugs? Is that why you spent time with me?"

"Not for an instant. I spent time with you because I couldn't stay away. Even when the evidence pointed to you, I didn't believe it. I thought someone had involved the center without your knowledge." She risked edging a bit closer.

"And that someone was Matthew Winston, my father's long-time friend?"

"Yes, I'm afraid so."

"I don't understand why he paid Martin Linen to write that story about the DRC when he knew it would result in a mayoral review or at least an audit. It doesn't make sense."

"Maybe he thought it would be easier to sidetrack a review than to distract you. He knew if you got any indication the center was involved with drugs, as your father had, you wouldn't rest until you found the truth. You're quite a formidable woman, Adena Weber." She took a chance and reached for Adena's hand, but she backed away.

"And you had no idea Sheriff, or Dennis Lowell, killed my father until the very end?"

"Not until that day at my apartment when he stabbed me, again. I promise you."

"Did Matthew have anything to do with Dad's death?"

"We're not sure yet. Lowell could've acted alone. Adena, I never meant to hurt you. I wanted to be honest with you from the beginning—"

"This wasn't a good idea." Adena started toward the door, but Colby blocked her path.

"Adena, please. I'm so sorry for everything. The minute I saw you, I knew I'd be torn between my feelings and my job. I just had no idea how hard it would be. Surely you understand how that felt. You deserved so much more. Haven't you ever wanted anything so badly but circumstances got in the way?" Adena didn't respond, but at least she didn't throw her out.

"Do you have any idea what it's like to be deceived by people you know and by some you've never met? I've known Matthew Winston all my life, considered him a friend and a patron of the

DRC. He'd been in my family's home often. Doc Raymond had worked with us for years. I guess helping others wasn't reward enough." The sadness in her voice made Colby ache. "Cowboy and that group of veterans…how could I have been so blind? And Martin Linen, a man I'd never met, tried to malign my father's reputation and put us out of business.

"Ollie and Lois were the only ones I could trust completely." Adena paused and Colby started to speak, but she held up her hand. "And then there's Colby Vincent, DEA agent playing homeless vet, alone and in need of help."

"You have no idea how much your friendship meant to me, Adena, how much you helped me. You gave the greatest gift to someone who was essentially invisible—your time. I wouldn't have made it without you and Sing Song." She forced herself not to move closer, though she was desperate to touch Adena, to make her understand.

"Every time I lied to you, it took a piece of my soul. Every time you tried to get me to open up, I died a little more because I couldn't tell you the truth. I finally had to stay away from you completely. I know how much it hurts to walk away from us, and I never want to again. But why should you believe me now? Because I'll do whatever it takes to convince you that I'm sincere." She was rambling, but as long as Adena was listening, she was making headway. "I'd like to show you who I really am, if you still want to know." They were so close she heard Adena's breathing quicken.

"Colby, I'm not sure I can."

"Because I hurt you?"

Adena finally looked at her, her eyes teary and dark. "Because you left."

"You wouldn't talk to me. I've called so many times. And I had to go back to New York to settle my affairs so I'd be free to return. If you have *any* feelings left for me, give us a chance. I'll do whatever you need." She wrapped her arms around Adena's waist. "Please. Look at me. Am I telling the truth right now?"

"How would I know?"

"Look at me." When Adena's eyes met hers, she felt a surge of love so deep tears streamed down her face. "Because I can't imagine my life without you."

Adena relaxed slightly in her arms, and Colby pulled her closer. "Please tell me we still have a chance. I'll win your trust back. I swear it." Adena was quiet for what felt like an eternity. Colby dug deep for the words she never thought she'd say, the words that had been buried inside her forever. "I'm in love with you."

"*What?*" Adena pulled out of Colby's arms and drew the scarf around her like a shield. "You can't just barge in here and blurt out something like that. It's…it's…"

"It's totally true. I'm. In. Love. With. You. I've never said those words to another woman." She waited, praying for a reciprocal declaration, but Adena continued to stare. The longer the silence, the more knotted Colby's insides became. When Adena finally spoke, it wasn't what she'd hoped or expected.

"Show me." Something sparked in Adena's eyes, and Colby wasn't sure what it meant. "Kiss me. I'll know if you're lying."

A powerful surge of adrenaline made Colby tingle all over. Her chest felt light, and her pulse thrummed. *Don't hesitate. She'll take your reluctance as uncertainty.*

She skimmed her hand down Adena's arm, entwined their fingers, and guided their joined hands behind her back, pulling them nearer. How many times had she imagined holding Adena like this, closely and deliberately? She caressed Adena's cheek with the back of her hand and held her gaze, praying Adena could see what she was feeling. She stroked her perfectly curved eyebrow and remembered seeing it arch when they looked into each other's eyes for the first time. Nothing had ever been more beautiful than the fire she saw there now.

"I love you so much." She bowed her head and licked Adena's lips before softly covering her mouth. The sweetness of their kiss was as she remembered, but the intensity of it burned hotter. She poured her soul into their joining, teasing and claiming Adena as if they were already lovers. "I am so sorry I hurt you."

Adena placed her hands on Colby's chest and forced her back. *What am I doing?* "Can't breathe." Her lips burned and her body ached as Colby rubbed against her. This little test of Colby's sincerity had flared out of control. She was satisfied Colby couldn't fake the emotions she felt pouring off her, but neither could she. She hadn't expected to ever see Colby again, but could she trust her? She desperately wanted to. Then she heard herself say, "Make love to me."

"What?" Colby searched her face.

"You won't see any hesitation this time. Make love to me, now." Her feelings for Colby hadn't diminished during their time apart, of that she was certain, but she needed to know if she could trust her—first with her body and eventually with her heart.

"We don't have to do this, Adena. I'll wait until you're ready."

She guided Colby toward the bedroom. "Do I seem unready to you?" She pushed Colby onto the bed and stretched out beside her.

"I want to be with you so much, but are you sure?" Colby asked.

"No, but do it anyway." Colby's eyes glowed like emerald fire as Adena ran her fingers through her strawberry-blond waves. Her longer locks were as soft as the stubble she'd touched weeks ago and filled her with an urge to grab handfuls of it and hold on as she came. "Undress me, slowly."

"I'll do anything you want."

Colby's whispered response made Adena realize she was orchestrating the seduction, but what would that prove? If she was going to trust Colby, she had to let go, even if it meant losing her. She raised her arms over her head. "How about you do anything *you* want?"

Colby nibbled the side of her neck, hot breaths alternating with cool licks up to her ear, and then she edged the delicate ridges with her tongue. Adena shivered as goose bumps melted into heat. She forced herself to lie still, unwilling to show Colby just yet how much she wanted her. Colby slid her hand slowly down her body, her touch barely discernable through the sheer fabric of her dress. She wanted to yell *touch me,* but she swallowed the words with an audible gasp.

"I want you so much, Adena."

Colby cupped her breast and gently massaged until her nipple hardened and pushed painfully against her clothing. They kissed again, and she sucked hungrily on Colby's tongue, urging her on. Every touch was too light, too tender to answer her need. She arched to meet Colby's hand.

"I'm...afraid," Colby whispered.

Adena opened her eyes, and Colby was poised above her, looking at her like she was something precious she feared breaking.

"I've never been in love, and I want to do it right."

The ragged edges of Adena's heart healed a little more. "Oh, darling, there's no wrong way. Just show me how you feel." She covered Colby's hand and guided it from her breast to the bare skin under the hem of her dress. "Touch me here."

When Colby's hand connected with her naked flesh and eased tentatively upward, something tore loose inside Adena. She strained as Colby teased higher and then down on the sensitive skin of her inner thigh. Her clit stiffened and her nipples tightened with each stroke. *I've waited so long for you, Colby.*

She yanked her dress up to her waist, rolled Colby on top of her, and brought their bodies together. "Oh yes." Colby caressed the outside of her thighs as she settled on top of her, undulating back and forth against her pelvis. "Harder." The rough jeans fabric aroused and chafed, and she pulled Colby's thigh snuggly against her center. "More." She bucked against Colby's leg.

"What can I do, baby?"

"Make me come."

"Are my jeans hurting—"

"Make me come *now*, like this. I can't wait."

Colby locked her arms on either side and watched as she rubbed her lower body against Adena in slow, deliberate strokes. Each pass of Colby's powerful thigh against her clit brought her closer to orgasm. She pumped faster. "That's it." Colby slowed, and her eyes sparkled with a mixture of mischief and desire. She was so beautiful, and Adena wanted to see her come while on top of her like this. "Faster, darling."

Colby moved against her more frantically, but her gaze never faltered. "Come for me, Adena. *Please*. I love you."

As Colby whispered her plea, Adena grabbed her shoulders and forced her down on top of her. With Colby so close and urging her on, Adena released and her orgasm flowed. "Oh, yessss! You gorgeous creature. Yes." Pleasure swept through her and she savored each ripple, feeling it might never end, praying it never would. She'd waited so long to be with Colby, but she'd never imagined anything this intense. Now she knew the truth.

When Adena opened her eyes, Colby's face was a mask of barely contained concentration. "Colby?"

"I love you so much. I could look at you all night, but I need to come right now."

She rolled Colby over and reached for the zipper of her jeans. "I want you in my mouth when you come." Colby's hips jerked as Adena pulled her pants down to her knees and stopped.

Colby tried to push them off. "Don't. I like you at my mercy." She wrapped a leg over Colby's thigh and ran a finger through her wet curls.

"I need you so much." Colby captured her lower lip between her teeth and bit down when Adena stroked her again.

Adena brought her finger to her mouth. "You taste so good."

"Please, baby." Colby raised her T-shirt and grabbed a taut nipple. The image was almost too much for Adena. Colby was trying to be patient, to give her what she wanted.

"I'm going to lick and suck you until you come. Is that all right?" Adena lowered her head but waited until their eyes met and Colby answered.

"Yes, please."

Colby cupped the back of Adena's head as she pressed her mouth against her. "Oh. My. God. Don't ever stop." *Is this really happening?* Adena looked up long enough to wink before sliding her tongue along the length of her clit. She wanted to spread her legs wide and thrash, but her jeans confined her, just as Adena had planned. If she needed to be in charge, Colby would gladly let her as long as she didn't stop what she was doing right now.

"Come back to me, lover. Where did you go?"

Colby caught a deep breath. "I was thinking how right this feels."

Adena captured her clit and sucked until Colby rose off the bed. "I love the taste of you."

She alternated between sucking and licking until the pressure was unbearable. Colby needed to come, but her lover had other plans. Just when she was about to release, Adena pulled back. "*Please, baby.*"

"How much do you want this?" Adena teased the base of her clit and then flicked back and forth with her tongue.

"So much." She tried to pull Adena up her body and rub off, but she resisted. "If you're trying to torture me, it's working."

"I just want you to realize what you've been missing." Another tongue swipe across her labia and down.

"I do. Trust me. *Please*, Adena."

"If you're sure." When Adena clamped onto her flesh this time, Colby tensed as sensation flooded her groin. Adena flattened her tongue against her clit, and when Colby started to spasm, Adena sucked until she came over and over again. When she thought she was finished, Adena drew more pleasure from her until she collapsed beside her.

Colby stared at the ceiling, trying to catch her breath. "Did that really just happen or was I dreaming again?"

"Depends. Which was better?"

"If that was a dream, they're definitely getting better." Colby rolled over and took Adena in her arms, sighing when Adena nestled her head into the dip of her shoulder. They lay caressing and kissing without words until the amber of streetlights filled the room. "What have you done to me?"

Adena snuggled closer. "Thought we covered that. I've shown you what you've been missing."

"You certainly did." She rose on her elbows and looked at their entangled bodies. Adena's classy dress was bunched around her waist, and her lace thong carved a swatch of black against her creamy skin. Colby's jeans and briefs were wrapped around her knees, and her T-shirt was gathered at her chin. She'd never been happier. "I love you so much, Adena."

"Show me."

"How?"

Adena got up, stripped her dress over her head, and shoved her thong to the floor.

"You're just as beautiful without clothes." And it was true, but Colby preferred to stare at Adena's face. Her golden-brown eyes glowed, and her face was flushed from their lovemaking. Her expressions revealed her heart, and when Adena's brow arched, Colby tingled with anticipation.

Adena held out her hand. "Take a shower with me. I want us both naked, slick, and rubbing against each other until we explode." She'd wanted Colby for so long it felt instinctual to have her again. Colby shed her clothes as she followed.

As Colby stepped under the warm spray, Adena brought their bodies together. Smooth, warm skin. Firm muscles. She wanted to uncover the secrets of Colby's body one at a time, but hopefully she'd have forever. She lathered her hands with soap and massaged the top of Colby's shoulders until she moaned. Moving her hands lower, she toyed with her erect nipples before sliding, covering the expanse of smooth skin with silky bubbles.

Colby kneaded her ass in rhythmic circles until her thighs slicked with arousal. "I knew those long fingers would get me in trouble one day." She moved against Colby and shared the bubbles that clung to her. "But can they get me out of it as well?"

"Depends on the trouble, I guess," Colby said, her kiss hungry and demanding.

She guided Colby's hand to her center. "You see, Agent Vincent, something's hidden here that only you can expose. Are you up for the assignment?"

"Definitely." Colby kissed her slowly, deeply before sinking her tongue and finger into her at the same time.

Adena rose on tiptoes and slowly lowered herself back onto Colby's hand. "Ahhh. So good." She pumped up and down while

Colby balanced her, each stroke bringing her closer to another orgasm.

Colby's arm tightened around her as Adena's vaginal walls spasmed and finally clamped onto her finger. When Colby rubbed her clit against the top of Adena's leg, they both climaxed in groans and laughter. Adena grabbed the shower wall as her legs weakened, but Colby was there to ease her to the floor. They huddled together in the stall until the water started to chill.

"That was long overdue. Thank you," she said and reached for the shower door.

"Where are you going?" Colby asked.

"Told you." Adena kissed her and ran a finger around her nipple before stepping out of the shower. "I have dinner plans. Guess I need another dress."

Colby reached out, but Adena was gone. "But..." *Is this it?* The sudden flash of disappointment gave her a chill deeper than the now-frigid water. "But I thought..." She'd told Adena she loved her. They'd made love, and now she was just walking away...to dinner with someone else? *Maybe all Adena ever wanted was sex.* Her heart ached with the sting of rejection.

"You thought I'd drop everything because you apologized and told me you love me?"

Colby didn't dare admit that's exactly what she'd hoped. "Guess not." She grabbed a towel and wrapped it around her waist. "Sorry." She retrieved her clothes from the bedroom and dressed while Adena rifled through her closet.

She felt awkward leaving without saying good-bye, so she waited in the living room until Adena came out, dressed in a red evening gown more stunning than the black one. "Wow. If it's possible, you're even more gorgeous."

"Thank you, Agent Vincent. Can I ask a question?"

"You can ask me anything, and I'll be a hundred percent honest, always."

"What do you see in me? I'm not one of your cultured, sophisticated New York jet-setters. I'm basically a homebody who prefers the company of the poor to boorish rich people. What's the attraction?"

"You're the most dedicated woman I've ever met, totally committed to what you believe and to your family. You're ethical, down to earth, and you have the courage to follow your heart, regardless of the circumstances. You cared about me when you thought I was homeless, but you didn't abandon your principles. I have tremendous respect, admiration, and love for you, Adena Weber. How could I not love you? You're the woman of my dreams."

Tears streaked Adena's makeup, and she patted her face with a tissue.

Colby held her arms out toward Adena. "Look at you. You're gorgeous and don't seem to know it. You cry at a simple compliment, and you're not afraid to stand up against injustice. Remember when you went after Wolf because you thought he'd beaten me up? You totally rock."

Adena wiped her eyes again and swallowed hard before responding. "Thank you for that. I've never felt anyone saw the real me before, only my father's daughter, the charitable attorney, or the do-good community servant. You get me."

Colby wanted to ask what happened now, but the doorbell sounded. "Must be your date."

"Guess so." Adena came to her, pressed their bodies firmly together, and whispered, "By the way, I love you too, so very much. If you're still here when I get back, we have a lot of talking to do."

Colby held tighter as a sense of relief and joy overpowered her. "Does that mean—"

"It means we have to talk honestly about our feelings and our lives. I've changed some things since you left. A relationship won't be easy, but I'm willing to explore the possibilities…if you are."

"Can't we start now?" Colby didn't want to let Adena go, now or ever, but certainly not until they'd agreed on a way forward.

"I have a DRC fund-raising dinner, and with everything that has happened lately, I can't miss it. Sorry, love. If it were anything else."

"Who's your *date*?" She'd never been jealous, but the tinge of green that colored her feelings was one more indication her feelings for Adena were genuine.

"Lois is an old law-school friend, and you don't need to be jealous. See you later. Be awake." Adena waved from the door and slipped out without letting Lois in. As the door closed behind her, Colby heard her yell, "I'm in love."

She pumped the air with both fists and yelled, "Me too!"

The End

About the Author

A thirty-year veteran of a midsized police department, VK was a police officer by necessity (it paid the bills) and a writer by desire (it didn't). Her career spanned numerous positions including beat officer, homicide detective, vice/narcotics lieutenant and assistant chief of police. Now retired, she devotes her time to writing, traveling, home decorating, and volunteer work.

Books Available from Bold Strokes Books

A Class Act by Tammy Hayes. Buttoned-up college professor Dr. Margaret Parks doesn't know what she's getting herself into when she agrees to one date with her student, Rory Morgan, who is 15 years her junior. (978-1-62639-701-9)

Bitter Root by Laydin Michaels. Small town chef Adi Bergeron is hiding something, and Griffith McNaulty is going to find out what it is even if it gets her killed. (978-1-62639-656-2)

Capturing Forever by Erin Dutton. When family pulls Jacqueline and Casey back together, will the lessons learned in eight years apart be enough to mend the mistakes of the past? (978-1-62639-631-9)

Deception by VK Powell. DEA Agent Colby Vincent and Attorney Adena Weber are embroiled in a drug investigation involving homeless veterans and an attraction that could destroy them both. (978-1-62639-596-1)

Dyre: A Knight of Spirit and Shadows by Rachel E. Bailey. With the abduction of her queen, werewolf-bodyguard Des must follow the kidnappers' trail to Europe, where her queen—and a battle unlike any Des has ever waged—awaits her. (978-1-62639-664-7)

First Position by Melissa Brayden. Love and rivalry take center stage for Anastasia Mikhelson and Natalie Frederico in one of the most prestigious ballet companies in the nation. (978-1-62639-602-9)

Best Laid Plans by Jan Gayle. Nicky and Lauren are meant for each other, but Nicky's haunting past and Lauren's societal fears threaten to derail all possibilities of a relationship. (987-1-62639-658-6)

Exchange by CF Frizzell. When Shay Maguire rode into rural Montana, she never expected to meet the woman of her dreams—or to learn Mel Baker was held hostage by legal agreement to her right-wing father. (987-1-62639-679-1)

Just Enough Light by AJ Quinn. Will a serial killer's return to Colorado destroy Kellen Ryan and Dana Kingston's chance at love, or can the search-and-rescue team save themselves? (987-1-62639-685-2)

Rise of the Rain Queen by Fiona Zedde. Nyandoro is nobody's princess. She fights, curses, fornicates, and gets into as much trouble as her brothers. But the path to a throne is not always the one we expect. (987-1-62639-592-3)

Tales from Sea Glass Inn by Karis Walsh. Over the course of a year at Cannon Beach, tourists and locals alike find solace and passion at the Sea Glass Inn. (987-1-62639-643-2)

The Color of Love by Radclyffe. Black sheep Derian Winfield needs to convince literary agent Emily May to marry her to save the Winfield Agency and solve Emily's green card problem, but Derian didn't count on falling in love. (987-1-62639-716-3)

A Reluctant Enterprise by Gun Brooke. When two women grow up learning nothing but distrust, unworthiness, and abandonment, it's no wonder they are apprehensive and fearful when an overwhelming love just won't be denied. (978-1-62639-500-8)

Above the Law by Carsen Taite. Love is the last thing on Agent Dale Nelson's mind, but reporter Lindsey Ryan's investigation could change the way she sees everything—her career, her past, and her future. (978-1-62639-558-9)

Actual Stop by Kara A. McLeod. When Special Agent Ryan O'Connor's present collides abruptly with her past, shots are fired, and the course of her life is irrevocably altered. (978-1-62639-675-3)

Embracing the Dawn by Jeannie Levig. When ex-con Jinx Tanner and business executive E. J. Bastien awaken after a one-night stand to find their lives inextricably entangled, love has its work cut out for it. (978-1-62639-576-3)

Jane's World: The Case of the Mail Order Bride by Paige Braddock. Jane's PayBuddy account gets hacked and she inadvertently purchases a mail order bride from the Eastern Bloc. (978-1-62639-494-0)

Love's Redemption by Donna K. Ford. For ex-convict Rhea Daniels and ex-priest Morgan Scott, redemption lies in the thin line between right and wrong. (978-1-62639-673-9)

The Shewstone by Jane Fletcher. The prophetic Shewstone is in Eawynn's care, but unfortunately for her, Matt is coming to steal it. (978-1-62639-554-1)

A Touch of Temptation by Julie Blair. Recent law school graduate Kate Dawson's ordained path to the perfect life gets thrown off course when handsome butch top Chris Brent initiates her to sexual pleasure. (978-1-62639-488-9)

Beneath the Waves by Ali Vali. Kai Merlin and Vivien Palmer love the water and the secrets trapped in the depths, but if Kai gives in to her feelings, it might come at a cost to her entire realm. (978-1-62639-609-8)

Girls on Campus edited by Sandy Lowe and Stacia Seaman. College: four years when rules are made to be broken. This collection is required reading for anyone looking to earn an A in sex ed. (978-1-62639-733-0)

Heart of the Pack by Jenny Frame. Human Selena Miller falls for the domineering Caden Wolfgang, but will their love survive Selena learning the Wolfgangs are werewolves? (978-1-62639-566-4)

Miss Match by Fiona Riley. Matchmaker Samantha Monteiro makes the impossible possible for everyone but herself. Is mysterious dancer Lucinda Moss her own perfect match? (978-1-62639-574-9)

Paladins of the Storm Lord by Barbara Ann Wright. Lieutenant Cordelia Ross must choose between duty and honor when a man with godlike powers forces her soldiers to provoke an alien threat. (978-1-62639-604-3)

Taking a Gamble by P.J. Trebelhorn. Storage auction buyer Cassidy Holmes and postal worker Erica Jacobs want different things out of life, but taking a gamble on love might prove lucky for them both. (978-1-62639-542-8)

The Copper Egg by Catherine Friend. Archeologist Claire Adams wants to find the buried treasure in Peru. Her ex, Sochi Castillo, wants to steal it. The last thing either of them wants is to still be in love. (978-1-62639-613-5)

The Iron Phoenix by Rebecca Harwell. Seventeen-year-old Nadya must master her unusual powers to stop a killer, prevent civil war, and rescue the girl she loves, while storms ravage her island city. (978-1-62639-744-6)

A Reunion to Remember by TJ Thomas. Reunited after a decade, Jo Adams and Rhonda Black must navigate a significant age difference, family dynamics, and their own desires and fears to explore an opportunity for love. (978-1-62639-534-3)

Built to Last by Aurora Rey. When Professor Olivia Bennett hires contractor Joss Bauer to restore her dilapidated farmhouse, she learns her heart, as much as her house, is in need of a renovation. (978-1-62639-552-7)

Capsized by Julie Cannon. What happens when a woman turns your life completely upside down? (978-1-62639-479-7)